INCURSION

BY STRENGTH AND GUILE - BOOK 1

PAUL TEAGUE

JON EVANS

IMAGINARY BROTHER

PROLOGUE

"Action stations, Mr Johnson."

"Ay, Captain," said Midshipman Johnson as he punched the command.

"Mr Wilkes, a message to the Admiralty. Let them know we have an unidentified threat," said Captain Nikolas Orwell, calmly formal as the klaxons blared.

"Ay, sir, message away," said Midshipman Wilkes.

"And an update on the probes, if you please."

"Working on it, sir," said Wilkes from the comms desk. "We've got two scanning probes in near proximity. I'm going to take a feed from Mitre1, I think it'll give us the best view. Placing a visual on the screen now."

Captain Orwell watched as his usual view of the stars was pushed out of the way by a fractured digital image of the fissure.

"Let's shut off the klaxons, shall we? I think we're all alerted to the situation." Wilkes nodded, and his hands flew across the console. "And we'll need something better than that, Mr Wilkes. What's wrong with the picture?"

Orwell frowned with annoyance. The posting to *Kingdom 10* was supposed to be a gentle downhill run toward his imminent retirement. Life was quiet out here by the Nebula, and this command was an ideal way to end his career.

Or so he'd thought. Now he was less certain, especially if Sol became involved. The last thing he wanted was the Admiralty crawling all over his command.

"Lens damage on Mitre1, sir," said Wilkes. "Placing it in repair mode now and switching to Legion3."

Wilkes ran his fingers expertly across the control panels. The pixelated images from Mitre1 were replaced by a much sharper view from a completely different angle.

"How large is that thing, Mr Wilkes?" Orwell asked, leaning forward to peer at the displays.

"Estimated size one kilometre and increasing, sir."

"What's the story from Sol, Mr Johnson? Anything?"

"They've received the message, sir, but no reply yet."

Orwell stared at the phenomenon playing out on the screen in front of him. The "anomaly" – there was no other word for it – looked like a fissure in space, a randomly-located gap in the fabric of the universe. It was a swirling mass of colour, as if someone was mixing paints in a giant hole in the darkness of space.

"What is it, Mr Brookes? And keep it simple, if you please." Like every science officer Orwell had ever worked with, Brookes had a tendency to give unnecessarily complicated answers.

"I have no idea, sir," said Brookes. "I've never seen anything like it."

"Great," grunted Orwell. At least he'd understood the answer.

Kingdom 10 had no records of anything that matched the description of the anomaly. In the decades since the space station's construction, it had never been involved in any type of hostile action, not even a threat from pirates or looters. Safe from the war with the Deathless, *Kingdom 10* had been the perfect posting for those who wanted a quiet life in the military.

"I have Admiral Staines, sir," said Johnson. "He wants to speak to you in your ready room." Orwell stared for a moment, trying to work out why Admiral Staines would be calling. Then he blinked.

"Patch him through, Midshipman."

Orwell handed over to his deputy and walked into his ready room. The low-fi avatar of Admiral Staines was waiting for him, shimmering in monochrome glory as it squeezed through *Kingdom 10*'s antique wormhole communicator.

"Orwell, what I'm about to tell you is highly classified," said Staines, getting straight down to business as soon as Orwell was alone. "In simple terms, the shit is about to hit the fan and *Kingdom 10* is going to get caught in the spray. We never thought this time would come, but Stansfield was right. He promised it would."

"Stansfield, sir? Admiral Thomas Stansfield?"

"The very same, Captain."

"What's going on, sir?" said Orwell.

"*Kingdom 10* is there for good reason, although it transpires there were highly classified reasons for it to be put into service," said Staines. "A plan was set in motion quite some time ago when an Astute19-class battleship called *Vengeance*–"

"Wasn't that was Stansfield's last command? I thought she was lost in action."

"That's what we all thought until we received your message about the portal. The coordinates activated an entire sequence of highly confidential file downloads. These files have been sitting in our systems, but out of view, for over half a century. We're sending them to your private console now.

"Stansfield's last mission on *Vengeance* was to pursue another Astute19-class ship, HMS *Centurion*, to the very point in space that you're now monitoring. The secure files reveal that an Ark Ship passed through that same point in space some years beforehand. What you have reported as a fissure is actually a portal of some sort, potentially even a wormhole."

"And is this where Stansfield and his crew lost their lives, sir?"

"No, Orwell. *Vengeance* wasn't destroyed. Her crew pursued *Centurion* to that very spot. *Centurion* passed through the portal, *Vengeance* did not."

"But what is the portal? Does it pose a threat?"

"Stansfield described it as the single greatest threat to Earth that we were ever likely to encounter. He didn't know about the Deathless when he made that statement, but Thomas Stansfield was not a man known for hyperbole. The Admiralty considers this portal to be one of the greatest potential threats that we've ever encountered, and that's why the files have been dormant on the system for so long. The moment those coordinates were entered into the system, it triggered a sequence of events that have been lying in wait since *Vengeance* encountered the portal."

"And what of Stansfield and his crew, sir? *Vengeance* was reported destroyed, wasn't it? If that's not the whole story, did the crew even perish out here?"

"No, Captain, they did not," said Staines, deadly serious. "Stansfield's final mission, at his own request, was to be put in stasis until the portal eventually opened. His entire crew were so committed to their mission that they volunteered to join him. They've been waiting ever since to finish their mission, and now that the portal has opened, they've awakened."

"But why do all this, Admiral? Why was Staines so keen to hunt down what sounds like mutineers? Especially at such great cost."

"The Admiralty is reviewing the original command decisions. I don't think anyone in the loop at the time is even alive now, and they're certainly not serving. I was read in to manage this situation because New Bristol is quiet at the moment, so keep me informed. I know that Stansfield described the reopening of the portal as the prelude to the end of civilisation as we know it, and the Admiralty believed him. He warned that the re-opening would be the beginning of the end."

Orwell nodded, not that he really believed any of it. The portal was there, but everything else was speculative.

"But *Kingdom 10* is no longer a military base, sir. We're strictly civilian, with only a small naval crew for oversight, and she was stripped of weapons and defences decades ago. We're not really in a position to fight a war. What do you need me to do, sir?"

"HMS *Colossus* has been despatched to reinforce you. *Vengeance* is en route from her holding position. Bring Admiral Stansfield up to speed, give him whatever assistance he requests. And Captain" – Staines paused – "make sure you keep me updated. Admiral Stansfield is taking local command of the situation, but I'm your first point of contact for any developments. Everything about this mission is obviously classified at the highest level. Remind your crew what that means."

"Yes, sir," said Orwell, "of course."

"Good luck, Captain," said Staines. Then his avatar disappeared, and Orwell was left alone with his thoughts.

1

Ten reeled as the sniper bullet tore a chunk from his left ear and sent him crashing to the floor for cover. Inches from his nose, a rat sniffed at him, then bounded away into the rubble.

Ten swore and eased himself around until he sat with his back against the wall. It felt good to have something solid between him and the sniper, but he'd been careless. Stripped of his HUD and power armour, his senses and reactions were dulled. This was raw combat, and he was completely outgunned.

He stared across the street at the crumbling balcony of the former Hotel Grande. The sniper had to be up there somewhere, hiding amongst the shattered wreckage. If he could take out that gun, he might have a small chance of containing the civilian body count.

A bead of blood ran along what was left of his lobe and trickled down his neck. It was a strange thing to notice among the oppressive sounds of hostile gunfire. Could they really not have spared a bit of backup?

"This fucking mission is cursed," Ten muttered to himself, frowning at a nagging doubt. Details of the operation buzzed through his head, but something was wrong. He tore the strip of severed flesh from his ear and tossed it across the room. He wouldn't be needing it anymore, and it would only annoy him. And now that the sniper was targeting him instead of civilians, his torn ear was the least of his worries.

A rat appeared from amongst the crumbling masonry at the back of the room, and Ten was briefly distracted as the rodent sniffed its way toward the discarded remnants of his ear.

"Slim pickings," said Ten, wondering what the locals were eating if even the rats were reduced to scavenging.

Then a bullet tore through the rat and sprayed blood across the shattered stone. Ten snapped back to the job at hand, recoiling from the sniper's display.

But this wasn't Ten's first duel with a sniper.

"Time to teach the bastard a lesson," muttered Ten.

He took a moment to focus and checked his weapon. He'd become lazy, relying on the tech to support him. Combat could be like a game at times, what with the constant flow of info to his HUD, the hi-tech kit, and the protective body wear.

But this was a bare-knuckle fight, like the old days. No fancy gizmos, nothing battery-powered, and only the wits that nature had given him. It would be enough too, but now he had to use his brain again and not rely on the computers.

Snipers were a special breed. They might lie for hours for the chance of a single shot, patiently waiting for their enemy to emerge. Always on the edges of combat, they never really felt part of the team. They were like the scared kids lurking behind the bushes, not the soldiers getting their hands dirty in the heat of battle. So it was with this guy.

But they were smart arses too, and only the very best were able to resist the temptation to show off. The sniper had taken the bait, just like the rat, and Ten grinned because now he knew where the sniper was hiding.

"Time to go to work," he whispered, frowning again because something wasn't right. Then he shook his head, pushing the doubt aside.

He unclipped a grenade from his belt and pulled out the pin. A heartbeat, a breath; then he moved to a crouching position, counted slowly, and threw the grenade to his right.

The sudden movement sparked gunfire, and Ten sprang off in the opposite direction, making for a doorway directly ahead of him.

The grenade exploded – he felt its blast even as he ran – and he used it to push him towards his destination. The firing was intense, but they'd been slow to see what he was doing, and he slid to the ground in the doorway, dodging a second bullet.

The sniper was above him, one of a band of terrorists within the building, working the city for some unknown reason. If the intel was correct, the civilians were in the heart of the structure, held in a central courtyard.

He slung his rifle and unholstered his pistol. He was low on ammunition after his previous encounters, but he couldn't remember why. The recent past was fuzzy, and that worried him.

Fresh magazine or not? he thought. Ten decided on a fresh one, then found he had none left. Strange. Six rounds left, for the sniper, then back to the rifle and its near-empty magazine. After that, it was a dagger, and then he was stuck with bare hands if he couldn't borrow a weapon from a corpse.

It wasn't often that Ten didn't fancy his chances, but today was one of those rare occasions.

He scanned the area. This was no way to run a military operation in a colony. They'd sent a tiny team, poorly-equipped with no support, and his fellow Marines were inexperienced and out of their depth. The war on the Deathless was squeezing resources, and Sol wanted this situation dealt with quickly, but he didn't like it.

Five of his team had been killed in the first hour. Sure, it was a stealth mission, but with only a single Marine left, the chances of success were not high. They were terrorists too, and Ten was more used to fighting soldiers of late. And wings – he'd had wings. This was just him, in a basic Royal Marine clone, no extras. It made him feel more vulnerable than he had in a long time.

"Fuck 'em," he said to himself. "Get the job done, go home. You know how to do this, Marine. This is what you used to do all the time. It's like riding a bicycle; you just jump on, and off you go."

He became aware of movement both ahead and behind him as the terrorists peered from their stations, trying to figure out where he'd got to.

"Over there, under the second balcony," one of them called.

Damn, where was covering fire when you needed it?

Ten tightened his grip on the pistol and moved towards an exterior cable conduit on his right. He gave it a tug to check it would hold his weight and grinned. Once upon a time, he'd held the cadet speed-climbing record for nine months.

He thrust his left hand forward and heaved his body up, jumping so that both feet were now in contact with the wall. He moved his left arm above his head, then pulled himself up a level. Difficult work, and after three reps he had to stop to deal with a couple of brave shooters who'd ventured from their cover to look for him.

"There," one shouted, spraying bullets as they slid to a halt in the open ground.

Ten took a cloud of brick dust to the face, then flinched as a voltage blast rippled through him, almost shaking him off the conduit. They'd hit the cable, giving him a solid jolt, but he clung on.

He was desperate to wipe the brick dust from his eyes, and his arm was being tortured by the voltage from the live cable, but he had to take out the shooters, or this crappy colony would get the better of him. He heard the click of rifles, his cue to act.

Clenching his eyes fast shut and whirling around, he fired twice at the first shooter, going on sound alone. There was the satisfying sound of a bullet tearing through flesh, a startled cry and a thud on the ground. He had moments to act, the voltage blast still numbing his left arm, and he'd have to let go if he couldn't finish the second shooter.

He listened again but heard nothing. His eyes were watering, and a few blinks helped clear the brick dust just enough that he could see. It itched like crazy. He needed time to sluice his eyes with water.

"Shit," said Ten, pushing back the other way, desperate to get clear. There was the *click-clack* sound of a jam being cleared, then swearing as the second terrorist wrestled with his weapon.

"Gotcha," whispered Ten, bringing his pistol up. Three shots, guided only by the sounds of the terrorist's panic. A loose cluster of fire, centred above the rifle sounds, then a pause.

There was a second thud – quieter this time – as a body slumped to the ground. Ten holstered his empty pistol and wiped the dust from his eyes. There were two corpses on the ground: one sprawled on its face, the other collapsed in a pile with a hole in its head. No pill in the universe was fixing that headache.

He gritted his teeth against the pain in his arm, and heaved himself up the conduit, towards the balcony. Above him, boots scraped on concrete as the sniper scurried away, looking for a new place to hide. These guys weren't made for close-quarters combat. Well, he was going to pay for the botched ear-piercing. Ten was coming for a refund, and he didn't deal in cash.

Eyes stinging from the dust, Ten reached the top of the conduit and swung himself over to the balcony. From all around came sounds of boots, weapons and orders. The terrorists were repositioning, getting ready to storm out of the building to try and pick him off before he got inside. He could hear them thundering up the stairs to head him off at the pass. And at the core of this unit were his mission objective, the civilians who they – *he* – was supposed to be rescuing.

He scooped up an abandoned automatic weapon from the balcony and checked it – plenty of ammo still – then aimed it directly at the doorway ahead. Two terrorists ran through, guns blazing, but he took them out cleanly, then shot both in the head again. If he'd learnt one thing from these sorts of operation, it's that you finish your enemies properly. Firing from below, and Ten spun to find more shooters. He returned the compliment, killing two outright and wounding the third.

"Careless," he said, cursing the lost seconds as he fired again to finish the wounded terrorist.

There were more of them coming up through the inside of the building now, disorganised and undisciplined. They moved quickly but carelessly as they hunted him. He killed another – a teenager – as he gawped at the bodies Ten had created only seconds before. He hated killing kids; they'd never get to learn the elements of battle like he had.

He walked from the balcony to the office beyond, where three bodies now littered the doorway. He could hear the terrorists whispering and shuffling into position on the other side of the entrance, waiting for him to show his face.

Fuck that for a game of soldiers, thought Ten, backing away from the door. He pulled the pin from his last grenade and listened to the terrorists counting down on the other side of the door.

Three, two, one.

He rolled the grenade when their count hit two and left it nestling amongst the three corpses. It exploded as the remaining terrorists tore into the room, yelling and firing their weapons as they came. A tsunami of guts and body parts spattered the walls of the room, and suddenly, the building was quiet.

"You boys are going to have to redecorate," murmured Ten, stepping up to the doorway. He paused on the threshold with the caution born of long experience. Then he kicked a severed hand out into the hallway and grinned at the panicked gunfire that erupted from either side of the door.

He burst through the doorway, shooting first to his left and then dropping to one knee as he turned to shoot the other way. After the gunfire, the sudden click of an empty rifle in the now quiet corridor was unnatural. Ten remained kneeling for a few heartbeats longer, listening as much as watching for movement; then he dropped the captured weapon and unslung his rifle.

At first, the building seemed clear, but then the sound of running boots led him to two fleeing guards. They'd obviously given up on their "higher cause," whatever ill-informed, anti-Sol bullshit had filled their heads. He shot them both as they ran, then followed his rifle down the steps of the ornate staircase.

For a moment, Ten had almost given up the mission, but experience had taught him there's always a last twist or a final play. What had they been thinking, teaming him up with a bunch of rookies?

He could hear the anxious murmuring of the captives in the central courtyard, terrified to step beyond the doors that held them in case their captors were still at large. These were government officials and administrators, of high value to Sol.

Ten kicked the double wooden doors open, ready to stride in like the cocky hero he was.

"You're safe, the building's clear..." he began.

Before he'd finished the sentence, a single bullet entered the space between his eyes, exploding his head all over the people he'd rescued.

In the milliseconds before he hit the ground, he had just time for one final profound thought.

Fucking snipers!

2

Ten blinked himself awake and sat up.

"A simulation?" he said bitterly as he looked around. "You know there's supposed to be a fucking command switch, right? An escape route to stop people losing their minds?"

"Get up, arsehole," said a voice, completely ignoring Ten's complaints. "You're about to be on the receiving end of rapid machine-gun fire!"

Ten hauled himself to his feet and followed the man...no, it wasn't a man, it was a woman. She was built like a brick shithouse, and they were on some kind of spaceship. Only moments previously he'd been in a virtual firefight with a bunch of terrorists. He knew they were running him through a series of high-intensity simulations, but he was struggling to keep up, or see the point of the exercise.

A special mission. We need your unique experience and skills, Staines had said, trying to flatter him. *A break from the Deathless, you won't be out of the New Bristol theatre for long*, he'd promised.

Well, so far he'd frazzled his arm, been shot in the head and fed a bit of his ear to a rat. The battle with the Deathless was beginning to look like a kids' movie in comparison.

"Where are we?" he said, shaky on his feet.

"It doesn't matter. Tool up and get ready for a firefight."

This was better. A Heads-Up Display, albeit an unfamiliar model, some decent weaponry and no place for snipers to hide. It was Sol construction too – definitely not Deathless. That made a change, at least.

Ten never thought he'd say it, but you could get enough of a good thing. Shooting lizards had been fun for a while, but terrorists and whatever this was made for a refreshing change of pace. In the world of Marine X, this had all the hallmarks of a relaxing break.

"Any body armour?" he asked hopefully. It had been a long time since he'd gone basic. He preferred things the modern way, with tech, gadgets and big kick-ass guns. Even better if there was something that belched fire at the enemy.

"That," said the woman, pointing across the room, "is Trooper Mason. I'm Corporal Conway, SBS. Mission details are on your HUD. Tool up, Marine, we've got some baddies to kill!"

"Baddies?" muttered Ten incredulously. "Are you a real person or just a badly scripted sim-character?"

Conway ignored him, and the HUD flashed into life. Mason and Conway were at the door ready to go.

"Who's Davies?" Ten asked, frowning at the squad list in his HUD.

"Over here!" came a reedy voice. Davies held up a hand, but the friendliness of his wave was drowned by the hostility in his face.

"What are you, the cleaner?" he asked.

"Enough of the smart arse attitude," snapped Conway, hostile and impatient. "Trooper Davies is about to unlock all the doors on this wretched spaceship. And when he does, you sure as hell had better have your finger on the trigger. These pirates aren't going to want to release this cargo."

Davies shrugged him off, used to the jibes of Marines. He was one himself, after all, so he knew how it worked. His skills lay elsewhere; they took a while to grow on brawns like Ten.

<Okay, are you up to speed, Ten?> Conway sent.

The message flashed up on Ten's HUD. <Yeah, I got it. Do you have anything for a headache?> he replied.

<You'll soon forget that once you meet these buggers. You'll be more concerned about a ball ache once Double-D over there gets the doors open>

<Double-D?> Ten asked, annoyed at the sudden introduction of new names.

<Dexter Davies over there. He's our tech specialist> Mason chimed in.

"Kill me now," muttered Ten, shaking his head.

"Okay, opening the doors in three, two one," said Davies. He was overjoyed with his own technical acumen.

The sketchy briefing said they were in a storage unit on a pirate ship, but with no explanation as to why. Ten hadn't figured out if they were in space or docked in a hangar. Either way, the bad guys were pirates, the ship was stolen, and they had some sort of collateral – as yet unknown – to seize as part of the simulated operation. They would receive that intel when they reached the internment cell where he, she or it was located.

The heavy black door slid open and rapid gunfire greeted the team. Shrapnel and bullets filled the air and pierced the metal walls, sending shards flying across the corridor as an assault of explosions echoed through the ship. It was only ten enemy guns, but it felt like an army firing at them.

"I thought these were low-budget rent-a-pirates?" said Ten. "Where'd they get tooled up like that?" He ducked back into cover to avoid the incoming hail of bullets.

"Concentrate, Marine," snapped Conway, her tone impatient. She said "Marine" as if it were an insult, and her attitude was beginning to annoy Ten.

Never one to chit-chat, Mason was already on the case. He'd activated a piece of kit about which Ten had heard only rumours from the research team.

"This is my kind of warfare," said Mason, like he was reading Ten's mind.

Davies was on his HUD now, gun at the ready, but he hung back, letting the others take the lead.

Mason activated a metallic disc that hovered just above ankle level. He gave it a nudge, shoving it through the doorway so that it floated off down the corridor toward the pirates; then he ducked back into cover. There was a bright white flash followed by a deep rumble that shook the walls.

"Go!" shouted Conway, charging down the left into the clouds of smoke. Mason followed on the right and Ten took the centre, with Davies following up behind.

As the smoke cleared at the end of the corridor, they found the bodies of ten pirates, all wearing unfamiliar body armour and carrying non-standard weaponry.

"This isn't military kit," said Mason. "Where the hell do these guys get this stuff?"

"It's a fucking simulation," muttered Ten, kicking at a corpse. "Who cares what they're armed with?"

"This is all illegal," said Davies, ignoring the Penal Marine and barely able to contain his excitement. "Some of this shit never made it out of testing, either inhumane or too dangerous. I'm taking one of these, who wants this piece of Sol crap when you can use one of these bad boys?"

He discarded his rifle and prised a heavy weapon from the hands of a dead pirate.

"So long as you use it, DD, I don't particularly care ... target right!" said Conway as she spotted movement.

They all spun to the side as a pirate ducked into the corridor, head-scraping the ceiling. He swung a huge multi-barrelled weapon towards the crew, and it whined as the motors spun.

"Cover," yelled Conway, diving aside as the team scattered.

But Davies was ready with his looted weapon, and it belched fire to punch a fist-sized hole in the giant's chest.

The pirate rocked back, weapon drooping as the strength left his arms. Then there was a dull *crump*, and the man's chest exploded, spraying the corridor with blood.

"Now that's what I call a weapon!" said Davies in a state of weaponry rapture.

"That's why these things are illegal," said Mason sagely. "They're just too much fun, so Sol won't let us use them. A kill is a kill, as far as I'm concerned. And the less effort I have to use to achieve that, the better."

"Simulation," said Ten wearily. "None of it's real."

"We'll do this in pairs," said Conway. "Ten and DD, take the right corridor. Mason, you're with me," she said, heading left. "Clear the decks, make for the elevator down to the internment area. Rendezvous in ten minutes. Go!"

Conway and Mason disappeared up the left-hand corridor, leaving Ten and DD to take the right.

"No shit from her, is there?" said Ten.

"She's good. She saved my arse a bunch of times. Don't doubt her, she knows her stuff," said Davies, jumping to Conway's defence.

Ten shrugged and followed Davies along the corridor. For all his lack of bravado, there was no doubt that DD was a soldier. As they moved stealthily along the darkened corridor, checking rooms as they went, his movements were skilful and practised. He was easy to work with, and Ten found DD's oddities strangely reassuring.

<Light contact. You?> sent Conway.

<Nothing so far. They'll be moving to protect the asset. Any idea what it is?> Ten replied.

<Only that it's a person, not a thing> sent Mason.

<How are we getting out of here?> sent Ten. <Excuse the questions, I was late to the party>

"Hold on, getting a warning," whispered Davies. Then he swore and dragged Ten into a side room, sliding the door closed behind them.

<Drones> Davies raised the alert.

<Taking cover> sent Conway. <Let me know when it's clear>

<Roger> sent Davies.

"Shoot them?" hissed Ten, his rifle aimed at the door. Davies shook his head and held his finger to his lips.

<Booby-trapped> explained Davies. <They explode>

Moving slowly, Davies drew a piece of electrical equipment from a compartment in his body armour.

<What are you going to do, fight them off with a calculator?> Ten teased.

<Watch and learn, newbie> sent Mason, keen to remind Ten that he was the new kid on the block as far as this team of Marines was concerned. <They gave us this mission for a reason>

<Ready to go in three, two, one> sent Davies.

<What just happened?> sent Ten.

<Drones are down. Opening door> Davies replied. He glanced at Ten, checking he had the door covered, then he trigged the release.

The clones were lying on the floor, crashed in a heap and rendered useless.

"How'd you do that?" asked Ten, frowning with suspicion.

"Jammed the control frequency," said Davies. "But it only lasts till they assign new codes. They'll reactivate in about thirty seconds. If we can make it to the main elevator by then, we'll outrun them."

A countdown appeared in Ten's HUD.

<Are you clear, Conway?> sent Davies.

<Clear, meet you at the elevator> Conway responded.

Davies began running.

"Shouldn't we just shoot them?" asked Ten, disturbed to be running from a prone but still dangerous enemy.

<Twenty-two seconds and counting> Davies updated the Marines. <Get moving!>

"Booby-trapped, remember?" said Davies as he ran. "They tend to explode if shot."

Ten ran, following Davies' lead. In his HUD he could see Conway and Mason making rapid progress, sticking to their plan to converge at the elevator where the two corridors met and then make their way down to the internment area.

They raced down the corridor, heedless of other potential threats. With ten seconds still on the clock, Ten heard the clones reactivating.

Conway and Mason were there before them, waiting inside the elevator.

"Hurry it up," shouted Conway, "or we go without you."

There was a deep rumble within the bowels of the ship.

"They're leaving the ship. Someone has taken off in a shuttle," said Mason, a frustrated expression on his face. "Mission failure. Fuck it!"

"Come on," screamed Conway as Davies and Ten pounded the last few metres. "They're right behind you!"

"Oh no they aren't," hissed Ten, giggling at his own inane joke as he and Davies fell at last into the lift. The doors began to slide shut behind them as Conway hammered at the switch.

"Incoming," warned Mason as the drones rose from the ground in a deadly act of resurrection and shot down the corridor toward the lift.

"Duck!" shouted Conway as the drones opened fire, rounds skimming between the closing doors to slap at the lift's inner walls. Conway slapped the elevator's activation button as bullets ripped at the doors. The lift lurched downward, then stopped, jammed in place.

Then there was a massive explosion, and the elevator was blown into a million tiny pieces.

3

"Your performance was lamentable."

Ten recognised the voice. Was that Staines? He wasn't in the same room, but he'd be ready to place a bet on it being the admiral. They were either in deep shit, or something big was about to kick off.

He looked around. Still the headache. Still the sore ear too, only it was back where it belonged now. All intact, once again. Bloody simulations. Sometimes he couldn't work out what was real and what was make-believe, which was why the sims had escape buttons.

The sore head was definitely real, though.

But at least now he was somewhere he recognised. A standard military briefing room. A crappy overhead projector. Seats that made your arse feel like it was on fire after only five minutes. This was what they were all fighting to preserve, their great tradition of freedom and shitty chairs.

Conway walked into the room, accompanied by Davies, Mason and another woman whom Ten hadn't met before.

"Oh, you're real," said Ten in surprise. "Thought you were training material."

None of them acknowledged his comments. They just took their seats alongside him, saying nothing.

Staines' avatar appeared in front of them, an immediate air of authority and status emanating from his very soul. The Marines stood up as he was followed in virtual form by other officers, none of whom they'd seen before. They all remained standing.

Admiral Staines launched straight into him. "Marine X, you're a bloody disgrace!"

"Sir," said Ten promptly, acknowledging the admiral.

He knew he'd blown the training missions. They'd been careless. He'd been careless. First the sniper, then the mined elevator. Leave the ship and booby-trap the exits was a pirate classic, and they'd missed it. Rookie mistakes in both simulations.

"You people are supposed to be the best we've got!" said Staines, spitting his words. He was not a happy man. "And we're out of time. We have to deploy you as an SBS team. Apparently the military hasn't got any better!"

As induction sessions went, they'd all had better.

"Permission to speak, sir?" said the new woman.

She looked like she'd rather rescue a cat from a tree than shoot the enemy, but Ten knew better than to judge a book by its cover. If she was in the same room as him, same as Double-D, they were highly-trained and effective killers. They probably had a few other hobbies too, like DD with his bag of tech.

Staines glared at her, then nodded.

"With respect, sir, the team was incomplete. We can do better."

"I hope you're right, Trooper Kearney, because this is a problem we can do without. We're still fighting the war with the Deathless, and we're seriously stretched. We don't have the time or the resources for an extended battle on a second front."

Ten screwed up his face as he looked towards Davies.

"Marine X, you're a hair's breadth away from being sent back to the front line!" Staines barked. Even in his virtual form, he still had a great military presence.

"I'm at your disposal, sir," said Ten, pitching his tone just the safe side of openly insolent.

"Yes, you bloody well are," snapped Staines, "and you'd better start acting like it."

If the admiral was appearing as an avatar rather than in person, he must have been light-years away. That meant Sol had actually put vital resources into creating this shitty briefing room, wherever it was. It was not money well spent.

Ten put on his serious face. Staines had picked him for this mission, and he wanted to be involved. Further down the command chain, they cut him the slack to play out occasionally, but the admiral and the parade of medals on either side of him knew him only as Penal Marine X.

And they'd chosen him anyway, in spite of failing two back-to-back simulations. Either times were tough, they were up shit creek without a paddle, or – even worse – both of those things. Staines glared at him for a moment before continuing with the briefing.

"We've assembled this team at short notice for a highly classified mission. Marine X, you're seconded to Charlie Team SBS as a temporary replacement for Sergeant Gallagher. You'll be joining Charlie Team."

"What happened to Gallagher?" Ten asked.

A frosty chill descended on the room.

"Drop it," Davies whispered to Ten, "touchy subject."

He could tell he'd entered delicate territory, but Staines ignored the interruption.

"You've been assigned a light patrol craft, *Solux IX*, to take you from this outpost to the staging point on *Kingdom 10*. There you'll receive your mission briefing and meet the final member of your team."

"Who's that going to be?" said Ten. Sometimes it was hard to keep his mouth shut.

"That's compartmentalised and even I don't know, but you'll obviously be told when you meet them. You'll receive your formal briefing from Admiral Stansfield."

There was a palpable ripple through the room. Stansfield was a name connected with military royalty. They'd all heard the stories and legends in basic training, but he'd been dead – or assumed to be dead – for a hundred and sixteen years. Maybe this was some relative? Ten frowned but kept his thoughts to himself; they'd find out soon enough.

"Needless to say, four of you know the high personal stakes with this mission. I don't need to remind you. Marine X, you are in a very privileged position; it's why we allowed you to experience real pain in the simulations. You need to remember that not everyone gets to return."

"How do we get to our final destination, sir?" Davies asked. He looked around as he said it, like he was asking for the rest of the room.

There was a pause. Staines looked like he was considering his words. "Conway will fly you out."

There was an uncomfortable shuffling from amongst the team. Ten looked at Conway, but her face gave nothing away.

"You need to get back on the horse after the loss of Gallagher," Staines said, an air of sympathy in his voice for the first time. "You're a most accomplished pilot, Corporal, but sometimes things go wrong, as you all know."

Marine X made a badly-timed attempt to loosen up the atmosphere. "Better hope we're luckier than Gallagher, eh?"

He'd barely finished the sentence when her fist came crashing across his chin with a force so hard it knocked him to his knees.

"Bastard!" she shouted.

Davies, Mason and Kearney turned in horror to the avatar of Admiral Staines. The virtual entourage surrounding him seemed equally aghast, looking to the admiral for a cue on how to respond to what had just happened.

"I'm sorry, we received some signal interference there," Staines began. "You broke up for a moment. You appear to have a nosebleed, Marine X. Get that looked at before you fly out."

Ten picked himself up from the floor and got back on his feet, feeling his nose to see if it had been broken.

"We're relying on you all, Charlie Team. I won't pretend this isn't a perilous mission, but I know you're up to the job. Good luck!"

As the admiral's avatar turned away, Ten caught the tail-end of his last words. *She can have that one on me. I've wanted to punch that Marine myself on many an occasion.*

"Too soon for a joke," muttered Ten in a rare moment of humility. He'd judged it wrong, come in too fast and too strong. These guys were a team, he was the outsider. It wasn't like a front-line Marine company where they worked with a large number of colleagues.

The Special Boat Service worked almost exclusively in small patrols of maybe half a dozen. They rarely fought at platoon strength. This was a tight team, and it seemed they'd somehow suffered a permanent loss, which was almost unheard of these days. He needed to give these kids time to adjust to his presence.

And if Conway drove a space shuttle half as well as she threw a punch, they were all in capable hands.

"Any idea who the sixth member of the team will be?" Davies asked. "We usually operate as five, I can see why Ten is here, but a sixth?"

"Don't look at me," Conway replied, rubbing her hand. Ten felt like she was made from concrete, but he deserved it even if she now had the swelling to prove it.

"So what do we know about our mission? And is that one of *the* Stansfields, do you think?" Kearney was speaking to the rest of the group for the first time. She was clearly at ease with these people.

"There's something serious going on in the Eagle Nebula," Conway replied. "Top secret, as Staines said, super classified. I know they're pissed off. They could do without it, what with the Deathless and all that. I take it that's where you've come from, Ten?"

He took his chance to do some bonding. It wasn't really his style, but he knew well how teams like this had to work. He'd suggest a group hug if it would help to thaw things with Conway.

"Yeah, front-line. Bit of a shitstorm. It's a long time since I've been cloned this far out in space."

"Hell, man, you're cloned?" Mason jumped in.

They all looked at him.

"Guess who just got lucky! It's curtains for us if we take a hit, we don't get to clone it out in this battle."

4

Staines was right to place his trust in Conway as a pilot. She handled the patrol craft with confidence and a sure hand. As *Solux IX* sat in the launch bay, Ten watched the stars on one of its displays and considered how much he missed by having his mind deployed through wormholes into a cloned body. It was a great way to dispatch Marines across the light-years, faster than a ship could get them there, but there was no time to take in the scenery.

And what spectacular scenery it was.

"Cleared for launch, *Solux IX*," said Control.

"Roger, launching now," said Conway, triggering the manoeuvring thrusters as the bay doors opened. The patrol craft was a small, sleek vehicle built for short-range missions. With space for a crew of twelve, it felt spacious with only the five of them on board.

Conway nudged the ship away from the outpost – Ten realised he hadn't even found out what it was called during their short time on the station – and set a course that would take them to a safe distance for the move to hyperspace.

"Manoeuvring thrusters for fifteen seconds," she reported, "then main engines at full power for sixty seconds. Hyperspace drive engagement in six hundred seconds. Buckle up, people."

"Nice ship, right?" said Double-D as he worked through the scanners, familiarising himself with *Solux IX*'s tech.

"Maybe," said Ten doubtfully, "when it's finished." He nodded at the gaping holes in the instrument and control panels, where some subsystems hadn't yet been installed. *Solux IX* wasn't new, and it looked like its refit wasn't even complete.

"It's a bit pokey," said Ten, frowning at the tightly packed command room where the team had congregated.

"You probably only travel on really big ships, right?" sneered Mason. "*Solux IX* isn't good enough for Mr Big Shot. What do you want, *Dreadnought*?" He barked a laugh, but Ten wasn't amused. *Dreadnought's* reactivation wasn't supposed to be common knowledge.

"What have you heard about *Dreadnought*, Mason?" he asked with a tone of quiet menace.

"Heard? Why would I have heard anything about that old relic? It was a joke, fuckwit. Get over yourself."

Ten settled back into his chair, unconvinced, and triggered his HUD to read the background material to their mission.

Kingdom 10 was an orbital space station, a former naval outpost so old it had been decommissioned decades before and turned over to a government-sponsored scientific mission. It was a throwback to the earliest days of Sol's exploration, a relic from an ancient age.

Much like me, thought Ten with a snort.

But *Kingdom 10* was holding up well, all things considered. The Mark 3 stations had been built at what were then the furthest reaches of explored space, and they were now merely staging posts, manned by skeleton crews of civilian scientists and technical personnel who were happy to be all but abandoned in the middle of nowhere.

Everything had changed when the Deathless had invaded New Bristol. *Kingdom 10* was no longer a holiday camp for anti-social civilians, and their peaceful existence had been disrupted by the arrival of a Royal Navy supply vessel laden with personnel, updated equipment and a plethora of new orders. Unusually for these isolated outposts, it now had a substantial military presence, and a hasty refit was underway to bring the structure in line with present-day military requirements.

"So why aren't they just sending clones out here to deal with this thing?" Ten asked Davies a few hours later as *Solux IX* slipped through hyperspace. They were in the ship's small mess, bonding over the shared horror of an indescribable microwave meal.

"Good question," said Davies with a bitter laugh. "We're all stuck in our original bodies because we were on our way to help establish a permanent military presence in one of the newer colonies. A sort of semi-retirement, a break after years of service. We weren't supposed to deploy to active service, but as you can see, in wartime there are no guarantees on that one."

"Okay," said Ten slowly, "makes sense, I guess, but why not switch to clones? You're backed up, right?"

"We are, but with a forty-eight-hour delay. No fucking clue why. Some mix-up somewhere, they said. No time to fix it or download to clones before we shipped out, apparently. We went straight into training, then briefing, then shipping out here."

"Briefing says *Kingdom 10* doesn't have cloning bays," said Ten.

"Or a decent wormhole communicator, if you can believe it. Low-bandwidth, audio and low-res video only. We're right out in the sticks, totally on our own."

"So if somebody dies...?"

"Yeah. If you die, you're fucked until someone walks your backup to a cloning facility several light-years away," said Davies.

Ten frowned and poked at his meal. "So you're stuck in these bodies till this is done?"

"Looks that way," said Davies bitterly. "At least you've got a proper RMSC clone, I'm in Human 1.0."

They finished their meals in silence.

"Why does Conway fly if she started as a Marine?" asked Ten as they headed back to the command room. "She seems to know how to handle this thing."

"Yeah, she wasn't always a Marine, let's just put it that way. Sometimes they need troopers who have a particular set of skills, right? I take it that's why you're here?"

"Probably," Ten murmured. "Though on my CV I would just list my special skills as *killing things and breaking stuff.*"

Davies seemed to find that funny, but when was the last time Ten had needed a CV? He couldn't remember. His personnel files were so heavily restricted that not even Admiral Staines had access to the full details.

"Dropping out of hyperspace in sixty seconds," announced Conway as Davies and Ten took their seats in the command room. "Then it's a nice easy run to *Kingdom 10.*"

"And another bloody briefing," moaned Mason. "Why didn't they just give it to us all at once?"

"Quit whining," said Kearney. "You're getting paid, aren't you?"

"Ha," said Ten, shaking his head. As a Penal Marine, he wasn't due to be paid for his services until his sentence was complete.

"Ah, right, you don't get shit, do you?" sneered Mason. "What did you do, in any case?"

They all turned to look at Marine X, not bothering to disguise their interest in the story of how he'd lost his name and ended up in the penal system.

"It's a long story," said Ten quietly, "and I'm not telling it now."

"Aw, come on," said Kearney, "we need to know who we're working with if we're going to trust you."

Ten looked at them all, then shook his head.

"Probably disobeyed an order," said Mason dismissively, turning away and picking up his data slate. "Or failed too many missions."

Ten said nothing.

Then *Solux IX* dropped out of hyperspace, and the plan fell apart.

"Mayday, mayday," squawked the comms system. "This is *Kingdom 10*. We are in urgent need of assistance. Please respond."

For a moment, the crew were silent. Then Kearney barked, and everyone moved at once.

Davies checked the comms system. "Looks like a genuine signal," he said. "They have the right security tags, and their broadcast has been authenticated by our system. Radio comms only, so it's purely a local call."

"No wormhole generator," said Ten. "We might be the only people to hear their call for months."

"I guess we'd better take a closer look," said Kearney, "and open a channel, see if we can get a little more detail."

Conway acknowledged the order. "Ten thousand klicks to *Kingdom 10*, firing engines at full power, sixty-second burn."

There was a roar from the rear of the ship, and it kicked forward, pressing the crew into their seats.

"Mason, find out what the hell's going on."

"Working on it," said Mason, all professional now that he had something to do. He tapped and swiped at his data slate, interfacing with the ship's sensors.

"Comms open," said Davies.

"*Kingdom 10*, this is the light patrol craft *Solux IX*. We are on course to dock with you in" – she paused to check the main display as the nav-computer updated their flight plan – "about thirty-five minutes."

"*Solux IX*, good to hear your voice." The man sounded stressed and afraid, but relieved to have someone to talk to.

"What's the nature of your problem, *Kingdom 10*?"

"We have a collision impact warning," said the voice of *Kingdom 10*. "High likelihood of major structural damage in ten minutes, medium risk of total destruction of the station. Anything you could do to help..."

Kearney muted the audio as a data package arrived. She opened it and flicked the contents across to the main display. It showed *Kingdom 10's* location in orbit around a large Earth-like planet, and the path of the objects that threatened to destroy the station.

"Shit," muttered Conway, "not good."

"*Kingdom 10*," said Kearney reopening the audio, "we're a long way off. Can you evacuate to the planet's surface?"

"Negative, *Solux IX*, we have three hundred people and only a ship-to-ship transport shuttle."

"Understood. We're working on it." She muted the audio again. "Mason, what's the situation?"

"Looks like a cloud of debris heading toward the station. Mostly small stuff, but there's a couple of larger pieces that could do a lot of damage."

"What the hell do we do about this?" said Kearney quietly.

"Delete the logs and head home? Tell everyone we arrived too late to help?" offered Mason.

"Three hundred people," said Ten into the sudden quiet of the command room.

"They'll be backed up," pointed out Mason, "and what can we do anyway?"

"We can try," said Kearney, and there was steel in her voice. "Conway, can you give us a flightpath that presents a firing solution on the largest pieces of debris? We can knock them clear or grind them into smaller pieces."

"Ballsy," said Conway with a frown. "I'll have a look, but it's not going to be pretty."

"DD, get our weapons systems online."

"Already on it. We have self-guided missiles and manually targeted railguns."

"Manually targeted?" asked Ten, incredulous.

"Weapons computer hasn't been fitted yet," said Davies, nodding at a hole in the wall. "It's in the hold if you're interested."

"No time," said Conway. "Plug yourselves in and get ready for action."

"Standing by," said Davies. Ten grunted his readiness.

There was a sudden and forceful collision that shook their vessel.

"Belt up, everybody!" said Conway. "Looks like we've found the edge of Mason's cloud of debris. I hope you cleaned your teeth and are ready for action, guys!"

"Cut the chatter," snapped Kearney. "Let's get a flight solution together that doesn't see us all smashed to shit out here."

"Got it," said Conway, flicking a plan to the main display. "We go right through the middle, shooting the larger bits to knock them clear of *Kingdom 10* or break them up. Should work."

They all stared at the plan for a few seconds, but it wasn't getting any prettier. Mason shook his head while Davies quietly whistled. It was a plan, but nobody liked the look of it.

"Grim," said Kearney, speaking for them all. "Let's do it." It wasn't like they had options. She reopened the comms channel and dumped their new plan down the link to *Kingdom 10*. "We're on our way. Hold tight, *Kingdom 10*."

Solux IX twisted and spun as Conway used the manoeuvring thrusters to re-orient the ship; then the main engines fired again.

"Three-hundred-second burn at full power," said Conway, straining against the forces that pressed her into her chair. The crew groaned until Conway snapped at them to shut up.

"That'll take us past the station in about eight minutes," said Conway. *Solux IX* rumbled and shuddered as the engines pushed her along. "If we don't break up on the way," she added as a panel fell off the wall and bounced across the cabin.

The command room fell silent as Charlie Team concentrated on keeping themselves in one piece while the brutal forces crushed them into their seats.

"How long till we have something to shoot at?" Mason asked when the engines finally cut off.

"We can hit the big bits with missiles," said Davies, his face shiny with sweat, "in about ninety seconds. Smaller stuff with the railguns as you see it."

Ten peered at his display. The ship's sensors highlighted the small pieces of debris, but without the targeting computer, it was hopeless. "Too fast, too small, too far away," he said, shaking his head.

"We have to try, dammit," snapped Kearney. Something bounced off the hull hard enough to shake them in their seats.

"He's right," said Davis, "this isn't going to work."

"*Solux IX*, we have a problem," said *Kingdom 10*.

"We're working on it," said Kearney through gritted teeth. "This isn't easy, you know." Behind her, Mason triggered one of the railguns and spewed rounds at a piece of debris as the ship tore past.

"Got it," he said with a mixture of surprise and satisfaction. In the corner of the main display, a zoomed-in video showed the fragment breaking apart and spinning off in a new direction as the rounds ripped it apart.

"I have missile lock on the main debris," said Mason. "Ready to fire in thirty seconds."

"Negative, *Solux IX*, do not fire on that target," said *Kingdom 10* suddenly.

Solux IX took another blow from a smaller piece of wreckage, jolting them in their seats.

"It's going to wipe you out, *Kingdom 10*," said Kearney. "We have to hit it soon."

"Negative," repeated *Kingdom 10*. "Scans show it contains a hyperspace engine core. Missile impact might cause a catastrophic explosion."

"Well, fuck," said Mason, throwing his hands up in frustration.

"How bad are we talking, *Kingdom 10*?" asked Kearney.

"It would kill anyone within a hundred thousand kilometres and sterilise this side of the planet," said *Kingdom 10*, "so pretty bad."

"We could try shooting it with the railguns," said Ten, but it was a shitty idea, and he knew it.

"What's our closest approach to the debris?" asked Kearney.

"About twenty kilometres, give or take, in just under three minutes," said Conway with a guarded tone. "Why, what are you thinking?"

Kearney was silent for a few seconds. "Three hundred people," she muttered; then she shook her head, decision made. "Put us on a collision course," she said firmly. "Not a direct strike, just bounce us off the debris and knock it off course."

"That's insane," said Mason. "We'll all be killed."

"Are you sure about that?" asked Conway, glancing at Kearney with a frown. "If we get it wrong…"

"Can you see another way of getting it done? Speak now," said Kearney forcefully. "Otherwise, get it done. We're wasting time."

"Environment suits?" suggested Davies. "Might help if we survive the impact."

"No time," said Conway as her hands flashed across the computer console, generating a new flight solution. "How's that?"

Davies looked at the plan and sucked in air through his teeth. "Trim the angle a few degrees," he said, "so we strike further up."

Conway's hands flicked over the console. "Better?"

"Yeah, should give it a gentle nudge," said Davies, although it was clear he wasn't happy with the plan.

"This is suicide," warned Mason, but nobody was listening.

"Program is laid in and ready to run," said Conway as they all stared at the main display.

"Punch it," said Kearney.

Conway hit the trigger. "Manoeuvring thrusters for ten seconds, then a sixty-second main engine burn. Impact ninety seconds after that."

"Impact velocity?" asked Kearney as the new flight plan flashed onto the main display. It showed *Solux IX* looping in toward the debris to strike it only seconds before it reached *Kingdom 10*.

"About fifty-five metres per second," said Conway. The manoeuvring thrusters stopped, and the main engines fired. "And now all we do is wait." She flicked the display to show the forward view, with flight trajectories over the top and a bright blue circle around the target debris.

"Sixty seconds," she said, although they could all see the countdown timer. "If this goes badly, just know that it's been fun working with you."

"*Solux IX*, your new course is taking you close to the target," said *Kingdom 10*. Kearney explained the new plan, and there was a brief silence. "Good luck, *Solux IX*. And thank you."

"Just make sure you've smoked the kippers, *Kingdom 10*," said Kearney, "and we'll be back for breakfast."

"Fifteen seconds," said Conway.

They watched *Kingdom 10* shake violently as three smaller fragments struck the station, one after the other, in rapid succession.

"Look at the size of that thing!" said Davies as the fragment filled the display. "What happened out here?"

"It's from one of ours, no doubt about it," said Mason, his tone grim. "That's no piece of space junk, it's from one of our newer battleships. Who the hell blew that to smithereens?"

"I've a nasty feeling we'll be finding out soon," said Ten.

"Five seconds," said Conway. "Losing power. That last impact must have hit something vital." Her hands flew over the console as she fired the manoeuvring thrusters to tweak their trajectory

"Fuck," said Mason as the debris filled the display. They all leaned away from the screen, as if that would do any good.

Then there was the most awful impact, and the crew were thrown against their restraints. The ship was filled with the scream of klaxons and the screech of tearing metal. Hull breach alarms flashed across the display before it went blank. Then the ship began to spin violently, the lights failed, and the last thing Ten heard before he blacked out was Conway's final update.

"Impact."

5

Ten came around first. His augmented clone comfortably outperformed Charlie Team's pure human bodies, and he blinked himself awake, ignoring the pain in his neck and head.

It took him a moment to get his bearings. The ship had stopped spinning, but only the emergency lights were on. The command room was bathed in a dim red light, and all the displays were off.

"Kearney?" he called, rubbing at his neck. "Davies? Conway?"

"I'm here," said Conway with a groan. She released herself from her chair and pushed herself free. "Gravity's off," she reported, then floated across to check Kearney while Ten shook Davies.

"Gngh!" said Davies as he woke. "Are we dead?"

"Feels like it," muttered Kearney. She looked around, wincing at the pain. "Check Mason."

Davies pushed himself out of his chair and checked Mason's pulse. "He's alive." Then he groaned as he hung in the air.

"How do we get things working again, Double-D?" said Kearney. "Everything's dead on my console."

Davies was quiet for a moment. "Need to restart the central systems. Looks like they're all offline."

"How do we do that?"

"Someone needs to get into the hold and trigger a manual reboot." He didn't sound enthusiastic.

"There's a manual reboot, but it's in the hold, not the cabin?"

"Yup. And yes, there should be a redundancy in the cabin, but no, there really isn't."

"And after we do that?" asked Conway.

Davies shrugged. "Depends what's broken."

"Get a move on, then," said Kearney. "Take Ten with you and get it sorted out."

Ten and Davies shared a look, but there was no way out of it.

"After you," said Ten, pointing at the door at the back of the command room. They floated over, checked that the pressure indicator was showing atmosphere on the far side, then worked the lever to open the door.

"Take this," said Conway, tossing a small flashlight to Ten. He flicked it on and shone it out into the dark corridor that led into the rest of the ship.

"Thanks," he said without enthusiasm, and then he and Davies pushed themselves through the doorway.

"Better close this," said Davies, working the lever again. "Don't want nasty things to happen."

"Ha," snorted Ten, playing the torch along the walls of the corridor. "Where are the environment suits?"

"Next door down," said Davies. "Storage cupboard." They floated over, pulled out a pair of suits, and spent the next few minutes scrambling into them.

"That's better," said Ten, flicking on the helmet lamps and checking that the communicator worked. "You can hear me?"

"Ay, loud and clear," said Davies.

At the end of the corridor, the door monitor showed vacuum in the hold beyond, and they paused to check everything was secure.

Then Ten operated the lever, and the door slid partway open. The atmosphere was quickly sucked from the corridor, and when the door was fully open, they could see why. A huge gash had been torn in the ceiling, opening the hold to the vacuum of space.

"Guess we won't be getting our deposit back," muttered Ten. "Where do we find this reboot switch thing?"

"Over here," said Davies, pulling himself into the hold. "Should be behind this panel." He whistled tunelessly as he struggled to open the panel in the suit's heavily insulated gloves.

"Do you reckon it worked?" asked Ten as Davies grappled with the panel's fittings.

"No idea," said Davies through gritted teeth. "Ah, got you, you bugger," he said as the panel swung open. "Let's give this a go."

He squinted at the controls, then flicked the big switch labelled "Power".

Nothing happened.

Davies toggled it back and forth a couple of times, then swore.

"Do you need to press that one as well?" asked Ten, pointing at a button labelled "On".

"Hmm, yeah, maybe," conceded Davies. He flicked the power switch, then pressed the button, and a small display came on. "Okay, says it's restarting."

"Job done," said Ten.

The screen flashed red and began to show alarms and warnings. Then the internal comms system came online, and Ten and Davies were able to link their HUDs to the main computer.

"It lives," breathed Davies, not daring to hope. "Let's see what we have left," he muttered, switching to diagnostics. He scrolled through the screens for a few moments, then jumped when Kearney called his name.

"Davies, we have comms back. Are you hearing me?"

"Loud and clear. Beautiful view of the stars back here where there should be a nice solid hull. Just checking for other damage. Looks like we might have a few systems that still sort of work."

"We need engines and thrusters, Double-D. Everything else can wait."

"Engines and thrusters," muttered Davies as he flicked through the screens. "Okay, here's the bill: multiple hull breaches, near-total loss of atmosphere, reserve tanks ruptured, nav-computer is a bit dicky, fabs are offline, and the coffee machine is fucked. Looks like thrusters are working, main power is at about fifteen per cent, engines are largely functional."

"Better than expected. Life support?"

"Er, no," said Davies unhappily. "The air scrubbers are toast, the artificial gravity is obviously offline, water recycling is fucked. Kitchen should be okay, but we'll die of lack of oxygen before food is a problem."

"Death is better than those microwave meals," muttered Ten.

"Anything else you can do from back there?"

"Don't think so," said Davies.

"Then get yourselves back up here," said Kearney. "Conway's going to point us at the station and try to get us home before we all expire."

"Ah, tricky," said Davies. "There isn't enough air left to flood the corridor. I think Ten and I are stuck out here for the moment."

There was a moment of silence from the command room, as if Kearney and Conway were having a private discussion.

"Find somewhere safe," said Kearney eventually, "and get ready for manoeuvring thrusters."

"Roger," acknowledged Davies, "give us a moment." He closed and secured the panel, then looked around the hold.

"Anything useful down here?" asked Ten.

"Sure," said Davies, "if we had enough time to make use of it. As it is..." He shrugged.

"Might as well get inside, then," said Ten, pushing himself back to the door.

Davies followed, and they closed the door behind them as soon as they were in the corridor.

"Manoeuvring thrusters in ten seconds," said Conway over the comms system. "Then everything the engine will give us for as long as it'll give it to us. Hold on."

∽

Forty-five minutes later, Conway announced that *Solux IX* had scrubbed its speed and was now accelerating gently towards *Kingdom 10*.

"We should arrive only a few hours after we run out of warmth and oxygen," she announced, "but at least Mason's awake. Seems he took a heavy blow to the head, but he should be fine until he suffocates."

"Good to know," said Ten. "Any chance *Kingdom 10* might rescue us in their shuttle?"

"Can't reach them," said Kearney. "Might be our comms, might be theirs."

"Or that little stunt failed, and they're all dead," said Mason bitterly.

"Or that," agreed Kearney. "Either way, we're on our own."

"We've got maybe fifteen minutes of O2 left," said Ten. He and Davies were floating in the corridor between the hold and the command room, moving as little as possible to conserve their air.

"Roger," said Kearney. "We're not much better off in here," she said, "and we're hours from *Kingdom 10* if they're even still alive. Been nice knowing you."

There was nothing to do but wait for the inevitable.

Then there was a chime on the comms system, and a new voice interrupted their silent thoughts.

"Patrol craft *Solux IX*," said the unidentified voice, "are you in need of assistance?"

"Fuck, yes," said Kearney trying to keep the relief from her voice, "welcome to the party. We're a bit short of O2. Any chance of a pick-up?"

"We're well ahead of you, *Solux IX*. Hang tight, we'll have you out of there in a jiffy."

∾

en minutes later the crew staggered from the wreck of *Solux IX* into a vast, dimly-lit hangar, with maintenance teams and engineering types rushing around like ants in their nest.

On the deck was a combination of craft. There was stuff they recognised – modern gunboats, a couple of shuttles and their associated paraphernalia, a collection of automated weapons platforms. But there were also old ships that Ten had never seen in person, or designs which had only been encountered in history lessons or in Space Corps handbooks. And there was new gear, stuff none of them had ever seen before.

"Welcome aboard," said an officer as they assembled on the deck, giving no sign at all that they were welcome. "I'm Lieutenant Alex Fernandez. I run the engineering teams on *Vengeance*. While you are aboard this ship, you will do precisely as instructed. No wandering off, no peeking into corners, no enterprising investigation. Is that clear?"

"What ship is this, sir?" asked Ten. He'd ditched his helmet, but he and Davies both still wore their environment suits.

Fernandez looked him over and clearly didn't like what he saw. "And you are?"

"Marine X, sir. The lasses and lads call me 'Ten'," as he gave Fernandez a quick salute. "The ship?"

Lieutenant Fernandez's eyes dropped to the tag on Marine X's uniform and its non-standard border. "You're a Penal Marine? Follow orders on this ship, or you'll be in the brig before you know what's happening, understood? The old man won't be happy they've sent you. You would have been briefed on *Kingdom 10*, if you'd made it that far," said Fernandez coldly. "Now you'll have to wait for answers."

"You can't tell us which ship we're on?" said Ten with a frown. "Why not?"

Fernandez ignored him. "Follow me," he said, leading them across the hangar.

"What about *Kingdom 10*, sir?" asked Conway at the door to a small mess hall as the rest of the crew filed in.

He gave her a hard stare, then said, "Better than expected. Some minor casualties, two fatalities, impact damage across four sectors and a hull breach, but your manoeuvre worked. We're clearing the rest of the debris at the moment."

"Thank fuck for that," muttered Kearney, closing her eyes and blowing out a long breath.

"What was the battleship?" asked Mason. "And what was it even doing this far out in space with the war on? Doesn't Sol have other fires to fight?"

Fernandez ignored him. "Wait here. Briefing in thirty minutes." And then he left them alone.

"I thought things were going to be boring around here," said Ten once they were alone, "but I think I can safely say you've piqued my interest."

"Good job on the flight plan, Conway," Kearney said. "And on getting the ship restarted, DD. How did you know to adjust the trajectory?"

"Do you really want to know the science?" DD asked. "I warn you, you won't like it."

Mason, Kearney, Conway and Ten looked at him; then Conway shrugged. "We'll pass, we learnt our lesson from that cloaking trick you pulled before they stationed us out here."

"Cloaking?" Ten asked, intrigued. He'd heard rumours of the research, but it had never gone anywhere.

"Seriously, don't ask," laughed Kearney. "Just think of it like this. DD plus science and shit equals amazing. He's got the Midas touch, seriously, this man can turn turds into gold. Though no, it wasn't real cloaking, he cheated. But it was still cool."

"Just don't rely on him in a firefight," Mason added, walking away to inspect the coffee machine.

"Hey, we're not killing machines like you, Mason," Davies protested. "Some of us prefer to use our brains as well as our brawn. Besides, it hurts less, and there's no blood. That's how I prefer it."

Kearney's data slate pinged, and she opened a call from *Kingdom 10*.

"This is Captain Nikolas Orwell, commander of *Kingdom 10*," said the caller. "The station is safe thanks to you, but you're about to enter a shit storm, ladies and gentlemen. The crew of *Kingdom 10* are immensely grateful for your service here."

"Thank you, sir," said Kearney. "That means a lot. Can you tell us where the debris came from?"

Orwell hesitated. "This information is highly classified, and I probably shouldn't tell you, but it was the battleship *Colossus*. She delivered supplies and equipment, then went to investigate the portal."

"*Colossus*? That's fresh from the shipyards, isn't it?" Ten tried to keep up with this stuff as best he could, in between befriending space monkeys and shooting at enemy clones that looked like lizardmen from a fantasy game.

"As new as they come," replied Orwell. "Her loss is a huge blow, that's for sure. *Colossus* was needed badly for the war against the Deathless. I have to go. Thanks again. Orwell out."

Mason passed around coffee from the machine, and they all sat down to await the return of Lieutenant Fernandez.

"Did you ever have a telescope as a kid?" Kearney asked Conway.

"Of course. I used to look up at the stars and hope I'd get to travel to them for myself one day."

"Me too. Sometimes I have to stop myself to appreciate the wonder of it all. In between shooting dickheads and avoiding exploding space debris, that is."

For Ten, the whole trip was a bore. The novelty of space travel had worn off already. He preferred deployment by clone. It was a lot faster, and you didn't have to wait around for any action. So why hadn't they just deployed his clone to whatever this ship was? Why all the diversions?

He sensed there was something big coming their way, so it seemed a great opportunity to get some shut-eye. One thing was for sure, HQ wasn't in the habit of arranging excursions or pleasure trips for new arrivals. If he knew his superiors, Charlie Team would barely get a chance to draw breath before they were back in the heat of action again.

"Wake me if anything happens," said Ten. He padded over to the edge of the mess, slid onto a long couch, and took his sleep where he could find it. He must have needed it too, because one hour and one full bladder later, he was awoken by some excitement.

"Look at this, Ten," said Mason, pointing at a large vid-screen in the mess, "it's *Vengeance*. It's only bloody *Vengeance*! No wonder they wouldn't tell us where we were heading, I can't believe it's still out here!"

Kearney was out of her mind with excitement. *Vengeance* was part of Royal Naval folklore, her exploits and successes well known by any Sol cadet worthy of their place in the military. The vid-screen showed a potted history of the ship and an image of her floating in space.

"Hacked my way onto their network," said Davies when Ten asked where the information had come from. "This is just the public stuff."

Vengeance sat like a mirage in space, a remnant of earlier explorations of the universe. She was seven thousand light-years away from Earth; that was still some feat at the time she'd been built. To her side was the spectacular sight of the Eagle Nebula, beautiful clouds of gas collapsing inward and dancing deep in space for millions of years.

"She's an Astute19 battleship," said Davies, "one of the originals. What a sight! What the hell is she doing this far out in space? How is she even still operational?"

"Looks like she's seen better days," said Ten. "They might have given her a lick of paint. I know the Navy likes to hang onto their ships, but *Vengeance* looks more like a museum piece."

"Don't underestimate her," Kearney answered almost defensively. "That ship has seen some shit, and somehow they always figured a way out of it. If this is the original vessel, we're in for a treat."

"Didn't somebody mention Stansfield earlier on?" said Mason. "It couldn't be *the* Stansfield, could it? Is that even possible, did they have cloning in his time?"

"I'm pretty certain they didn't," said Kearney. "It must be some descendant or something like that. Naval families like that tend to keep it in the family. I'll bet it's some great-great-great-great-great nephew or something like that, riding on Admiral Stansfield's coat-tails. Lucky bugger, imagine having a pedigree like that in your family."

"Yeah, imagine," Ten muttered.

Then the door slid open, and Fernandez marched back in.

6

"For anyone who has already forgotten, I'm Lieutenant Fernandez, Engineering Officer," said Fernandez unnecessarily. "Welcome to almost certain death. We also call it *Vengeance*."

Mason began to speak, but Fernandez shut him down immediately.

"Everything you see or experience from the moment you arrived on this ship to the moment you see it disappear – if we live that long – is highly classified. The admiral will explain that to you himself at the briefing. Admiral Stansfield doesn't like smart arses," Fernandez warned them. "So park any attitude, and you'll find him easy to get on with. As easy as your average ogre, that is."

He paused as the doors to the mess opened again, and a small group of officers came in.

"This is Commander Vernon, second in command to Admiral Stansfield, and Executive Officer of *Vengeance*. Believe me, you're honoured."

Vernon's face looked like it had previously belonged to three careless owners. What hair he had was completely grey and cut short. The uniform he wore – in fact, all the uniforms on this ship – were

British standard from a previous generation, with washed-out fabric and his dulled medals.

"Commander Edward Vernon, he's a legend too," Davies whispered to Ten. "But how is this guy even here? He must be hundreds of years old! Possibly even older than you."

"He looks it, too," Ten replied. "I hope they've got some paint left over, because he could do with a couple of coats."

Kearney stifled a laugh and straightened up as the commander approached.

"Welcome aboard *Vengeance*, Charlie Team, your sixth team member is here already."

Davies looked at Ten, who shrugged. They'd almost forgotten the extra member. After the shoot-out in space and the near-death experience on *Solux IX*, they were beginning to feel like a proper team. A new addition might throw things off, particularly if they were straight into action.

"Admiral Stansfield has requested that I escort you to the briefing room. He's waiting for you there. Keep your questions to yourselves until the briefing."

With no further ceremony, Vernon led them out of the mess and into the ship's corridors.

The more they saw, the clearer it was that this ship was as old and battered as it had looked from the outside. There was a faint but persistent rumble, presumably from the engine rooms or the heating system, and an all-pervading smell of age and oil. Everything was consistent with Royal Navy history and tradition, but *Vengeance* seemed out of place, a relic from another time. It was like nothing they'd experienced in their lives in the Commonwealth and allied fleets.

Vernon and his small entourage said nothing as they made their way along the oppressive corridors of the battleship. Ten took it all in, watching, learning, absorbing.

The rest of the team were also hyper-vigilant. They continuously scanned their surroundings, familiarising themselves with the layout, the signage, probable points of entry during a boarding action, and so on.

That was a good indicator for their level of professionalism. The SBS – Special Boat Service – were elite specialists, and the selection process hadn't really changed since World War II.

Most troopers were recruited from the Royal Marines, so they were already trained to a standard well above the rank and file of the British Army. Even though the applicants were serving Special Forces personnel or Marines, the selection process was so tough that it weeded out more than half the applicants in each intake.

The SBS required the highest standards of physical fitness and mental toughness, particularly in terms of endurance, intelligence, cunning and combat proficiency. Most applicants had a specialism like sniping or demolitions, and anyone who didn't would undoubtedly pick one up after their training completed.

Just knowing these were experienced members of the SBS meant Ten could trust them to be qualified. That didn't mean he wasn't reassured by seeing their skills in action, but it boded well for the mission.

But none had served as long as him, of that he was certain. He was the old hand, the most experienced member of the team even though he was the newbie.

At last, four levels up, they arrived at the briefing room. Vernon entered first and indicated that they should remain standing, even though there was a perfectly adequate number of seats. Ten missed Vernon's cue and pulled out one of the chairs.

"Stand, Marine!" Stansfield barked, without looking up from his data slate.

Never one to give the stripes the complete upper hand, Ten opted for a relaxed lean instead. It was upright enough not to make Stansfield interrupt proceedings again, but casual enough to draw a smirk from his colleagues in Charlie Team. He didn't want the others to think he gave too much of a shit now, did he?

Admiral Thomas Stansfield was grey-faced and worn. He looked like a man who'd been asleep for hundreds of years and was no less pissed off than if his alarm clock had just gone off to wake him up for this briefing only five minutes earlier. He emanated an air of impatience and bad temper. His hair, unlike Vernon's, still had streaks of black hanging on within the untidy mess. He looked like a forgotten retiree left on duty by an inattentive commander.

"Welcome aboard, Charlie Team," he said finally, his voice rich and deep. "And congratulations on what you did for *Kingdom 10*."

Oh, he's not so bad!

The thought ran through their heads at the same time.

"... but you'll need ten times that level of commitment if you're going to be any use to me here."

Damn, not so good.

Stansfield looked at Vernon. "Is he ready?"

Vernon nodded.

"Bring him in."

Vernon touched a device on his lapel. "Okay, let's have him."

Stansfield didn't bother to fill the awkward silence. He sat motionless, examining their faces as if wondering what kind of shower of shit he'd been handed this time. The wait took five minutes, but it felt like an hour. Ten almost exploded. He was dying to make a wisecrack, but even with his poorly tuned sensitivities, he could see that now wasn't the time.

The door opened. A completely bald man entered the room, ducking as he did so. Ten tried to guess his size. The doors were smaller on *Vengeance* than on more modern ships, but if Conway was built like a brick shithouse, this guy was the extension on the extension. His right sleeve was torn off to reveal a cybernetic arm.

A cyber-bloody-netic arm!

Again, the same thing went through their heads.

He was cuffed, muzzled and followed by two armed guards.

"This is Marine Rick Hunter, the sixth member of your team."

They moved their eyes off Hunter to face Stansfield directly.

"That thing on Hunter's arm is a highly illegal but cybernetic enhancement. The technology was outlawed by Sol, but Hunter had it fitted regardless. The Navy will neither endorse nor acknowledge

Hunter's weaponry, but for this mission, permission has been granted at the highest levels for us to deploy him into combat. That device makes him useful to this particular mission, and it will give you access to technology that is likely to come in handy.

"Like Marine X, Hunter is serving in the Penal program. He's formerly a Royal Marine but technically still an SBS Trooper. If he doesn't complete this mission successfully, he'll be a dead Trooper, and I'm not sure anyone will bother redeploying his last backup, which was some time ago. Quite frankly, if he does complete this mission successfully, I'd still quite like to eject him into space. It seems the Royal Navy has become soft during my... absence."

Ten had worked for some difficult bosses in his time, but the admiral was shaping up to be one of the most prickly he'd encountered in a good long while. He seemed to have had a sense of humour bypass.

"You should know that I have very little time for convicted criminals taking active duty roles. In my experience, prison is the best place for you. However, there have been some very rare cases of your type being able to turn around their lives and do something useful. You were highly recommended by Admiral Staines, but you start from nothing with me, understood?"

"You won't be–"

"Shut up!" Stansfield exploded. "A simple 'Yes, sir' will suffice. I don't need to hear *War and Peace*, understood? That goes for Hunter too, while we're at it."

Ten narrowed his eyes, but he was used to overbearing officers. "Sir," he said. Any shit from him at that point might land the others with a harder time, so he kept his mouth closed.

It all reminded Ten of a sorry episode at school on one of the rare days he'd decided to turn up. Only that time he'd locked a teacher in a store cupboard, and he was just as much in the dog house. There was no way he was locking Stansfield in the storeroom. Besides, from his ashen face, it looked like he'd been kept in the dark long enough already.

"Kearney, Mason, Conway and Davies, I specifically requested you for this mission, your reputation within the Navy is excellent."

For a moment, the four team members relaxed a little, basking in the warmth of Stansfield's small compliment. But their relief was short-lived.

"This mission is dangerous. Your chances of survival are slim, but success is critical and, if we fail, the Commonwealth itself is at risk."

The Troopers nodded grimly; the admiral wasn't telling them anything new.

"Permission to speak, Admiral?" Conway asked.

"Go ahead." He was different with Conway, respectful.

"What are we doing here? I mean, I know it's highly classified and all that. But what's the mission, in a nutshell?"

Ten detected the faint hint of a smile of Stansfield's face. He looked down at his slate, then up at the Marines with an earnest look on his face.

"You're here to help me prevent the annihilation of Earth."

7

Ten was no stranger to planetary annihilation. He'd been bang in the middle of a slight disagreement with the Deathless when he'd been temporarily extracted for this mission, but there was something about the way Stansfield said it that made him pay particular attention.

"The enemy that we're fighting is formidable," the admiral continued. "I've received briefings about the Deathless, but they can at least be engaged off-planet and present no real threat to the citizens of Earth."

Ten frowned. The Deathless were a long way from Earth, but they were a dangerous, unpredictable enemy, and he was uneasy at the way Stansfield dismissed their threat.

He looked hard at the admiral, scanning his face. The man was weary and worn out. It occurred to Ten that the Admiral might be a bit past his best, though he was a fine one to talk at his age. However he'd managed to be sitting in front of them now, whether it be as a clone or a cryo job, the admiral had the demeanour of a man who was tired out by life. The deep furrows in his brow were like the rings of a tree, each one marking a crisis or dilemma he'd been forced to confront during his military life.

"We've never encountered an enemy like this one. Nor have we dealt with a force quite so intent on destroying us. Ed, start the sequence."

Commander Vernon swiped twice across a console, and a 3D virtual render appeared in the middle of the large table.

"We're on the edge of the Eagle Nebula, seven thousand light-years from Sol. In this view, you'll see a green point marking *Vengeance's* current position. To the right, you'll see *Colossus* and the orbital station *Kingdom 10*."

Ten noted the time stamp. Only fifty-six hours had elapsed, so this event had happened just over a day before they'd set off for *Kingdom 10*.

"What are we looking at, sir?" said Mason.

"Just watch!" Stansfield barked impatiently.

As the reconstruction played out, Charlie Team followed the sequence of events as a yellow pin-prick appeared out of nowhere to the side of *Colossus*, growing in size at an accelerating rate until it became a massive circular fissure shimmering in space.

"What the fuck?" Davies asked.

There was no answer. Playback accelerated, and in a few seconds, *Colossus* had moved until it was almost on top of the fissure.

"They took two hours to approach," explained Vernon, "and then this happened."

Playback resumed at normal speed. *Colossus* began to enter the illuminated ring of colour, moving so slowly that she hardly seemed to be in motion at all.

Then there was a massive explosion, the vessel ruptured along its spine, and debris was sent hurtling into space. The crew groaned. It was a difficult thing to watch.

"The fissure – or portal – remained open for another five hours," said Vernon as he closed the render. "Then it shrank back to nothing and closed."

"That's what we're up against," said Stansfield. "It's nothing we've ever seen before. Not officially, at least."

Vernon picked up the briefing. "What you're seeing is some sort of portal, we think, a more advanced version of our communication wormhole. Where we can only transmit data, this wormhole – or whatever it is – seems capable of dealing with entire ships. *Colossus* was to penetrate the portal and find out what was on the other side, but you saw what happened. That was our best shot, to send one of our finest battleships in to see what was beyond the wormhole and pre-empt any aggression that might be heading our way. You can see how well that worked."

"If that's a wormhole that can move whole ships on demand, with an opening from only one end, it's a game-changer," said Stansfield. "If we can get our hands on this technology, it would give us a huge advantage in the war."

"So what's on the other side?" said Mason, asking the question they all wanted answered.

"That's what you're here to find out. You saw what happened to *Colossus*, we can't risk sending in any more ships like that. What's more, the debris from *Colossus* was thrown directly at *Kingdom 10*, and we don't think that was a coincidence. Whoever triggered the portal, they used the destruction of our warship to try and take out *Kingdom 10*."

"So why not *Vengeance*?" Kearney asked. "You're the most immediate threat. Why not take you out after *Colossus*?"

"That's what we'd like to find out. The portal hasn't reopened since we arrived, but we have to assume they know we're here, and know that their attack on *Kingdom 10* failed."

Vernon looked at Stansfield. It appeared as if they were agreeing between themselves on what they would reveal and what would remain hidden for now.

"We're under pressure from the Admiralty to get results," Stansfield continued. "The portal has been opening and closing like this for the past month. We think it's a test for something, a kind of trial run. We need to assess the level of threat and see what can be done to repel it. Needless to say, this far out in space, we could do without this headache in the middle of a war with the Deathless."

"Could it be anything to do with the war, sir?" asked Conway. "An opportunist move, perhaps?"

Vernon and Stansfield exchanged a glance.

"Very possibly," Stansfield replied. "Watch this, Charlie Team."

Vernon took his cue and reactivated the 3D render. This was now a simulation, with a projected time stamp displayed and six new objects added to the scenario.

"This is your first objective," Vernon began. "We're sending you in SEVs to investigate the outer perimeters of the portal, next time it opens."

"SEVs?" said Ten.

"Space Exploration Vehicles," Vernon replied. "You're familiar with Exploration Pods, but these SEVs are from an older generation entirely. They're what we used before the Navy developed our current Raleigh Class Exploration Pods. The controls aren't much different, so you shouldn't have any problem with them."

"Yeah, I know what SEVs are, sir. My thing is, they're bloody antiques. What possible reason could we have for pulling them out of stores? Where did we even find some in working order?" Ten asked.

Stansfield frowned at his vulgarity, but stopped short of reprimanding him further. "Ah, I see. There are specific engineering reasons we want to use the SEVs, plus there's a time constraint. *Vengeance* has plenty of them in working order, and the few more recent alternatives available in *Kingdom 10* aren't likely to work for us."

"But why not use pods, sir?" Conway asked. "Why go in there with old technology? Do they have extra functionality we don't normally have now? I've never been in one."

"Lieutenant Fernandez and his team have been modifying our SEVs, and we have good reason to think that they will out-perform the more recent alternatives for this mission."

Before he'd completed his answer, there was a bright flash from beyond the windows that illuminated the room.

"Permission to look, troopers," Stansfield said, giving them the nod to move. "That's better than any simulation we can show you."

Charlie Team gathered around the windows to view the phenomenon. They watched as the blinding white light expanded in size, circular in shape, and then became a shimmering mass of beautiful colours, taking in a vast area of space.

"It's magnificent," Davies said, shaking his head in wonder. "To be able to generate and contain enough energy to tear open a wormhole of that size, that's quite incredible. Whoever is on the other end, they have scientific and engineering knowledge that blows away our progress in the field."

"What you have to remember, Davies, is that their science was once ours. We use our wormholes for data only, but since the Koschei left Sol space, this group have pushed the boundaries of the technology. Nevertheless, it began as a British research project, if you don't recall your history. There will be a straight line between our current technology and this portal, and if we can get the data to understand how they're doing it, we'll be able to replicate it." Stansfield said.

"Or steal it," said Ten, as much to himself as everybody else in the room, "or have it stolen from us by the Deathless."

"The portal is opening more regularly now," said Stansfield, ignoring the interruption. "It opens at three-hour intervals, and remains open much longer, with increased activity. Whatever the portal openers plan, it will happen soon."

"But what makes you think anything hostile is coming over from the other side, sir?"

"Er, *Colossus*, Davies," said Kearney.

"Yeah, but they might have seen *Colossus* as a threat. Who says they're coming to annihilate Earth? They might take a right turn or a left turn when they come out the wormhole. They might just be on a day trip to the Eagle Nebula, it is pretty impressive. Who says they're the bad guys?"

"Enough!" Stansfield interjected. "At this moment in time, we're not at liberty to divulge all details of this operation. You don't need to know the details. Take it as read, a hostile enemy is coming out of that portal, and they'll be heading straight for Earth. "

Stansfield touched his lapel, and the voice of Fernandez came through his communicator.

"SEVs are ready to go, Admiral. We have seven prepped, and I'd like to request permission to go with the teams, sir."

"Denied, Fernandez. The Admiralty has asked that we deploy Lieutenant Woodhall on any fact-finding missions."

"Woodhall?"

It was the first time they'd heard Hunter speak. He tensed his body and pushed against the cuffs that restrained him.

"I'm well aware of your past with Lieutenant Woodhall," Stansfield answered, a flash of contempt on his face. He could barely look at Hunter. "But this is a military operation. You know how this works, Hunter, and I want to be very clear about one thing. If I get even an inkling that you have anything other than this mission on your mind, your colleagues have my permission to take you out before they fire on the enemy. Is that understood? One suggestion that you're not fully engaged in this operation and they put a bullet through your head. Am I clear?"

Hunter subsided with a curt nod, but he clearly wasn't happy. Ten wondered if he was equally disposable to Stansfield. What was it that Stansfield had against Penal Marines? Was it something in particular, or just a general dislike for the idea? It wasn't as if all the reprobates in the forces got duty like this, just a handful of unusual cases. *Never waste good people* was an excellent rule to live by, Ten thought. Apparently Stansfield had other ideas.

"Lieutenant Woodhall is here at the request of the Admiralty. He's a Royal Navy science officer, so make use of him. But always be aware, he's reporting back to the Admiralty, and he mustn't get in the way of your mission."

"Is our mission not the same as the Admiralty's?" asked Ten, but it was as if he spoke only to himself. He glanced at Kearney, who gave a tiny shake of her head.

Stansfield had turned his attention to Hunter. "Take off the cuffs. Remember what I said, Hunter; from this point onward you're working for the Commonwealth. You cut the crap, do your job, you have every chance of avoiding the death penalty. You screw this up, I'll blow up that thing in your head myself!"

Conway, Mason and Davies looked at him.

"Hunter has an explosive implant embedded in his skull. If he goes on the run or disobeys an order, he dies immediately, no paperwork. He already has a death sentence. This mission is his only chance to avoid it being carried out."

The voice of Fernandez came from Stansfield's communicator. "All clear for launch, sir. The portal will reach full expansion within the next twenty minutes. The team needs to leave now."

8

"Now this is what I call retro," declared Davies, eager to take the SEV out for a spin. The team were wearing lightweight power armour suits that would protect them in the event of a hull breach or power failure.

"Not that we expect that, of course," said Fernandez. "This is a straightforward flight, and these are the same basic layout as a standard Exploration Pod, even if they handle a little differently."

"A little differently," snorted Ten. "You could say that." Davies looked at him quizzically, but he didn't elaborate.

The pods were small, only seven metres long, and purely short-range. One pilot, no additional crew or cargo, and a huge wraparound diamond-glass window at the front. Most of the hull was taken up with sensor equipment, engines and life support.

"Any armaments on these things, sir? Can we defend ourselves?" Ten was always eager to get his hands on the weapons.

Fernandez gave him a cold stare. "Survey only. We're not expecting to be engaged on this mission; you're simply required to get as close as you can to the portal, gather as much data as possible, and support Woodhall in making his assessment for the Admiralty. No shooting required, okay?"

"Yeah, of course," said Ten, wondering how many times he'd heard similar statements from backroom officers.

"*Vengeance* is moving closer to the portal," Fernandez went on, "so you'll be only a few kilometres away when you launch."

He flicked at a slate and sent them all the flight plan.

"Here's Lieutenant Woodhall," said Fernandez without emotion. "The man's a prick and Stansfield hates him, but has to kiss arse. Woodhall is all that's keeping the admiral from permanent retirement."

Ten frowned at Fernandez's sudden and unexpected revelation, sharing a suspicious glance with Davies before they watched Lieutenant Woodhall approach.

"We all answer to somebody, eh?" said Conway.

Woodhall made his presence felt immediately. His hair was slicked back, his facial grooming impeccable, his build slight and his attitude one of entitlement. This man's natural habitat was an office, his greatest foe a data slate with a flat battery. He'd done his military training, then taken refuge behind a desk. It was clear from the get-go that he wasn't going to be one of the team.

"Is there a reason my power armour has a red circle on the derriere, Fernandez? I seem to be the only person here who has one."

Fernandez let slip the tiniest of smirks, but managed to keep his face straight. "Nothing to worry about, Lieutenant Woodhall," he replied. "We had to make last-minute repairs to the suit when we learnt that you were joining the team on this mission. It's nothing personal."

Ten knew otherwise. Woodhall looked like he had a big red target on his arse., and Ten sensed that he was going to end up wanting to kick it at some point. Woodhall wasn't the kind of man a fighting team needed, and Ten could see him ending up as a dead weight, an annoyance, a thorn in their sides.

Still, at least he didn't have a skull implant like Hunter. That was exceptionally unusual, even given Hunter's conviction. There must be a good story behind a security precaution like that. It wasn't just a matter of failing to show contrition during the court-martial. Things could have been worse.

"Okay, let's clear the bay, people, we need to get this team out of here before the portal begins to contract. Are you sure you're okay with the SEV? There's no shame in delaying this trip until you've accumulated more hours on the simulator."

Woodhall bristled at Fernandez's comments.

"I'm perfectly capable of handling one of these museum pieces. Just make sure they work; I don't want to end up calling a rescue tug," said Woodhall with a derision he didn't attempt to hide.

Hunter made a fist, then loosened it. Ten saw him do it and nodded to Mason, who'd also seen it.

"You reckon Hunter's safe out here?" said Ten quietly.

"He's a great Marine, according to his record. I'm surprised you don't know him. He made a bad choice, that's all. That thing on his arm, that was his mistake. That and leaving the battlefield before he should have. But he's a good soldier, or at least he was at one time."

"I take it he doesn't use that arm of his to blend smoothies?"

Mason laughed. "Shit, no! Let's put it this way; if that's what I think it is, Hunter's going to be a very useful man on this mission. That thing's like a Swiss Army knife of weaponry. You wait and see."

Ten nodded doubtfully. "Good luck," he said as he climbed into his SEV.

There was an electronic hum as Conway's SEV powered up and raised off the ground. The burners fired and she was off, expertly taking the unit out of the vast opening to the bay. Davies followed, then Kearney and Hunter.

"It's a long time since I've flown solo, so this should be fun," said Ten on the team's comms channel.

"You're Marine X?" said Woodhall.

"Yes, sir. People mostly call me Ten," Ten replied, wary. Sometimes he grew tired of proving himself to sceptical or suspicious officers.

"I've read all about you, Marine X," said Woodhall, which marked him down as a damned liar, "and while you're working alongside me, I expect ultra-focus and no attitude, is that clear?"

Ten was thinking about that target on Woodhall's arse again. "Understood, Lieutenant," he replied. "By the way, sir, you need to release that catch to open the door."

"Don't patronise me, *Penal* Marine!" Woodhall snarled. "I know what I'm doing." He fumbled with the catch some more and finally managed to climb into his SEV.

Ten shrugged. Woodhall was a pompous prick, but Ten had seen plenty of officers just like him who'd hit the invisible ceiling once their superiors had grown to know them. He wouldn't last.

Ten switched his focus back to the controls of his own SEV and expertly activated the control panel. "Just like the man said, standard configuration. Thrusters, navigation, manoeuvring and monitoring. Yup, it's all there. Let's take this thing out for a spin."

Ten powered up the SEV, raised it three metres above the cold floor of the hangar, and triggered a gentle forward thrust. As he was belched out into the limitless expanse of space, he felt the same rush of adrenaline that he'd experienced the first time he'd done this. There was nothing quite like it, and the basic design of the SEVs made it feel like he could reach out his hand and touch the stars.

"We have it too good these days," said Davies. "This is what I called extreme space travel!"

"I love it," Ten replied. "How old are these things? It's a bit shaky, but it puts me in touch with my softer interstellar side."

Conway had come up on his rear, and pulled level with Ten and Kearney. "Steady, Ten. I'm guessing it's some time since you've been out in space like this. Take your time, get used to the handling. These feel a bit sensitive to me. If we're not careful, they'll wrench about the place."

Hunter spotted something in the distance.

"Did *Vengeance* just take a dump, or is that Woodhall finally on his way?" Hunter asked over a channel that didn't include the self-important lieutenant. It was the first time he'd addressed them all, and as far as Ten was concerned, it was a pretty solid start.

"Steady, boys," Conway cautioned them. "He runs the show out here. Remember who pays your wages."

"Wages?" scoffed Davies. "Who gets wages? I've been away from home so long I could retire on the amount of leave I've accumulated."

Woodhall's SEV approached the cluster of craft. He moved jerkily, with exaggerated movements as he overcompensated for every error, but he was at least managing to keep up.

"That's one hell of a sight, even if Stansfield is right about it being able to destroy the Earth and end civilisation," said Mason with amusement.

About half the team's communication was being sent to a channel that included everyone but Woodhall. He must have thought they were being really good boys and girls by sticking only to vital comms.

Stansfield's voice came over the team's private comms channel. "Lieutenant Woodhall may be listening to only one channel, but the bridge team is monitoring all comms. Keep the chatter to a minimum, like the professionals I know we all are."

Ten looked across at Mason in his SEV and wagged his finger at him. Mason gave him the finger.

"The portal is now at its maximum recorded expansion, it's time to go in, team," came Fernandez's guiding voice from *Vengeance*.

"We take a sector each," Conway picked up. "Ten and Hunter, top and bottom, me and Kearney left and right, Davies takes the centre. I take it you'll be operating as a free agent, sir?"

"Affirmative," Woodhall replied, acknowledging the deference. "I want to take some energy readings and get a sense of how they created this thing."

"It's pretty, so so pretty!" sang Ten, testing the vocal cords of his clone.

"Steady, Marine," came Stansfield's warning voice over the radio. "I'm sure we've got one of those skull implants left. Just give me an excuse, and I'll happily get you retro-fitted."

"You can fucking try," murmured Ten to himself, adding Stansfield to his ever-growing list of people to avoid in the future.

Hunter flashed his finger, but Ten shrugged off the insult.

"We have a visual on you, Hunter. If you're waving to your friends, you might want to be a little more careful about who sees you!" came Vernon's voice.

"Taking exploratory formations in three – two – one," said Conway.

The SEVs headed for their allocated sectors. Woodhall lagged behind as his vessel moved fitfully after the others.

The portal had transformed from its initial white light to the shimmering array of colour that indicated it was now at its full expanse.

A warning came from the bridge.

"Do not, repeat, do not cross into the mouth of the portal. *Colossus* had barely broken the skin before it exploded. Caution is your friend here," Vernon said.

Ten was getting along with his new transport just fine, his old skills coming back to him. It was exactly like riding a bike: you absolutely forget how to do it well, but practice was returning his old confidence.

The movement controls were good, and it was easy to manoeuvre the tiny craft just where he wanted it to go. It was fast, too, and he was itching to take it out into space for a blast. He wondered idly if there might be time to race the SEVs across *Vengeance*'s hull. He reckoned Hunter would probably be up for it.

Then he sighed and focussed on the job. There was always a job to do; he just hoped there would be something a bit more interesting than taking sensor readings. Captain Warden would be furious if this was all he was asked to do.

The team moved around their assigned sectors while the sensors captured their readings, assessed energy levels and performed spectral analyses. The information was stored in the on-board systems, then conveyed straight back to *Vengeance*, where the science team immediately began to crunch the numbers.

Vernon came back on the radios. "Lieutenant Woodhall, you're getting dangerously close to the outer skin. I recommend you withdraw some."

"I know what I'm doing, Commander, thank you!" came the dismissive reply.

Ten wasn't certain he hadn't imagined it, but he thought he heard Vernon in the background muttering the word 'tosser.'

"Moving in a little bit closer," Woodhall updated. "I'm sure I see something mechanical in there. I'm closing the gap so you can get a better visual."

"You're too close to the skin, sir," came a second warning from the bridge. "Recommend immediate withdrawal. You're metres away; initial data from the *Colossus* incident indicates critical safety distance is now breached!"

"Are you getting this, Admiral?" Woodhall responded, oblivious to the alerts. "It's a probe of some sort, I'll move just a fraction closer ... damn it!"

Woodhall was so intent on moving in right up to the skin that he nudged his craft a little too much to the left. He was about to plunge his SEV directly into the portal and, in a panic, he took massive corrective action, sending his craft hurtling out into space.

"Woodhall's in trouble," Conway alerted them calmly, her pilot's instincts and training keeping her steady in the face of the sudden emergency. "Ten, you're closest, can you keep on his tail?"

Unaccustomed to the stress of battle and the need for fast, calm decision-making, Woodhall was now in full panic mode, pressing every button that he could to steady the trajectory of his SEV.

"Yeah, no problem. Moving to assist," said Ten wearily. Five minutes into the mission and Woodhall was already proving unreliable. He wondered if the lieutenant had any useful skills; maybe he was just socially inept and an incompetent pilot.

"I'll back you up," Davies offered. "Look at him go, Ten. He's a magnificent man in his flying machine."

"Steady him up, Charlie Team, we can't have SEVs racing out of control like that," Vernon said over the channel to the team. Then he broadcast wide, "Lieutenant Woodhall, cut your speed and calm down."

Davies' voice interrupted, alarmed. "Lieutenant, you're heading straight for me, pull out, pull out!"

"Right thruster, Lieutenant," Ten advised.

He closed his eyes as Woodhall's SEV crunched the glass of Davies' vehicle. The two craft spun away from each other.

"I'm breached, *Vengeance*," said Davies angrily as he wrestled to pull his vehicle out of a spin.

"If your helmet isn't up already, Davies, get it on and if you can't regain control, cut your engines completely. We'll come and get you," said Conway.

Davies touched a button on his power armour, and the visor of his helmet slid into place just as the diamond-glass in his craft shattered and blew out into space. A second later and he'd have been in serious trouble from the vacuum alone. He took Conway's advice and powered down his SEV and sat dead in space, waiting for a tow.

Woodhall's craft, bounced by its collision with Davies, was now heading at great speed back towards the heart of the portal.

"You all good, DD?" Ten said.

"Affirmative," Davies replied. "Move your arse, Ten, he's heading directly for the centre."

"Let's see how fast these things go!" Ten said cheerily. "Remind me how to power down fast, Conway, I saw you skimming the manual earlier."

"Above your head, yellow button. It'll kill the engines immediately," came her reply.

"Lieutenant, yellow button, press it now and power down," Ten instructed. "We'll rescue you."

"I don't need to press the button!" Woodhall protested, although it was clear he had no control over his craft.

"With all due respect, Lieutenant Woodhall, do as Conway advises and press the damned button. She's on this mission for her skills as a pilot!" said Stansfield, unable to contain his impatience.

Woodhall pressed the button. The SEV fired its thrusters to stop the spin, then powered down.

Ten pushed his SEV to maximum forward thrust. "Hold on, Lieutenant, and don't shit your panties, it'll be unbearable in your suit if you do and I'm coming in fast," he said, intentionally disrespectful of the young officer.

"Twenty seconds to portal contact ... nineteen ... eighteen ..." came the warning from *Vengeance.*

"I'd close your eyes if I were you, sir," advised Ten. "I'm going to bounce you back to safety."

"You're going to do what?" Woodhall demanded, the fear in his voice crystal-clear to everyone over the excellent comms of the SEVs.

"Conway, any more juice to be had out of the thrusters on this thing?" Ten asked, getting ready to thrash the SEV.

"Now at ten seconds ... nine ..." came the countdown from *Vengeance.*

"Left switch, below thruster," Conway instructed. "No, damn it, right switch, right switch!"

She was too late. Ten's SEV struck Woodhall's vehicle at just the right angle to do the job he intended. The impact was bone-jarring, but it deflected the impulsive lieutenant away from the portal. Once he stopped wailing into the open comms channel, he'd realise he was safe, and Conway and Mason could snag him to tow him back to the safety of *Vengeance's* hangar.

But for Ten, his thumb hit the left switch in the brief moment between his SEV slamming into the side of the one piloted by the Navy's biggest fuckwit, and Conway changing her mind about the correct switch.

Instead of a punishing deceleration from extra retro-thrusters, Ten had a last-second burst of speed from the thrusters. The collision had pushed him off course in about the worst way possible.

As the bridge crew of *Vengeance* breathed a sigh of relief that they'd managed to keep the Admiralty's pain-in-the-arse emissary alive, Ten's SEV hurtled right into the heart of the portal.

9

"Get yourselves out of there, Charlie Team, the portal doesn't like foreign objects," came the concerned instruction from *Vengeance.*

"Ten? Ten? Are you out there? Are you okay?" said Conway, yelling into her helmet mic.

"Are you getting anything from Marine X, Control?" asked Mason.

"Negative," came the update from *Vengeance.* "All comms have gone quiet. Any visuals on him?"

"Negative," said Kearney.

Stansfield's voice could be heard in the background. "Why did Sol have to send us their biggest prick? If we've lost one of those Marines already, I'll lock him in his quarters myself."

There was silence. The crew on board *Vengeance* were scanning intently, searching for life signs, radio contact or a visual. Conway too, releasing Davies and Woodhall to the care of Kearney and Mason, shot across the mouth of the portal, searching for some indication that Ten had made it through alive.

"Conway, any sign of debris? *Colossus* blew up like a bomb," Commander Vernon asked.

Then, from the silence, Ten's SEV crossed the threshold and emerged from the portal.

"Wheeeee!" came Ten's voice, seemingly out of thin air.

There were sighs of relief on the bridge, and Conway relaxed her hand on the thruster. She hadn't realised quite how tense she'd been.

Ten performed two spins, then levelled his SEV with Conway's. "Did you miss me?" he asked. "Go on, tell me you missed me."

Conway delivered the third finger of the day through the glass of her craft.

"Report back, Marine. How did you manage that?" said Stansfield, forever focussed on the mission.

"It goes straight through," said Ten, elated at his discovery. "I passed to the other side. It's incredible, it hopped me to another universe. It's amazing out there, you should see the colours!"

"What was out there, Marine X?" asked Vernon. "Any craft or defensive apparatus?"

"Not that I could see, sir," said Ten. "How stable is the portal? Do we have time before it closes? I say we go back and take a proper butcher's."

"But how come you got through?" said Conway.

"Best estimates give you at least fifteen minutes before the portal closes. Hold for orders," Commander Vernon replied.

"Let's find out, shall we?" said Ten. "Who's coming?"

"Aww, don't leave me," Davies pleaded sarcastically.

"*Vengeance*, if we leave these two in their SEVS, can you bring them back in?" Mason checked. "Requesting permission for me and Kearney to follow Marine X through the portal."

There was a pause before Stansfield answered. "Permission granted. Conway, Marine X, Mason and Kearney go through. Take initial readings, stick close to the portal and come back within eight minutes. Do not push that window. Good luck."

Woodhall protested. "Admiral Stansfield, I insist that the team wait for me before they go into that portal!"

"Sorry, Lieutenant," said Fernandez, sounding not even a little remorseful, "we need to check your craft for damage before you go any further. We'll send drones to pull you and Trooper Davies back into the launch bay."

"Okay, Conway, let's go through. You good?" Ten checked.

"At your side, Ten. Let's a take a closer look at this thing," she replied, eager to get started.

The multi-coloured array at the mouth of the portal looked from afar like it might be a collection of gases, but as they passed through it became clear that it was some interference or interface between what was on one side of the portal and what was on the other.

"Damn, Ten, look at this," Conway marvelled. "Do you recognise the star patterns?"

"This is not Sol-explored territory," Ten remarked. "The computer doesn't recognise anything here. I've triangulated already, and we're a long way from home, but we don't have contact with *Vengeance* on this side. We'll have to run it on the ship's computers when we get back."

Kearney, Hunter and Mason had made it safely through the portal.

"It's beautiful," said Kearney as her ship crossed the threshold. "This is absolutely stunning, I've never seen anything like it."

They took a few moments to admire the vast expanse of uncharted universe before them. In the near distance, a red-hued cluster of planets; close by, a green planet, silent and friendly-looking.

"How come we got through?" said Mason. "Whatever happened to *Colossus* seems to have passed us by."

"I've no idea," said Conway. "I suggest we don't push our luck for now. Let's just take readings from this side of the portal and head straight back. When's the portal next due to close?"

"Soon," Ten replied vaguely.

"Be quick then, Marines," said Conway. "Let's gather as much data as we can and get out of here."

The team worked around the perimeter of the portal, taking readings as they had on the other side. Without warning, there was a red flash that washed like a wave across the whole of the portal's mouth. It then created a peak in the centre, which emitted a power surge.

Hunter was directly in its path. His SEV powered down; his helmet sensed the life-support emergency and unfurled over his face to deliver oxygen.

"Heap of shitty junk, I'm dead down here," said Hunter.

"The portal's beginning to close," said Conway.

"Shit, now? We should have had another ten minutes. Are you sure?" asked Mason.

"Of course I'm fucking sure," snapped Conway.

"Are you completely out of power, Hunter?" said Ten.

"Yeah, I've got nothing, I'm a sitting duck. The controls are dead."

Kearney gave a second warning. "Time to go. The mouth is beginning to contract, we need to get out of here."

"Any ideas, guys?" Hunter asked. "I don't like Stansfield very much, but I'd sooner be stuck on *Vengeance* than stranded on my own out here."

"Conway, you and I are closest, said Ten. "We have limited options, I reckon. We can't bump him, we'll have to bust him out of there and give him a lift."

"You're kidding. You are kidding, aren't you?"

"Do I sound like I'm kidding, Conway? You keep an eye on the portal and count me down. This is going to be close."

"Ha! It won't be the first time I've been busted out by a couple of pals!" said Hunter with a nervous laugh. "You are my pals, aren't you? I'd be heartbroken if you weren't."

"I'm not ready to go steady with you just yet, Hunter, but I am happy to get your arse out of there," Ten joked.

Conway's voice interrupted, serious and focussed. "Portal closure at seventy-eight per cent. Mason and Kearney, get out of here, head back to *Vengeance*."

"Are you sure?" said Kearney. "You might need us."

"Do it," said Conway. "We've got this."

"Roger," said Kearney before she and Mason powered up their SEVs and disappeared through the mouth of the portal.

"Seventy-three per cent closure, Ten, you need to be moving in now," Conway warned.

Ten was on the case already, moving his SEV directly alongside Hunter. He pressed the button on his power armour and helmeted up, then unlocked a protected switch to his right and opened up the glass. He felt the pressure change even within his suit, and he checked that he was securely clipped to his seat.

"It's going to be tight in here, Hunter," said Ten, grinning.

"I ain't sitting on your lap, if that's what you're suggesting," said Hunter, playing along.

"Cut the foreplay, gentlemen," Conway cut in, serious and intense. "The portal is now at fifty-two per cent."

"That's over halfway, right?" Ten teased. "I was never good at maths. Plenty of time. Hunter, I need you to clip yourself to a high tensile rope and hop on over here. You all right with that?"

"Why wouldn't I be?"

Conway was becoming anxious now. "The portal closure is accelerating, guys, we're at forty-six per cent. Get a move on!"

"My canopy won't open," said Hunter, a slight trace of panic in his voice. "I've got no power. Is there a manual override, Conway?"

"I'm going to have to consult the manual on that, Hunter. Can you see a catch or anything?" she responded.

"Screw that!" he said, now impatient.

Ten watched as Hunter clenched his cybernetic fist and a sharp spike shot out between his knuckles. A projected matrix shone onto the glass, a red dot appeared in the middle, and he stabbed the spike precisely where the dot was. The glass shattered completely, freeing him from the SEV.

"Fuck me, Hunter, remind me to call you next time I need a bottle opener," said Ten.

"And you ain't even seen my real party trick yet. Just make sure to retract before you scratch your arse," said Hunter.

"Nice chat, guys," came Conway's voice, uncertain whether to be irritated or amused. "We're at thirty-eight per cent now. At ten per cent, I'm not even certain we'll get through before it closes on us."

"Okay, Hunter," said Ten, getting back to business. "Clip the rope on, keep it nice and tight, then unbuckle your straps."

"Affirmative!" Hunter responded. "It's a great day for a spacewalk." Carefully, he allowed himself to rise up from his seat, assuming a horizontal floating position. "Can you grab my ankles and haul me in?" he suggested.

"Only if you promise me you washed your feet!"

"Twenty-nine per cent, I don't think we're going to make this," came Conway's urgent warning.

"Get yourself out of here, Conway, there's no point all of us getting stuck. Go! Go!" said Ten.

"Twenty-five per cent and the portal closure is accelerating, Ten," she said, pushing her SEV towards the portal. "Good luck, boys, see you on the other side."

Ten leaned across from his SEV, reaching out as far as he could to get hold of Hunter as Conway's SEV disappeared through the portal.

And just like that, the two men were alone.

10

Conway ran through in her head the steps that Ten and Hunter would need to take to get out of there. There was no way they'd make it, surely?

As she emerged from the portal, her radio crackled back into life. Kearney and Mason were waiting, ready to step in and assist if necessary.

"Status report, Conway?" came a voice from the bridge of *Vengeance*.

"The portal's closing, fast. Hunter's SEV is down, Ten's pulling him out, but there's probably no more than half a minute until they're stuck in there," Conway replied, a resigned tone in her voice.

"Acknowledged," came the response from *Vengeance*.

Conway watched anxiously as the collapse of the portal accelerated. The entire team were willing Ten and Hunter to get out of there. Even if they could survive on the other side of the portal until it next opened up, their SEV power wouldn't last them that long. Nor their oxygen supplies, come to that.

"Anything to report, Conway-Davies-Mason-Kearney? Anybody?" came the ever-present voice from the bridge of *Vengeance*.

"Nothing yet, keeping my fingers crossed," said Conway. "I don't think Ten's big on punctuality!"

The swirling mass of colour was now collapsing on itself. By Conway's calculations, there would be a critical point at which the portal was still open, but the SEV wouldn't be able to make it through.

"Davies," said Conway, "you're the mathematician. What do you think, how much more time have they got?"

Davies, now safely back on *Vengeance*, could be heard slightly off the speaker on the deck, where he'd joined Vernon and Stansfield to monitor the ongoing operation.

"Tricky," he said. "We have so little data about the portal, and the information we do have is inconsistent. This thing doesn't seem to follow any predictable patterns, so it's anybody's guess how long until it's completely closed. And even then, I don't really know what happens if it closes on them."

Kearney took a close look at the contracting fissure. "How big a ship might pass through that thing?" she muttered to herself. Even this close, it was difficult to estimate size and scale.

It didn't matter anyway, because at that very moment, just as she'd convinced herself that there wasn't enough space to squeeze a cargo box through, let alone an SEV, Ten's voice came crackling on the radio as he emerged from the portal.

"Sorry to keep you," he said as his SEV emerged from the collapsing portal. "Hunter got a little tied up back there, and we reckoned we'd got a few extra seconds to bring back a souvenir."

Ten emerged directly from the core of the fissure, the glass casing of his SEV blown off by the momentum of his vehicle, with only his power armour and helmet providing protection from the lack of oxygen in the expanse beyond. Fastened to the headrest of his SEV was a bright red external inspection rope, and moments later came Hunter, still clipped to the rope and hanging on to some foreign object for dear life.

"There were no seats left," said Hunter. "I had to travel third class."

Mason chuckled as they watched the ridiculous sight of an SEV towing a Marine on a high-tensile wire rope at a speed that would have paralysed most people with fear. Instead, Hunter looked like he'd just taken a ride on a Big Dipper at the fairground. But more interesting than that was the thing he was clutching.

"We have a partial visual on whatever that is that Hunter is holding," came Vernon's voice. "Can you confirm the nature of the item?"

"Well, let's put it this way," said Hunter. "If it's a bomb, we're celebrating our escape from the portal a little too soon. Please parcel up the bits of my body and send them to my family to help them remember me by. If it's not a bomb, I think we just grabbed ourselves a bit of alien technology. Only if you asked me to guess, bearing in mind I'm being towed by a spaceship, using my finely-tuned observation skills, I'd say this is human technology."

"What makes you say that, Hunter?" Stansfield asked, taking a conciliatory tone with the Penal Marine for the first time.

"Well, I'm no space scientist," he began, "but there's a little lid at the side of this thing that reads *Open Here*. Unless that's some alien language and I'm mispronouncing it, I'd say that's human!"

Ten slowed the SEV, making sure that Hunter didn't come crashing directly into his rear thrusters. The cable, built to withstand extreme stresses in space, was glowing red at his end, and he was pleased that he hadn't shared his doubts that it might actually melt in the burners before it brought Hunter to safety. Not that it seemed to bother Hunter, who shared Ten's sense of adventure. Ten was almost jealous that he hadn't been the one hanging on to the rope and getting a tow through space.

"I'd appreciate a lift from somebody. Conway? Kearney? Mason?" Hunter pleaded. "It's all right, you just hovering there in space enjoying the spectacle, but some of us could do with a ride back to *Vengeance!*"

"Moving in, Hunter," said Mason. "That was some stunt out there. Nice work, troopers. It's a long time since I've enjoyed watching a couple of pros at work like that."

"Agreed, good work, Hunter. Reckless, dangerous and aggressive, but keep that up and I might feel inclined to take my finger off the trigger for that thing in your skull," Stansfield added.

"Stop, sir, you've brought a tear to my eye, I'm all choked up now," said Hunter, making his best effort to sound a bit emotional. For the first time since Hunter had arrived on *Vengeance*, Stansfield cut him a moment of slack.

They'd made progress. Stansfield had been able to move things on without having to sustain the massive loss of a battleship this time around. The Admiralty had been too gung-ho in entering the portal. Stansfield had warned them but, impatient to bring this matter to a close and focus on the battle with the Deathless, they'd been careless and assumed they could send in their latest technology and have everything wrapped up by sundown.

"Get yourselves back to *Vengeance*, Charlie Team," said Stansfield. "Let's let the techs take a look at that thing."

Twenty minutes later, the team were back in *Vengeance*'s main bay. Fernandez was there to greet them, wearing what they were coming to recognise as his customary pissed-off look.

"I sent you out with seven SEVs, and you've destroyed three and damaged one. At this rate, we'll run out. I don't want to sound like I'm ungrateful," he said coldly, "but I really would appreciate it if you'd look after our property."

"Yeah, sorry about that," said Ten. "I failed my driving test and never quite got the hang of using my mirrors. You can patch them up, can't you, sir? You have spares?"

The rest of the crew looked at him. "Driving test? How fucking old are you?" murmured Kearney.

"I honestly can't remember, Kearney. You could ask your mother, I suppose," Ten replied.

"Yes, Marine X," said Fernandez with a glare, "we should be able to patch them, but I'd still appreciate it if you took a little bit more care. Now, where's that thing you brought in? We'd best give it a scan before moving it into the heart of the ship, just in case it is a bomb or something like that."

"A bomb?" asked Conway incredulously. "Why would anyone booby-trap a portal?"

"It pays to be cautious," said Fernandez as two technicians removed the device from Ten's SEV.

"Yes, well," said Fernandez when the device was set on a table, "this is clearly some sort of sensor, and that," he said, pointing at a part of the device, "is a comms device, so I think this has the capacity to relay data back to a ship, device or location. It looks benign, but we'll take a closer look in case it helps give us a better idea of what we're dealing with."

"I'd like DD to take a look, sir," said Conway. "He's pretty good at this kind of thing."

Fernandez frowned, then gave a curt nod.

Davies arrived from the bridge a few minutes later with Woodhall in tow. The lieutenant had tried to regain a little of his dignity by antagonising those around him and detracting from his incompetent work piloting the SEV, but no-one was buying it.

"I shall be reporting to the Admiralty," said Woodhall. "I know exactly what you did when you ignored my instructions not to go into the portal, and the sooner you understand that this is an Admiralty-led mission, the better. *Vengeance* does not have command."

"Your diligence does you credit," muttered Fernandez. Then he turned away to supervise the small team of technicians who were going to strip down the device. The team worked swiftly, removing the metal casing from the contraption and getting into the electronics so they could assess its purpose.

"These things were all over the other side of the portal," said Hunter. "I just grabbed one."

"I think I saw one on this side as well," said Woodhall. "I did," he protested when the others gave him sceptical looks.

"I have a theory," said Davies quietly. "They're monitoring the mouth of the portal. They alerted whoever created the technology to the fact that *Colossus* was passing into their territory, and that triggered either a defensive system within the portal itself or offensive weaponry on the other side."

"That makes sense," Fernandez said with a grudging respect.

"So how did the SEVs get through them?" Conway asked.

"That's just it, that's what tipped me off. *Vengeance* and the SEVs are old kit; the Navy changed its propulsion system years after *Vengeance* was built. The SEVs, *Vengeance* and some of the older craft on this ship give out a different signature. I think these gizmos detect old-style ship signatures and destroy anything that doesn't match their records when it attempts to cross over the portal. If I'm right, the SEVs got through because they have an old, obsolete signature, so these devices just didn't notice them. In effect, Ten was invisible when he went shooting through the mouth of the fissure."

"So, if I'm following your train of thought," said Fernandez, eyes flashing as his brain worked overtime, "we could actually go through that thing with *Vengeance* next time the portal opens?"

"Precisely, sir," said Davies, "that's exactly what I'm talking about. If we can prove that theory correct, we should be able to send *Vengeance* right through the heart of that thing and send whoever's sniffing around our territory back home with their tail between their legs."

The members of Charlie Team exchanged glances, smiling, excited at the prospect of taking a battleship – even if it was *Vengeance* – into uncharted enemy territory. Not only did it give them the necessary firepower to greet any foe, it meant they didn't just have to sit and wait for whatever was heading for the portal. There was a spark of excitement in the air until Woodhall interrupted and threw a bucket of cold water on the lot of them.

"After what happened to *Colossus*, we will be sending *Vengeance* through that portal over my dead body!"

"I'm sure that can be arranged," Fernandez mumbled as the spark of energy on the bridge was extinguished by the rude intrusion of the Admiralty and the tedious necessity of sticking to the rule book.

11

Within the hour, Fernandez and his team had learned three things. Firstly, the design of the device was rooted entirely in Earthly origins. The similarities were clear, but multiple generations of development had taken this device down a different technological path. It was as if somebody had taken sensors from the *Vengeance* itself and then developed them in a completely different way – the same starting point, but a different endpoint.

Secondly, it was definitely a scanning and sensory device. There was no question that it was in any way an offensive weapon, nor could these mechanisms have been the means by which *Colossus* was repelled and destroyed.

"Part of a sensor array," said Fernandez. "It has a database of *Vengeance*-era Royal Navy engine signatures. They're watching for us. Sentinels."

So it seemed Davies was right. The reason the SEVs had got through the portal safely was that they were ancient pieces of junk, and whoever had created the sensors had no expectation that Sol would be sending museum pieces into their universe. There seemed to be other data sets in the code, but they were heavily encrypted.

It wasn't until Davies and Fernandez were discussing the Sentinels near Ten that they had their answer.

"It's obvious, isn't it? Dormant code. We found the same thing in the Deathless gear. They have their own language, right? But once you know enough of it, you can go into a settings menu on their power armour or ships, and literally flip the switch to set it to English, or Russian, or French. They never bothered removing all that stuff. Storage isn't an issue for them, and when they left Sol, they had scientists and engineers from all over the world. So they just left it in."

Fernandez and Davies stared at him in amazement.

"What? Why are you looking at me like that?"

"Just surprised, is all," said Davies with a shrug. "I wouldn't have taken you for a tech specialist."

"Yeah, I get that a lot," sighed Ten. "I haven't managed to shut out Gooders when she's yammering away about her latest discoveries. Then there's this group of surveillance pilots in New Bristol who insist on coming to me with their stories. You wouldn't believe the way they drone on and on about, well, drones. Nice kids. Bloodthirsty, but nice in their own way." He trailed off, frowning down at his data slate.

Davies opened his mouth to ask more, but Fernandez gave a subtle shake of his head and mouthed, "Let him be."

And now, with the final clues from Ten, Fernandez was able to make some headway with the software and run some tests on the older, unencrypted Royal Navy scan data. He quickly demonstrated that the sentinel detected signatures, ran them against its database, encrypted or otherwise, and sent reports to some central service, the nature of which was still unknown.

They gathered the rest of the team for an update on their findings.

"They're basically fully-automated electronic snitches. They watch the portal, categorise every ship they see, and relay the details to a hidden master service," said Fernandez. "So the big questions are, who or what is receiving this information, and how did they manage to repel a ship the size of *Colossus* with such apparent ease?"

"I think that if we could answer those questions, we'd quickly get a sense of what we're up against," said Conway. "Is Admiral Stansfield completely signed up to the fact that this is a hostile force? Other than the fact that they destroyed *Colossus*, of course? I mean, that might have been a defensive manoeuvre, we did send a kick-arse war machine right through their front door, after all. I think I might be a bit pissed off if somebody did that to me."

Fernandez opened his mouth to reply, but the ever-present Woodhall spoke over him.

"This is good work," he said. "I will send a glowing report back to the Admiralty. Send your data and a summary of your conclusions to my console so that I can pass it over for immediate analysis and recommendation. Needless to say, we won't be taking any action until we hear from Earth."

Woodhall marched off self-importantly, and the atmosphere relaxed the minute he stepped out of the hangar, allowing the team to speak freely once again.

"Stansfield seems convinced that this presents a huge risk to Earth, though I've seen nothing to support that so far," said Fernandez, breaking the silence. "However, I'm new here, not original *Vengeance* crew. A bit like Woodhall, I'm a modern-day Admiralty crony. Only I'm not averse to a bit of creative rule interpretation from time to time to get the job done. I can't say I subscribe to Woodhall's reading of the guidelines."

"Stansfield is a tough geezer," said Hunter. "And much as I resent his attitude, men like him are warhorses, they know the heat of battle, the fear of defeat and the terror of losing good men. I gotta tell you, if he tells me that he's shitting bricks about what's coming through that portal, I'll happily shit a few with him. Besides, I've heard him and Vernon talking, and those two know more than they're letting on. In fact, this whole crew feel like they're manning a ghost ship."

He paused to check that they weren't being overheard, then lowered his voice.

"I've been on *Vengeance* for three weeks now, and if you asked me to wager on it, I'd say these guys know exactly what we're dealing with. Only they're not letting on."

"So how about a test to move things on?" Davies asked. "Let's not get bogged down with red tape, we can leave Woodhall and Stansfield to squabble about that. I say we send in two shuttle ships, one of those beat-up old things over there, and, if you've got one, a modern Sol cruiser."

"Risky," said Fernandez, "but it would test the hypothesis, and I think I agree. If any good came from *Colossus* being this far out in space, it was that they delivered some decent bits of kit and spare parts to *Kingdom 10*. And some of that stuff is now on board, so we're not restricted to the limited technology that came with *Vengeance*, and we have some decent weaponry available. All of it's ready to go right now, but at least we're not stuck with stripping old vehicles for parts."

"We should send in the newer ship first," Davies advised. "But let's strip it first so that we salvage as much kit as possible. What do you think Stansfield will say? Is he going to be happy to sacrifice a shiny new space vehicle in the name of science?"

But Davies had missed the tangible change of atmosphere in the hangar, and he turned to find Stansfield and Vernon standing behind him, listening to him speak.

"Sir," said Davies with a slightly green expression.

"I concur with your thinking, Davies. I suspected as much when *Colossus* was destroyed. I agree with you, it would make sense for the technology around the portal to be scanning for Royal Navy signatures. Permission granted to strip down one of the shuttles and send it in remotely to the portal. How long until you can make this happen?"

"If I assign enough engineers to the team, within the hour, sir. Will you be waiting for Woodhall's response from the Admiralty before proceeding?"

Fernandez couldn't have been more obvious about his body language if he'd had his fingers crossed behind his back.

Stansfield gave him a steady look. "Let me worry about Woodhall and the Admiralty, Lieutenant. In the meantime, make your preparations. I want the second shuttle ready to go through immediately after the first. If we prove the theory, we take *Vengeance* through. I'm not waiting here like a lame duck. Let's get those shuttles launched into space, ladies and gentlemen."

Stansfield had barely finished the sentence before Fernandez began assigning the teams to their respective shuttles and the preparation process had begun.

He was as good as his word. Only an hour later, the test ships were been manoeuvred into the front of the launch hangar. Everything useful had been stripped from each vehicle to the extent that they were basically skeletons, a simple metal framework carrying only its means of propulsion and anything else that couldn't be removed without welding or cutting.

"Conway, I'd like you to remote-control the shuttles," said Fernandez, "You've got a good handle on getting through that portal already. Besides, there wasn't even a scratch on your SEV, you're my favourite safe driver at the moment."

Davies shared a meaningful glance with Mason and Kearney. It was clear Fernandez knew bothing of Conway's past.

"I'd like to attach monitoring equipment to the front of the first shuttle, sir," said Davies. "I want to know what's firing on the other side of the portal. We need to understand what we're dealing with here."

"I think you're right," Fernandez replied. "If we start to gather data about their armoury and overall ability to fire on us, that at least gives us some kind of advantage if we end up getting into a scrape with these guys." He gave the nod, and his engineering crews rushed off to locate some monitoring equipment to be lashed to one of the seats of the shuttle.

After another fifteen minutes, the shuttle was ready for launch, with Conway sitting at a remote console deep within the launch hangar. Fernandez, Charlie Team and a group of eager engineers gathered around the monitoring screens to watch the operation. With the sure confidence of an experienced pilot, Conway took the first shuttle out and guided it towards the part of space where the portal had been.

"How long do we have to wait?" asked Conway, staring at the stars from the cruiser's viewpoint.

But before anyone could answer, the portal observed its regular opening times and obliged them by opening, right when they were expecting it. As before, it began with a bright white dot in space, then quickly expanded to create the wonderful array of dancing colours that they had all marvelled at previously.

"Sending in shuttle one," said Conway. "Distance of four kilometres and closing."

"Look!" Davies erupted. "There are monitors on this side of the portal," he said, pointing at one of the screens. "They know we're here already. Those contraptions around the mouth of the portal, look at them, they're talking to each other!"

"We're getting all of this on the bridge," Stansfield's voice came over the intercom. "Do you see the purple lights flashing on those units? They know the shuttle's there, they can sense us."

"Two kilometres," said Conway. "Damn, look at those things, you can see them transmitting data to something, they look like they've gone into overdrive!"

"How are they sending data through the portal?" wondered Davies, leaning forward. "We lost all contact with you guys after you passed over."

"Conway, go faster," said Ten. "If they're going to blow up that thing, let's at least get it through the portal so we can see what they're throwing at it."

"Taking the shuttle to maximum acceleration now. By the look of those devices, we're about to get a big bang any moment. Let's hope it's fast enough."

Conway pushed the shuttle as fast she could make it fly, directly towards the heart of the portal. Using the close monitoring that the shuttle gave them, they were able to see the array of lights of the monitoring devices as they detected the intruder, confirmed its size and shape with each other, then transmitted that data to an enemy unknown.

As the shuttle entered the skin of the portal and began to disappear within its centre, there was a massive explosion. The shuttle was belched back out of the portal, smashed to smithereens by whatever had shot at it from the other side, and all that was left in space was a cloud of debris from a Sol shuttle that had just taken its final flight.

12

"**D**ammit!" said Fernandez. "We're no wiser than we were beforehand."

"We have evidence to support our hypothesis, sir," pointed out Davies. "Our modern ship was destroyed, just as we predicted."

"I'm going in on the second shuttle," Ten said. "We need to recover the monitor, and if we get a glimpse of what they're firing at us, we have some hope of defending ourselves."

"And what if we're wrong about the shuttle signatures?" Conway asked. "You'll end up as a piece of floating space junk just like that first shuttle."

"I'm happy to take the risk," said Ten. "I like to know what I'm shooting at when I go into battle, so I want that monitoring equipment back if it's out there."

"Get yourself on board the second shuttle, Marine X," Stansfield's voice came over the intercom once again. "Lieutenant Woodhall is in conversation with the Admiralty as I speak, and I do not want that man hindering our operations. The sooner we can get this done, the better."

"On my way, sir," said Ten, needing no further prompt. Still wearing his power armour, he checked his oxygen levels, ensured his helmet was still operational, then ran over to the landing platform and strapped himself into the second shuttle.

The craft was old and battered, like it had just been retrieved from a scrapyard. It looked like it had seen much better days, and had all the signs of a craft that had served Sol well. No sooner had Ten strapped himself in, the burners fired, and Conway launched the ship into space. Ten got some sense of what it must have been like for Hunter being towed along the back of his SEV.

The engineering team had left very little but the shell of the shuttle. It was much like taking a trip on a bed frame, but this bed frame had a pair of blue burners at its rear and was hurtling through space at speed towards that portal.

Looking down at *Vengeance* below him, Ten thought he saw the ship begin to move. Until now, it had sat there in space, idle and static, safely monitoring at a distance from the mouth of the portal. But now, even whilst distracted by the shimmering lights of the fissure, Ten was certain that it was turning to follow him. Surely Stansfield wasn't planning to come in directly after him? That showed an enthusiasm for engagement that put even him to shame.

His musings were interrupted by Conway. "You sure you're happy for me take you through?"

"No reason not to," Ten replied. "I'm certain that Davies is right about this. Well, I'm mostly certain, anyway. It's a risk someone has to take, so let's just crack on, shall we?"

The second shuttle moved slowly through the mouth of the portal. The bridge crew on *Vengeance*, Conway and Ten monitored the sentinels to see if they had sensed his movement, but all was as it had been with the SEVs. As far as these devices were concerned, he was invisible.

"Going through," said Ten, his voice crackling as the massive interference from the wormhole disrupted his comms. The moment he passed through the portal, the channel went abruptly silent.

~

PAUL TEAGUE & JON EVANS

"Okay, I've lost control, he's on his own now," Conway said. "You'd think that a man could get too much excitement in one day!"

"Are we moving?" Davies asked, looking up from his screens in the hangar.

"The admiral is moving us closer to the portal," said Fernandez. "I'm not sure what the old man is up to, but my guess is he's playing cat and mouse with the Admiralty."

"Just how close?" Conway asked, frowning hard.

"Don't ask," said Fernandez. "I think the minute Ten comes back with the shuttle intact, *Vengeance* will be heading straight through the portal. Stansfield has had itchy feet for days, ever since the Admiralty lost *Colossus*."

The portal hung on the vid screens, a giant mess of colour against the blackness of space.

"Come on," said Davies, as if he might pull Ten home by sheer will alone. "Don't let me down."

The minutes dragged on. The hangar was quiet, every eye focussed on the screens, waiting.

"How long do we wait?" someone asked, but nobody answered.

And then the colours shifted, and the battered nose of an ancient shuttle nudged slowly out of the portal. There was a cheer in the hangar as the tension broke.

"Did you miss me, *Vengeance*?" said Ten as the shuttle cleared the portal.

"What took you so long?" asked Conway.

"Well, I didn't I stop for tea and biscuits, if that's what you're worried about," said Ten. "The monitor had been ejected, just as we planned, but it took me a while to find and snag it."

Charlie Team and the engineering teams watched as the shuttle made its way sedately toward *Vengeance*.

"It's as you said, Davies," said Ten over the radio. "It has to be the signatures. There wasn't one moment of recognition from those devices, we're completely invisible on the other side of the portal. They can't detect us."

"Acknowledged," said Davies calmly, as if he'd never had any doubts about his hypothesis.

"We have a connection to the monitoring equipment," said Fernandez. "Downloading the files now, I'll let you know what happened to that first shuttle as soon as we can."

Fernandez was excited. The retrieved files would give them a glimpse of the hostilities that waited for them on the other side of the portal.

Stansfield's voice boomed out across the loudspeakers positioned throughout the battleship as he made a ship-wide announcement.

"*Vengeance* crew, this is what we waited for. This is why we lay hidden for so many years in this part of space. I've seen enough to convince me that it's safe to go through that portal and that our need to proceed with our mission is urgent. I'm not waiting for it to open up again in another three hours. We cannot risk the future of our planet by sitting out here in space and idly waiting.

"I've given the order for us to go through. We'll be at action stations alert until we are safely on the other side. Five minutes until we enter the portal. We don't know what's waiting for us out there, but whatever it is, I trust that the crew of *Vengeance* will be more than up to the challenge. Stansfield out."

"We've got our footage, ladies and gentlemen," said Fernandez. "It's being rerouted to my console now."

Ten powered down the shuttle so that he hovered in space between *Vengeance* and the portal, and waited for the file to hit his HUD. It was there in a moment, and he braced himself, eager to get a first glimpse of their foe.

The poor-quality footage showed the view from the front of the first shuttle as it emerged through the portal. The moment it did so, the sentinel devices began to scan the entire ship, and the camera was ejected, flying away from the doomed spaceship.

Moments later, before the shuttle was even fully through the portal, it was blasted by some remote device outside the camera's view. The shuttle was destroyed, and they watched as it was pushed through the portal, back to where it had come from.

Then everything was silent, the portal shrinking as the camera moved slowly away, and nothing else happened until Ten's ship appeared. Fernandez zipped back to step slowly through the images.

"Not a lot to go on there," said Hunter.

"As far as I can see," Davies picked up, "those devices scan whatever goes through the portal, then something else destroys it. They're gathering intelligence as well as wrecking our toys."

"Yes, but it's the signatures they're detecting," said Kearney. "They're only as good as the technology they're made of. If they're not looking for us, they're not likely to find us." She had been quiet for some time, as was her way. She was a Marine who performed better in the silence, but like the rest of the team, she was anxious to know what they were dealing with.

Stansfield's voice came over the intercom. This time he spoke only to the team in the bay and to Ten, still sitting in his shuttle. "We're about to go through the portal with *Vengeance*. Marine X, I'd like you to follow us through and join us on the other side."

"Acknowledged, sir," said Ten. He moved the shuttle out of *Vengeance*'s path and positioned it so that he'd be able to enter the hangar as soon as they passed through the portal.

On the bridge, Woodhall blustered around, demanding that they cease their mission immediately.

"The Admiralty will be issuing a direct order not to enter the portal until more research and surveillance has been completed," he shouted at the admiral. "That order is being sent in an encrypted message to you right now. If you go through that portal, you will be disobeying a specific directive. I'm sure that even you, with your rich history of military achievement, would not want to put all that at risk, Admiral."

Stansfield held out his data slate and stared directly into Woodhall's eyes.

"So you're saying the order will arrive at any moment now, direct to my slate?" Stansfield took a step forward so that he was mere inches from Woodhall. "I agree, Lieutenant Woodhall, that once I receive your rumoured order, I'm bound by Admiralty regulations to obey it," he hissed. Then, without looking away, he asked more loudly, "How long until we're through the portal?"

"Passing through at the moment, sir," said the midshipman at the navigation console, looking like he'd rather be anywhere else. "A few minutes at current speed."

Stansfield looked at his slate and held it up for Woodhall to see.

"It seems we've just lost all communications with Sol. I would be delighted to obey their orders, but due to the technical interference caused by passing through the portal, I'm unable to confirm that the order was in fact issued," hissed Stansfield, his eyes burning with the light of madness.

Woodhall opened his mouth to speak, but Admiral Stansfield held up his hand and cut him off. "Take a deep breath, Lieutenant, and unclench your arse-cheeks. You're along for the ride now."

13

As *Vengeance* slid through the swirling colours of the portal, all radio communications on the bridge fell silent. For the crew, it was an eerie sensation. Crackles of conversations between them and Sol had punctuated every hour of every day, and the termination of contact felt very much like losing a safety blanket.

Having put Woodhall back in his box, for the time being at least, Stansfield took the conn from Vernon and began to monitor their progress through the phenomenon. He was hungry for information.

"Place the portal view on full screen," he said. "I'd like to get an idea of how they're achieving this."

"Initial analysis suggests the ability to harness and sustain a massive power source, though how it's being done beats me," said Lieutenant Yau.

Davies was analysing the stream of data from *Vengeance's* sensors at a console on the deck.

"I've never seen anything like it," he murmured. To his knowledge, Sol was nowhere near capable of a technical breakthrough of this magnitude.

Stansfield opened a channel to Fernandez. "We have attack craft ready in the bay, yes?"

"Two attack craft readied and primed, sir," said Fernandez from the launch hanger. "I have Conway, Mason, Kearney and Hunter in the old Raptors, and ten of our own people on standby in the HR2s. Raptors use old Sol signatures, that's our safest response strategy if we encounter any problems."

"Agreed, Fernandez. Stay at action stations until we're through safely."

Ten's voice came over the comms unit. "Hey, don't forget me out here on this floating bed frame."

"What do you see out there, Marine X?" asked Stansfield.

"Nothing worth reporting, sir. There are no signs of alert or defensive action. *Vengeance* is passing through unseen, I think we're all good here."

The ship moved slowly through the mouth of the portal. The crew was tense; every factor that could be monitored was being examined by engineering, defensive and science teams.

Ten had significantly more movement capability than *Vengeance*, so he used the time to check out the guardian devices that had detected – the ones that had caused the destruction of *Colossus* and the first test shuttle.

The massive hulk of *Vengeance* was able to pass through without them batting an eyelid, though still the guardians floated there in space, waiting, watching, seeking. For some reason, it made Ten uneasy.

"Might go off at any time," muttered Ten. *Colossus* had been a significantly larger and more capable ship than *Vengeance*, yet whoever had created this wormhole had made light work of the Navy's newest ship. *Vengeance* would be no match if it came to a game of *whose weapon is biggest?*

Then the portal began to shrink, and Ten sat up in his seat. "We may have a problem, *Vengeance*, are you seeing this on the bridge?"

"Affirmative, Marine X," Stansfield replied, intently focussed on the task in hand. "We're seeing fast and sudden portal contraction. Current estimates at a five per cent reduction in circumference. Can I get a projection on how long until total closure, please!"

"It's closing much faster than before, sir. *Vengeance* needs four more minutes to pass through completely, it's going to be a close thing."

"What are you seeing, Marine X?"

"Sentinel activity, sir. It's like they're chattering to themselves, but no indication yet of defensive action. If you asked me to make an assessment, I'd say they've seen us."

"So why aren't they taking offensive action?" Stansfield asked aloud. "Can we increase speed, Fernandez?"

"Affirmative, Admiral, but if we increase speed, we'll reduce our capacity to fast-launch the Raptors if we need to…"

"Advice, please," Stansfield said.

"Suggest maintaining a suitable Raptor launch speed and monitoring progression of wormhole closure," said Fernandez.

"Launch Raptors, then increase speed," came Conway's voice from her position in the bay.

"I agree with Conway, sir," said Davies. "I've not seen the portal close as fast as this, and it's going to catch our tail if we don't accelerate."

"You must turn back and wait for orders from the Admiralty, backup, and authorisation to proceed further," said Woodhall.

"Three minutes to portal closure," came a voice from the bridge.

"No, we're committed, and this is a one-way trip," said Stansfield. "Launch Raptors, Charlie Team, and get through the portal. Helm, increase speed the moment they've launched. Calculations please, Davies."

"A twenty-five per cent increase in speed at ninety seconds will get us through, sir. You've got a minute to get your butts out of that bay, Charlie Team."

"I'm seeing stars already, DD!" came Conway's voice. She'd been itching to launch and had fired her engines before Stansfield had even completed his command.

"Me too," Hunter's voice followed, then Kearney, then Mason.

"Charlie Team are clear," said Fernandez. "HRs at the ready if we need them."

"Why not just increase speed and launch the Hostile Response craft?" asked a frustrated Woodhall. "What's the point of giving you that capability if you stick to using your outdated technology?"

"Let me remind you that our 'outdated technology' is what got us this far," snapped Stansfield. "Those Raptors use old signatures, they won't set off anything nasty going through the portal."

"Yes, but once we're through the portal, what does it matter? Surely we should be using the best we have, not crappy old attack craft that should have been mothballed decades ago!"

Vernon interrupted this time.

"Those crappy old Raptors have saved this ship's arse on more occasions than I care to remember. They've saved my own life on at least fifteen separate occasions. Don't knock a Raptor, Lieutenant, they're built of strong stuff and a delight to handle in battle."

Woodhall was silenced at last, but Stansfield could see he was going to be a constant problem. They watched him slink off, away from the bridge, no doubt to plan his next snitching call to the Admiralty if they ever managed to re-establish comms.

"Speed increased by twenty-five per cent as requested," said Fernandez.

"Raptors, maintain escort pattern for *Vengeance*. Keep your eyes open wide, ladies and gentlemen," said Vernon. "If anything moves out there, I want to know about it."

Davies jumped up like he'd had sudden inspiration. "I've got an idea, sir."

"Speak," said Stansfield.

"That shuttle Ten is in. We can use it to open a data wormhole to Sol and hop signals out of the portal when it opens."

"Thirty seconds," came the countdown from the bridge.

"Park that idea, Davies," said Stansfield. "Are we getting through?" he asked.

"Increase speed!" Davies shouted. "Now, by fifty per cent.""

"Do it!" Stansfield commanded.

"Ay, sir, adjusting now," said the midshipman at the helm.

"Are the instrument calibrations correct on this ship?" Davies asked. He'd gone from inspired to flustered in ten seconds flat.

"We tend to allow a little extra here and there," Vernon, frowning at Davies" excitement.

"What do you mean by that?" Davies asked, completely oblivious to the expressions on his superiors' faces.

"Well, if a dial reads ten," said Fernandez, "it probably means somewhere between nine and eleven, but it could be anything from six to fourteen."

Davies frowned.

"Don't take anything on *Vengeance* as an absolute reading," said Fernandez. "We tend to add in a bit of buffer when making calculations."

"Portal closed, we're now through safely," Vernon issued the update.

"Bring us to rest four kilometres clear of the dead centre of the portal," said Stansfield, "then let's take a look at what's out there. And get me some data on that portal closing, that's the shortest window I've seen for as long as we've been observing that thing. Vernon, get me a scan of this star system, I want to know if it's known to Sol."

"It's all quiet out here," said Kearney. "Not that I'm bored or anything, but it's as dead as night."

"Yeah," replied Ten, "but have you seen what ugly creatures come out to play at night? Permission to bring this piece of crap back to the hangar and get my butt into the seat of one of those Raptors?"

"Permission granted," came Stansfield's voice over the comms. "Charlie Team, maintain your escort array pending a full scan of the area. Marine X, get yourself out back out there in a more suitable vehicle. I'm interested in this idea of yours, Davies. The one with the shuttle."

"Listen in, Fernandez," said Vernon.

"If we send out Marine X's shuttle when the portal next opens, we can rig a line through the portal to a comms buoy and talk to *Kingdom 10*."

"Like a short-range walkie-talkie?" Fernandez asked.

"Exactly, sir," said Davies. "And if *Kingdom 10*'s new wormhole communicator, courtesy of *Colossus*, is up and running, we'll be able to talk to Sol. It'll be no use to use when the portal is closed, but the minute it opens, we can hop signals from *Kingdom 10* to the shuttle, down the line to the buoy, and then to *Vengeance*."

"And security?" Stansfield asked. "It can't be an open comms line from *Vengeance* to the shuttle."

"We could assign a dynamic encryption protocol to everything leaving *Vengeance*. Once it's hopped from the shuttle, it would be secure by default. At least we won't be on our own out here."

"Do it," Stansfield said. "Davies, work with Fernandez. I'm taking you away from your team while you sort this out. Make it a priority, I want to test it next time that portal opens."

<Later, suckers> sent Davies to Charlie Team's HUDs.

"We've got the report on the star system, Admiral," said Vernon as he stepped over to Stansfield. "You may like to see this before we share it."

"In my ready room," said the Admiral. "Anybody else need to see it yet? Operationally?"

"I think you'll want to see this privately first, sir, before we communicate to the team."

They moved to the side of the bridge into Stansfield's sparse and neglected ready room. It looked much like it had been under dust sheets for some time.

"Okay, Ed," said Stansfield when the door had closed. "What is it?"

"We know why *Vengeance* is *here*," said Vernon darkly, "but we don't know why we're here *right now*."

"No clues in the report?" said Stansfield with a frown.

"Nothing, sir," said Vernon. "It's like the rest of the Navy just forgot about this place. They built *Kingdom10*, ran it as a military base for a few decades, then turned her over to a civilian scientific project. Nothing's happened here for over a century."

"Figures," grunted Stansfield. "Bloody desk-pilots. They wouldn't know a threat if it smacked them in the face."

"Anyway," said Vernon, ignoring Stansfield's cynical observations, "the point is that the Navy has no other resources in the area. It's us and Kingdom10, that's it."

Stansfield frowned and looked up, surprised. "You're sure? Just *Vengeance*?"

Vernon nodded, and Stansfield frowned even harder.

"Then we'd better make sure we're up to the challenge, Commander, because things might get a bit difficult if it's just us."

"Aye, sir," said Vernon. "I guess we're just in the right place at the right time."

"Exactly as we planned, Ed," said Stansfield. "Exactly as we planned."

14

"Permission to take a look around, sir?" said Conway over the comms system.

"Permission granted," came Stansfield's voice, now back on the bridge. "Steady out there, Charlie Team, I can't believe they don't know we're here."

"Defensive cluster, Charlie Team. No day-trips, Ten, understood?" said Conway.

"Yeah, of course," he replied, now comfortably ensconced in his own Raptor. "Though it does look kinda pretty over there."

"Has anybody ever flown one of these things before?" Mason asked.

"I used to VR them at the academy, they're lovely machines," said Conway, allowing her mind to wander back to simpler days. "I don't know why the Navy moved onto the HR craft, they always felt a bit flimsy to me."

"Somebody told them that small craft were a boon for space combat," said Ten acidly. "As if anyone would ever bother to use the bloody things in anger."

Hunter joined in the conversation. "Decommissioned Raptors are used by space pirates and smugglers these days. They love 'em 'cos they're fast, small and have space for both a few passengers and a little cargo. Did anybody play *Deadly Mission 3* in VR when they were younger?"

"Yeah, I loved that game," said Mason, joining Hunter on the trip down memory lane.

"The Gazelles in that game are a direct rip-off of Raptors," said Hunter. "The Navy tried take legal action over it, it was so close. Military secrets and all that. It was a great game, though."

Ten's voice interrupted the nostalgia trip. "Incoming! What is that thing?"

"It's coming straight at us," Conway responded. "Shit, there are five of them. Action stations, Charlie Team, spread out. Be warned, *Vengeance*, we are under attack."

The five Raptors dispersed from their cluster and spread out.

"Has anybody got a visual yet?" asked Kearney.

"I see them," Mason confirmed. "Five black spheres, active mines or heat-seeking missiles, I'd guess. Technology unknown. They're not heading for *Vengeance*, repeat, not heading for *Vengeance*."

"Balls," exclaimed Ten, "five of them, and that's not something I thought I'd be able to put in my mission report. Right, watch this, I may need your backup."

"Steady, Ten," Conway cautioned. "Oh, too late, I see."

Ten had accelerated hard in his Raptor and acted as bait for the approaching missiles. As he'd done so, one of the spheres had broken formation and moved to intercept him.

"We've got one each," said Mason. "Did anybody see if those things were fired or if they were sitting there already?"

"My guess is they're Sentinel Mines," said Kearney. "Sol used to deploy them, but they get a bad rep because they have a habit of taking out friendly craft. Whoever left these out here doesn't give a crap about the risks."

"We were ten kilometres out from the portal centre when they activated," said Conway. "Looks like we breached some perimeter or stepped on a tripwire."

"Err, excuse me guys," Ten interrupted, keen to remind them of his present predicament. "It's all right you all having a nice chit-chat, but some of us have a Sentinel Mine right up their arse."

"On it, Ten," Mason responded, snapping into action. "Prepare for a bump, I'm going to have to shoot it just beyond your burners."

"Bracing."

"Wow, I love this targeting system," Mason said, excited at piloting the unfamiliar craft.

"What's the shooting like?" Ten asked sarcastically. "Seriously, you might want to give that a try too. Like sometime before I get blown up by this thing?"

There was a massive purple explosion at Ten's rear, and his Raptor was showered with shrapnel. Alarms blared and the monitors flashed damage reports, but the critical systems were undamaged.

"Got it," Mason declared.

"That scorched my arse, it was so close," said Ten. "Damage is minimal, though. If that thing had caught me before Mason smashed it, I'd have been toast."

"I love these Raptors," said Mason, delighted to be getting some action. "Conway, you're next, I recommend evasive action."

"I see it, Mason. Kearney, have you got this?"

"I'm on it," she replied. "Mason and Ten, stay alert, we've all got one of these things on our rear."

"I could do with your help, Kearney," Conway reminded her, watching the mine getting closer.

"Damn it, Mason, you're right about this targeting system," said Kearney, getting into the swing of piloting her Raptor. "Watch this, and brace for impact, Hunter."

There were two purple explosions in rapid succession: first the mine that was tracking Conway, then the mine that had moved to intercept Hunter.

"Whoa, careful, Kearney," Hunter mock-protested. "At least warn a man before you stick a firework up his behind!"

Conway wasted no time getting straight back to her objectives. "Mason and Kearney, continue using evasive flying patterns, those things are getting faster."

"I've got yours in my sights, Mason," came Kearney's voice. "It's almost on you. Damn, these things are good, it's predicting your movement pattern."

"Try the random evasive option," Hunter suggested. "Scroll down, it's at the bottom of the options. They fixed that bug on the VR Gazelles, but never did it in real life, by the look of it."

"Yeah, I've got that now," Mason responded, checking his controls. "Neat, it can't keep up with me now. Thanks, Hunter, good tip."

"Brace for impact, Mason," said Kearney. "Damn it, it missed. Are these things *learning*?"

Kearney's missile flew past the dark, spherical object and exploded well away from its target.

"I think that's an affirmative, Kearney," Conway confirmed. "Move to evasive now, your Sentinel Mine is too close for comfort. Deploy the random evasive option like the nice man said."

"Gee, no one ever called me a nice man before."

"There's a first time for everything, Hunter," Conway said, a smile in her voice. "How about you take a shot at one of these things and show us how good you were playing *Deadly Mission 3*?"

"My pleasure!" Hunter exclaimed. "Watch and learn, Charlie Team, this is how you fly a Raptor."

Hunter drew away from Conway and Ten and positioned himself above Kearney and Mason, who were both in a random evasive array pattern. He plugged his finger into one of the data transfer ports on the ship's console, and a green light pulsed to confirm that his download had been completed.

"Oh, yes! It took the mod. Watch this shot, Ten, you're gonna pee your pants over this." Hunter was getting carried away with himself now. "Kearney and Mason, you'll see a code on your HUDs. Enter it into your consoles now."

Hunter confirmed his targeting options, waiting for confirmation that Kearney and Mason had done as he'd told them, then launched two missiles, one after the other.

"Not a hope in hell, Hunter," Ten said. "Those missiles are going wide."

"Agreed, Ten," said Conway. "The Sentinels are getting too close for comfort."

There were two explosions in the distance. Conway and Ten checked that the right thing had exploded. It had; Hunter had just taken out the last remaining Sentinel Mines.

"How the hell did you do that?" Ten asked, genuinely impressed. "Those mines were all over the place, what with your random evasive pattern, or whatever Conway called it."

"I downloaded a game mod from *Deadly Mission 3* into my Raptor," Hunter beamed, relishing in the admiration. "It's called *Random Array Replicator*. It allows missiles to track the randomised movements of Kearney's and Mason's craft, then predict to ninety-eight per cent accuracy the resultant actions hostile weaponry will take. It got it just right, it usually does."

"Jeez, Hunter, no wonder the Admiralty was pissed off about that game," said Mason.

"It was made by the same guy who built my arm," Hunter revealed. "That man knows his stuff when it comes to tech. If the Navy weren't so sniffy about human rights and shit like that, they'd be able to deploy this tech to the troops."

"But can you pick your nose with it, eh, Hunter?" asked Ten. "Because if a man can't pick his nose with his robo-arm, what use is it?"

"Sorry to break up this fascinating insight into the mind of a grown man who plays games for kids," Conway interjected, "but there are more of those things on their way. Can you patch that mod though to the other Raptors, Hunter?"

"I don't know how Fernandez would feel about that," Ten said.

"Lieutenant Fernandez is busy working on a comms project with Trooper Davies in the bays," came the voice of the Engineering Officer on their radios. "I guess he won't know. Nice shooting work, by the way!"

"Does he monitor everything?" asked Hunter.

"Yes, I do," came the reply.

"Sending the mod now," said Hunter.

"Humour me, Charlie Team," Conway picked up. "I want to test my new ten-k theory with these Sentinel Mines."

"I'm always in the market for a bit of creativity, Conway. What's your vibe?" Mason asked.

"Those mines weren't triggered until we were ten kilometres from the portal," Conway explained. "Ten thousand metres, dead on, and that's no coincidence. That's something human engineers would do."

"Careful, Conway, I'm still monitoring," came the voice of Fernandez.

"No normal person would fuss that much," Conway continued. "They'd mark a perimeter in a rough spot, and that would be that."

"Do you think that's what this is? A perimeter?" said Ten, intrigued by her suggestion.

"I hope so," Conway replied. "If not, we've got fifteen of those Sentinel Mines to shake off. I don't fancy our chances of getting all fifteen, even with Hunter's mod."

Mason thought it was a sound theory. "Agreed, let's pull back to ten-k and see if Conway is right."

"Kearney," said Conway, "you're too far out, come back in closer." Kearney had become separated from the pack; she had a couple of kilometres to make up.

"Get out of there, Kearney..." Conway warned.

Mason, Hunter, Ten and Conway spun their Raptors back towards *Vengeance*. Kearney did the same, monitoring the Sentinel Mines as she did so. Three of them had split off from the main pack, heading her way now.

"This is going to be tight," said Kearney, doubt in her voice. "I might need your help, guys, stay alert, please."

"Watching those fuckers like a hawk," Ten reassured her.

"Same here," said Hunter. "I've got all three eyes on those critters."

"Three eyes?" said Mason, alarmed at the thought.

"Don't ask," warned Conway. "I need your minds on the job at hand."

One by one, the Raptors came in over the ten-kilometre line. As each craft entered Conway's theoretical perimeter, three of the Sentinels broke off and switched to target Kearney's Raptor instead.

"Well, thanks for nothing, guys," said Kearney. "I've got fifteen of those things chasing me now!"

"Hellfire, what are they?" said Conway. "We're coming out to assist Kearney."

"No, I can do this," she protested. "We need to test your theory. If I make it to the ten-k line and these things still have their noses up my sphincter, then you can help!"

Kearney moved to full throttle and patched in the evasive array option. She could see all fifteen of the deadly spheres on her monitoring screen, getting closer – closer – closer by the second.

"Have we got radial armoury on these things?" said Kearney. "Does anybody know?"

Hunter knew the answer. "Yep, scroll down, it's one of the few criticisms pilots had of these things. Counter-intuitive labelling in the menus. You say *radial*, Raptor says *360*. It's first in your menu."

"We've got to go out and help Kearney. There's too many of them, even with random switched on. You're outgunned, let us help."

Conway was genuinely concerned that Kearney would be outpaced.

"Negative, Conway," Kearney insisted. "I can do this. It's going to be tight, but I'm certain I can make it. Where's DD when you need his maths skills? One thousand metres from the perimeter, engines at max burn, fifteen Sentinels...fuck!"

There was a massive purple explosion, the wreckage from Kearney's Raptor went hurtling out of control over Conway's perimeter, and then it went deathly quiet in space.

15

"Kearney? Kearney? Damn you, Kearney!" Conway was frustrated and disoriented.

"Chill, Conway, it's all good," Hunter reassured her.

"Stick your chill where the sun don't shine," Conway was genuinely angry. "I can't lose another – *we're* not losing another member of the team."

"We're not losing any team members today, Conway," said Ten, anxious to put her out of her worry. "Look out there."

Conway steadied herself. She'd let down her guard, which was rare for her, but after what had happened with Gallagher, she was tightly wound. She looked out into space and breathed a sigh of relief. Far off in the distance, maybe three hundred metres beyond the perimeter, Kearney floated in her power armour, still in her pilot's seat. Silent, still and waiting were the nine remaining Sentinel Mines, lined up obediently around the perimeter as if waiting for permission to step over an invisible line.

"I told you," said Conway, greatly cheered now. "Engineers love round numbers, they just can't help themselves."

"I'm still monitoring," came the voice of Fernandez once again. "And that's another spacecraft destroyed. I am counting, you know."

"Whoa," said Kearney, feeling a little exposed.

"What is it, Kearney?" Conway asked.

Conway looked out on her colleague with relief as she deployed another of the features that a previous generation of Sol pilots had loved so much: an ejector seat option with the ability to get some basic propulsion in space. Every time she boosted the seat to move herself closer to the perimeter, the Sentinel Mines jumped but didn't re-target her. The trace from her boosters wasn't enough for her to be targeted.

Kearney spoke again. "Hey, Fernandez, seeing as you're listening in anyway. The SEVs must give out a similar negligible trace. Surely that means we can get in close and disarm these things manually?"

"That's good thinking, Kearney, you're right," said Fernandez. "They give a minimal trace, nothing like a fighter or a shuttle. I'm not sure if I'd like to be in your space boots diffusing a line of alien Sentinel Mines, though."

"Who says they're alien?" said Conway. "Kilometres are a human unit of measurement, and this perimeter is ten kilometres dead. Somebody said *I want a perimeter around that portal at ten k*. We said it already with the Guardian units, these things originate from Earth tech. That perimeter has every sign it was put up by humans. I'd say this is the work of an Ark ship crew. Does anyone know if any Arks headed out this way?"

"You're right about that ten-kilometre limit, Conway," said Mason. "Hey look, Kearney's back. You looked like you were paddling back to shore on that thing."

"Ha," said Kearney, not laughing. "It's not the most elegant way of getting through space, but it saved my neck. And it proved Conway's theory."

"Sorry to butt in, guys," said Ten, "but am I the only one excited by the prospect of disarming these things from an SEV? Come on, everybody – party!"

"I've got a right arm that'll help with that," said Hunter.

"Is there anything that tin arm of yours doesn't do?" asked Ten with genuine interest.

"Saving kittens," Hunter replied unexpectedly. "It's not good at saving kittens. When I'd just got it fitted I tried to save a kitten. I hadn't got the hang of my strength at that stage, so–"

"Oh no, what happened?" said Conway.

"I'm pleased to tell you I was fine," said Hunter. "I learnt to handle the arm."

"I meant the kitten," said Conway , exasperated. "What happened to the kitten?"

Mason laughed.

"Come on, Hunter, we're on tenterhooks here," said Ten.

"Well, yes, the kitten survived, after the initial shock of a tight squeeze. She went on to live with my mum in one of the colonies. She still yowls at me whenever she sees me on a video screen."

Vernon's voice crackled over the radios. "This is all very entertaining, Charlie Team, but let's get you back to *Vengeance* and out on the SEVs. There's work to do!"

<Don't tell, but Davies wants to know what the kitten was called> sent Fernandez, wanting to keep a low profile.

<Now, don't laugh. It was my mum's cat, okay? I had nothing to do with it. It was called Fluffykins>

Charlie Team burst out laughing in unison.

"That's fricking priceless, Hunter." Mason was laughing his head off. "The meanest-looking bastard in Sol and he has a cat called Fluffykins."

"Hey, it's not my cat, I told you that," Hunter protested. "And I *am* the meanest bastard in Sol space, don't you forget it."

"Reading you, Fluffykins!" Ten teased.

"We're ready for you in the bays when you have a moment," said Fernandez. "And don't forget Kearney."

"Yeah, who's clipping me on?" asked Kearney. "Conway, come and get me, will you? I'll get the smoothest ride with you."

The Raptors enabled an ejected pilot to clip on externally at the rear of the craft, so Kearney got a decent ride home courtesy of Conway, who – for a moment or two at least – had had to face the prospect of her friend being dead.

"I'm gonna get some close-in footage of these Sentinel Mines and give DD and the tech team a better idea of what we're dealing with out there," said Mason.

Mason stayed behind a few minutes, capturing details, diagnostics and visuals, then returned to the bay with the others. As an explosives geek, it was bliss for him.

"Do we think it's safe yet to send out a Sol signature ship? I mean, those things would track anything with a pulse," said Conway as the team assembled back in the hangar.

"Hey, are you saying my SEVs don't have a pulse?" Fernandez replied, mock wounded by her comment.

"I think we need to hang fire on that," Mason picked up. "Let's deal with the mines first, then explore beyond the perimeter. After what happened to *Colossus,* we can't risk it. We've made great progress."

"Agreed, Marine," said Stansfield, striding into the bay with Vernon at his side. "Solid work out there. Too much dicking around for my tastes, though. Hunter, what was that shit you put into the Raptor?"

"It was a VR game mod, sir. From *Deadly Mission 3,* they use it on the Gazelles. It's a great game."

"Enough, Hunter! Did you ever consider how a piece of black hat code from that action arm of yours might compromise the ship? Has it been checked for viruses or malware? Do you know where the mod came from?"

Hunter had been caught with his dick in his hand. He considered telling Stansfield that Fluffykins had gone on to live a full and purposeful life, filled with adoration and plentiful mice, and that it was cause to celebrate. But even he didn't need a fancy cybernetic arm to tell him to keep his mouth shut.

"You give me one inkling that you're going to endanger our people with that thing," said Stansfield, "and I'll tear it off and give it to Fernandez for scrap. You got that?"

"Understood, sir."

"Now, that said, how can that cybernetic arm assist with the mines?"

Hunter snickered under his breath. Stansfield resented him, but recognised that he couldn't do without him. And however suspect the code, he'd got them all out of a scrape.

"My arm has been designed for complete steadiness, sir. High-speed auto-stabilisers make it excellent for taking detonators out of mines." He picked up a screwdriver and balanced it on the tip of one finger to demonstrate. "It can interpret my thoughts and compensate for the vibration of the ship, and my breathing and me speaking, and remain perfectly balanced."

"My ship does not vibrate," muttered Admiral Stansfield defensively.

"I have the data from my arm's sensors, sir," said Hunter. "It vibrates." He was going to add *also good for safe-breaking*, but thought Stansfield might tear off his lower arm and have Fernandez add it to one of the SEVs as an indicator if he provoked him any further.

"You've picked out your next role already, Charlie Team. Marine X and Hunter, I want you out there on the mines. This looks like an ideal task for two smart-arse criminals looking to pay their debt to society. Kearney and Mason, you take them out in your Raptors and provide backup if it's needed. Bring them back if they survive."

"We don't get our own Raptors, sir?" Ten asked.

"No, you don't. I want some left for later, and at the rate you SBS Jonnies are destroying my complement of ships, I'll soon have nothing but empty hangars," said Stansfield.

"We'll take the SEVs, then," Hunter said.

"You certainly won't. If you screw up the disarming, we'll lose a valuable vehicle. No, for you two it's a few kilometres of travel, safely secured to a Raptor. You're more than trained enough to handle that, and you've just ably demonstrated it's perfectly feasible with Kearney. Switch to engineering power armour, though, it's more capable for the task," Stansfield ordered.

"How about me, sir?" Conway asked, visibly pissed off at being left out.

"You're with Davies and Fernandez. Next time that portal opens, we're going to try and re-establish comms with Sol. We need our best pilot on that. I want you on standby in case the window is shorter this time again," Stansfield replied. "That's if it opens at all," he added.

Stansfield looked around at Charlie Team and nodded. "Good luck, troopers." Then he was gone, with Vernon following in his wake.

"Careful out there, boys," Conway said to Ten and Hunter, who were already itching to head out.

"Hey, what happens to the world if two of the Commonwealth's finest Penal troopers get blown up by nine motherfucker alien mines?" Hunter joked.

"I don't know," Conway replied. "Make sure it doesn't happen, right?"

"We mourn the loss of the mines," said Kearney quietly. Hunter glared at her, but she stared back, face blank.

"Bugger me, that was dark," said Ten.

"And it's not funny," said Conway as Hunter grinned. "Do you see me laughing?"

"Stansfield's a prick," said Hunter with a shrug. "We did good work out there, and he's on my case fretting about shitty mod code. It got the job done, no lives lost. What's his beef?"

"I hate to sound like your wise Aunt Lucy–" Ten began.

"I don't have an Aunt Lucy."

"Hey, I'm bonding here, Hunter, cut me some slack. I'm loathe to admit it, but Stansfield's right. Even as a one hundred per cent dyed-in-the-wool, break the rules kinda guy, it was reckless to put untested code on the network that risked bringing *Vengeance* down and crippling our mission," said Ten, and the bay fell silent as they watched the two Penal Marines square off.

The moment lasted only a few seconds, then Hunter nodded, and the tension bled away.

"Yeah, point made," said Hunter, hands raised. "I'll get it checked out, cleared for combat and all that. Truth is, Stansfield doesn't know half the stuff I can do with this thing."

"Your private life is your own business," said Ten, "but if it affects the mission, we need to know, right? So how about you let all of us know what it can do for Charlie Team, eh? Other than help us play decades-old games."

"Right," agreed Hunter. Then he grinned. "Are you ready to get your hands dirty with some explosive alien shit?"

Ten shook his head, "You're the one with the magic wand. I'll bring the toolkit, and you can play with the bombs." He was warming to Hunter, but he could see why Stansfield considered him a loose cannon. Ten had furrowed the brows of many a superior officer in his time, but Hunter was a new level of agitation.

But Hunter was good in the field, he played nice with the others, and he was a good laugh. As far as Ten was concerned, he could talk all the bollocks he wanted, as long as he did the job of an SBS team member. There was something that still bothered him, though.

"Can you lot stop calling this crap alien? We thought the Death-less were aliens for a day or two, but they weren't either. Everything we've encountered is based on human tech, so unless you find something with a tentacle or six eyes, it's not likely to be alien, okay?" Ten said.

"How about Advanced Line Iterated Equipment Non Sol, then?" Davies suggested.

It took a second, but he got a good round of laughter.

16

"Have you any experience with mines?" Hunter asked on a private channel.

"Anti-spaceship mines and their disarmament, anti-personnel mines and their use in ground warfare, denial of access using anti-vehicle mines, or just mines in general?" Ten asked.

"Any. All. Anything that you can do other than just watch me work would be handy to know. If I'm going to explain my arm to you all, you could do the same," Hunter replied.

"I've done plenty of demolitions and bomb disposal in my time, but mostly landmines and terrorist weapons. I've done courses on minefields in space, but the plan was always about how to get through them to reach a target. I've never had to disarm anything like this. How about you?"

"Some. I'll bet Stansfield read my criminal record. That's probably why he looks so tired and grey-faced all the time."

"No judgement here, Hunter," Ten reassured him. "We've both done some serious shit to get where we are. I wish Stansfield didn't have such a downer on us brig-bunnies, though. I mean, what's not to love?"

Hunter and Ten were closing on the ten-kilometre perimeter.

Fernandez had warned them not to take too many detours. The suits were designed for use outside a ship, but they weren't suitable for flying through space for long periods.

Mason and Kearney had dropped them off as close as possible, then retreated five kilometres to wait for them. If the Sentinel mines were somehow kicked into a different operational mode and crossed the threshold to pursue the Raptors, they'd need a head start to respond and make their escape.

"Not that I don't trust you boys," said Kearney, "but we'll sit out here well beyond the blast zone. Shout if you need a hand. Mason will be happy to come to your aid."

"I'd rather be out there with them," said Mason, genuinely pissed to be left out of an explosives situation. "It's a bit dull just sitting here in space. I've got this lovely Raptor at my disposal and nothing to do with it."

"Stay alert, Charlie Team," Stansfield's voice came over the radio. "We've got the portal opening once again, we're going to try and establish a radio link hop while you're out there. Keep your eyes wide open, we'll shout if we need you."

Hunter and Ten arrived at the Sentinel Mines. They looked even more sinister up close.

"Are you seeing this, Kearney? Mason?" said Ten. "These things look like tricky devils."

The Sentinel Mines were small, jet-black metallic spheres. They were dotted with propulsion vents and sensor arrays, but the engine mechanics and power source weren't immediately obvious. Each had two red lights at the front, and it was these that gave them their demonic appearance. All nine remaining mines had clustered together on the perimeter, sitting in a holding pattern and waiting to seek their next target.

"Where do you think they came from?" Hunter asked. "Do you reckon they were just waiting there for us? Or do you think there's some kind of mine-laying ship out here?"

"No idea," said Ten. "Doesn't matter. Are you ready to tether and eject?"

Hunter and Ten checked their gear was all securely attached to their power armour. Ten would have been happier if they'd had SEVs, but in truth, if the mines went active, they weren't likely to have time to respond.

The engineering suits were ancient, much older models than either Ten or Hunter were used to, but so similar that using them wasn't a problem. They weren't fast or nimble, but engineering suits were designed to let wearers spend hours in space.

Fernandez had insisted they wear nappies in case the mine disposal task took a long time. Zero-G toilet facilities weren't a lot of fun, but nobody wanted fluids floating around inside their suit. The armour was less snug than the combat power armour suits normally used by the Royal Marines, but they were still pretty comfortable.

Attached to their power armour were accessory belts, with additional tools for bomb disposal in case the mines were booby-trapped. They were also armed with personal defence weapons. Each had an assault carbine and a pistol, both specially designed for ship-boarding actions and vacuum operation.

"There's no fucking way I'm going out there again without being properly tooled-up," Ten had said before they left *Vengeance*, and nobody had been inclined to make an argument of it. The mass of the weapons wasn't going to impact the flight time of the engineering suits significantly, and if a man was about to try and defuse anti-starship mines, he was probably entitled to a comfort blanket.

"Right," said Hunter, readying himself to get stuck in. "Let's take a look at these things. Fernandez wants us to bring one in, if we can work out how to disarm them. I told him not to hold his breath."

The troopers manoeuvred themselves to the closest Sentinel Mines, having already attached themselves to each other with a standard high-tensile cable a few metres long. In the event of an emergency, they could pull in to each other, or use quick-release mechanisms to separate.

Hunter placed his hand on the nearest sphere and began to rotate it confidently. His cybernetic arm was bare below the elbow. His customised suit ended and the ring seal clamped directly to the arm, rather than the forearm section the power armour usually held. If the suits hadn't been modular, his arm would have been largely useless.

"Hellfire, Hunter, careful," said Ten. "If we're going to be tethered together, I'd appreciate a heads-up before you grab the explosive devices."

"It's fine, Ten, relax. These things detonate on impact, they're not movement sensitive. They wouldn't have been able to chase us around like that if they were."

Hunter pointed to an area dotted with small pins.

"That's what triggers it." Hunter pointed towards the device. "The moment those come in contact with your Raptor, it's BANG! Seriously old-school, none of this messing around with proximity sensors or vision systems. Touch and go."

"I get it, so no touching the pins. How come these things don't just float away in space? I've never seen something like this before."

"Engine ports," said Hunter, pointing at the mine again. "My guess is some kind of ion-drive based stabilisation technology, with built-in high-efficiency solar panels. It's neat, in something this small. The thrusters are used for target pursuit, but general repositioning is slow; it doesn't matter if it takes hours. These things just sit there, gathering sunlight and moving slowly to their positions. You only need to refuel them in the rare instances that they've pursued a ship but not detonated. Definitely human tech."

"Good to know," muttered Ten as he leaned in to take a closer look. Hunter was right. It was the same as the Guardian devices. Below the two red lights was the writing *Armed When Lit.*

"More English," muttered Ten. "Not good."

"I want you to hold this thing while I work some magic with my CyberPort," said Hunter.

"Is that what you call that thing? A CyberPort?"

"Yup. Cost me an arm, and Sol put a stop to them before they went mass production."

"You got any more? Asking for a friend."

"That's why Sol are so pissed," said Hunter, picking up the story.

"They got their hands on me, but the others are still out there. They hate these things. Personally, I'd say they're pretty useful."

As Ten gripped the Sentinel Mine, Hunter used his cybernetic arm to open up a panel at the back. From his central knuckle, a device appeared that enabled him to insert an instrument into the heart of the sphere's operational system.

"What's that doing?" said Ten. "Do you never get confused about what pops out where? I mean, it could get a man in big trouble!"

Hunter grunted, but his concentration didn't waver for a second.

After a moment, his intense concentration eased, and he replied, "My brain and spinal column are linked to an operating system located at the top of my arm. It's shielded and protected, but it enables me to work at several times normal brain capacity. Only when it's enabled, mind, it can frazzle your brain if you run it too often or for too long."

"I'm beginning to see why Sol don't like these things." Ten had seen some serious shit in his time, but this beat pretty well everything.

<Hey boys, we've got company> Kearney sent on the team channel.

Woodhall had taken it upon himself to join them in one of the SEVs, keen to ensure that the Admiralty wasn't denied any of the latest data from this mission. It was surprising, because Ten was pretty sure Admiral Stansfield didn't want Woodhall out here. The lieutenant must have got out without actually asking.

Crafty little sod, thought Ten.

<Shiteballs, a supervisor. That's all we need> sent Mason.

"Anything we can do to help, sir?" asked Ten, eyes locked on the mine in front of him.

Woodhall's voice came over the radios, superior and threatening. "I'm monitoring these messages, Hunter, and you'd do well to remember who pays your wages and provides all this technology that you're using. I want to make sure you're recording this operation in line with Admiralty protocols."

<I wish everyone would stop banging on about wages> sent Ten. <Penal Marines don't get paid>

"We're all good here," said Hunter, ignoring Woodhall completely. "I just sent a 3D model of the inner workings of this mine to *Vengeance*, and I'm now going to deactivate these things."

"I'm keeping a copy for the historical record, sir," said Ten, in the hope it might give them a little insurance. He wasn't particularly keen for this jumped-up little tit to distract Hunter from his work and find out what it was like to be vapourised by a mine.

Heedless of his safety or theirs, Woodhall moved his SEV as close to the heart of the action as he was able with his limited piloting skills.

Probably using the magnification systems in his HUD to spy on us, thought Ten, *as if we're operating outside our orders.*

Ten strongly suspected Woodhall had been ordered to keep an eye on things and was grasping for any chance to be relevant. It was clear Stansfield wasn't in the least bit interested in cooperating, and who could blame him? Woodhall had already proved to be completely obnoxious, and Ten had only known him a short while.

Woodhall just hovered there, oblivious to the fact he was no more useful than a dangerous distraction. He was just trying to score brownie points with his superiors back at the Admiralty by being the first to report any developments. No doubt he was practically wetting his lingerie at the prospect of the work Davies and Fernandez were doing to establish a communication link through the wormhole. If that happened, and a usable signal route back to Earth was established, Woodhall could make reports, and the Admiralty could give new orders to Stansfield.

For Woodhall, that could mean a promotion, especially if it embarrassed Stansfield. The admiral's return must have ruffled a lot of feathers, especially amongst the officers waiting for an admiral's position.

Ten sighed to himself. Admiralty politics had never been a good thing, and he'd long wanted to stay far away from it.

"I've never seen tech like this before," said Hunter, interrupting

Ten's pondering. "It's human, no doubt about that, but it feels different, like someone's taken something familiar and fiddled with it. Actually, what kind of people would invest so much effort in making a better mine?"

"Yeah, that's a bit of a worry. The Deathless and these guys together, what a bunch of malcontents. I hope we don't hear from any more Lost Ark colonies for a good long while," Ten replied.

"Seconded. Right, time to see if I've got this right. Hold steady there, cross everything you have," Hunter said with the typically dark humour of the bomb tech.

"What's the worst that could happen?"

"Deactivation in three, two, one ... and it's safe."

"You sure?"

"Look at the red lights. Gone."

To illustrate the fact, Hunter pushed the sphere into Ten's chest so that the pins were fully depressed. There was a mechanical click, and Ten's head jerked back.

Ten wasn't amused. "Thanks, Hunter, now I have to clean out my suit. Talk about a brown trouser moment."

"Yeah. If you die, though, you don't lose much. I actually have something to lose, and not just the time since my last backup. I'll lose the arm and everything that goes with it. They're not going to attach it to a new clone for me."

"You should die more often, Hunter," said Ten sharply. "Stops you relying on trinkets like that arm, puts everything in perspective. Doesn't matter if you redeploy, dying still hurts."

"Yeah, right, I'd rather keep my beauty here than go back into a completely organic body," Hunter said, dismissing Ten's case. "Let's get these things finished off, I'm ready to be out of here, and I think I've got the hang of it. Should be much quicker now."

Carefully, painstakingly, Hunter and Ten worked methodically through the Sentinel Mines, with Woodhall monitoring the entire process and observing that these two arseholes actually worked well together. Finally, they got to the last unit.

"Nice job, Ten and Hunter," said Woodhall. "I'm going to leave you and check out the radio link progress. Do you need me to take one of those mines back to *Vengeance* for examination?"

"We're good, thanks, sir," said Hunter. "We'll take one back for stripping and full analysis and leave the other eight out here, disabled."

"Very well." Woodhall fired up his SEV and begun his manoeuvre. Ten held the final Sentinel Mine, and Hunter began to open up its casing.

But Woodhall, more familiar with driving a desk than a spacecraft, botched the turn and drifted his SEV over the invisible perimeter as he tried to turn toward *Vengeance*.

The last Sentinel Mine twitched, and its engine fired, jolting it free from Ten's grasp. It shot towards Woodhall's SEV.

"Woodhall, full throttle, now!" shouted Ten.

"What? Why?" blustered Woodhall. Then he twigged and hit the throttle. His SEV shot away.

"Kearney, Mason, we've got a problem. Requesting immediate backup for Woodhall," said Hunter, urgent and suddenly alert again. "Sentinel Mine on Woodhall's craft."

"Affirmative," Kearney responded.

"I see it, on his tail," said Mason.

Woodhall had now spotted the Sentinel Mine at his rear and was in a state of panic. His craft was at full throttle, but his rudimentary knowledge of the SEV put him in no position to outrun the predator on his tail.

"There's not enough speed in that SEV. The Sentinel Mine is almost on him," said Kearney.

"We're too far out to get in close quarters, we're going to have to go long-range," said Mason.

"Do it," said Ten, unable to help. "It's his only chance, do it now."

Hunter and Ten looked on helplessly as the spherical black device shot after Woodhall like a cheetah chasing down its prey. It was far off in the distance, and the two Raptors had only just passed overhead.

"He's not going to make it," said Hunter.

"He'll be a very lucky man if he does," said Ten , bracing himself for the shit-show if the lieutenant didn't make it back to *Vengeance*.

Then, in the distance, there were four flashes and the distinctive purple explosion.

"Sit rep," came Stansfield's voice over the radio. They'd been monitoring it all on the bridge of *Vengeance*, flitting between the two ongoing operations.

"Mason? Kearney?" said Ten.

Woodhall's voice came over the radio. "I'm fine," he said, "but I'd appreciate it if I could get a tow back. That was a close-run thing back there."

"What happened?" said Hunter. "How'd you manage that?"

"Two shots each," said Mason smugly. "Just ahead of the Sentinel Mine. Then I triggered remote ejection for Woodhall. Two seconds more and he'd have been toast."

"Good job," said Ten, "but I think you woke something up out there."

17

"Are you seeing this, *Vengeance*?" said Ten.

"Affirmative," said Stansfield. "Kearney and Mason, get Woodhall out of there. Conway, I need you out with the other two Raptors straight away. Get Marine X and Hunter back to *Vengeance* as quickly as possible. Flight deck, all attack craft on standby."

"All types, sir?" the voice of Fernandez came over the radio from the bays.

"Everything we've got. I want another ten Raptors out here straight away and twenty HRs on standby for immediate launch."

"Affirmative, Admiral."

Stranded in the vastness of open space with their escort, Hunter and Ten watched in awe as, no more than twenty kilometres away, a vast mechanical orb at least the size of *Colossus* was revealed.

"I guess we know where the Sentinel Mines came from."

"Yeah, but what the hell is it?" said Ten.

"I don't even know what to call it, but it's bloody massive, and I don't like the look of it," said Hunter, scanning the intruder. "Let's get this bloody mine stowed, then we can get back out here in Raptors and give it a proper look, eh?"

"Oh yeah, sure, I'm looking forward to it," Ten grumbled.

"Confirming that Woodhall is retrieved and safe," said Kearney. "I'm joining the defensive screen around *Vengeance*."

"Heads up, Ten, Hunter. I'm closing fast on your position, get ready to latch on," said Conway.

Hunter and Ten waited until Conway's Raptor drew to a halt; then they powered toward her as fast as their suits would go, dragging the mine between them. They secured it to the hull of Conway's Raptor, then clipped on themselves, and they were off.

Ahead of them, well within the ten-kilometre perimeter line, *Vengeance* launched ten Raptors to lead the response, with Mason and Kearney amongst them after they'd dropped off Lieutenant Woodhall.

As Conway brought her Raptor to a stop in the docking bay, Ten and Hunter moved away, dragging the mine to the waiting engineering team. Conway was back into space before they had cycled through the airlock.

The bulky engineering suit was far too large for the cockpit of a Raptor, so Ten and Hunter had no choice but to change into the standard combat power armour used by Marines and SBS alike. On their way to the armour lockers, they passed Woodhall, who was strapped to a medical gurney and ranting at two medics who wanted to sedate him. Ten gave them an encouraging thumbs-up, hoping they'd knock him out while whatever was about to happen went on. The last thing he wanted to hear was that pillock moaning about his orders and what the admiral should do.

The enormous sphere was undergoing some kind of activation process, as if the caretaker was walking through a building, firing up the boiler and switching on the lights. And all the while it advanced.

"*Vengeance* Raptors, Charlie Team have the lead in the field; repeat, Charlie Team have the lead," said Stansfield. His voice came across the comms channel clearly and calmly, as if the situation was completely normal.

A massive spherical spaceship turns up just as you finish disarming a minefield? No problem. Business as usual for Vengeance *and its commanding officer,* Ten thought. He could well imagine the palpable air of tension on the bridge as the officers braced themselves for battle and went about the tasks they'd been rigorously trained to implement when they were ordered to action stations.

He and Hunter raced to get into combat power armour. There was no time for bullshit, so they helped each other as they went. On land, an improperly-fitted suit was bad. In vacuum, it was fatal.

"Good to go?" Hunter gave him a two-handed thumbs up.

They headed for the launch bay at a jog and then came to an abrupt stop.

"Er, Conway, where are the Raptors?" said Hunter.

"All Raptors were launched. What, did you think there were spares?"

"We had rather hoped to be out there with you," said Ten.

"Yeah, well, I need pilots out here, not you two numpties."

"Hey!" protested Hunter. "Kearney and Mason are out there!"

"Sorry, chaps, you'll have to sit this one out. Smoke us a kipper and all that." Conway closed the channel.

"The bitch," said Hunter incredulously. "She's bloody abandoned us." There was a noise behind him and he turned to see Ten grabbing weapons from a nearby rack. "What the fuck are you going to do with those?" he asked.

"Shoot them at anything that looks unfriendly," said Ten as he stacked the rifles into his SEV.

"How? You going to get out of an unarmed SEV and stand on the roof, shooting at attack craft with a small arm?" Hunter scoffed.

"Don't be daft," said Ten, "I'm going to use a rocket launcher. The rifles are just in case we get to board anything. You coming or what?"

Hunter stared at him for a moment, a look of incredulity plainly etched on his face. Then he shrugged and jogged over to the armoury. "All right, fine, but if I get killed doing this, I'm blaming you."

"Fair enough, if you and your non-backed-up arse die, and get redeployed having lost weeks of memories or months or however long it is since you were last somewhere civilised, I will absolutely bring you up to speed and accept the blame for your untimely demise," Ten said.

"Damn right you will," Hunter agreed.

"As long as I get the credit when this moment of tactical genius works and we get to tell the story in the canteen, deal?" Ten said with a wolfish grin.

"Oh yeah, sure, that's the most likely outcome of this venture, you getting to regale the crew with stories of your military prowess rather than the officers delivering a sad speech about how we were suffering from oxygen deprivation due to faulty power armour," Hunter scoffed sarcastically.

A moment later though, despite Hunter's scepticism, they were hurtling into space at the maximum acceleration the unarmed SEVs would allow. Hunter continued to mutter and grumble over their buddy comm channel, and Ten just soaked it all in.

"Weapons are active, Raptor teams, let's see what they throw at us," said Stansfield.

"That thing reminds me of the Sentinel Mines far too much. I'm really hoping it's not the universe's largest bomb," mused Conway.

"Thanks, Conway. That's a thought to give me nightmares for a week," Kearney replied.

"It could be worse," said Ten, "there could be five of them spread out in a front for a showdown of epic proportions."

"Someone likes their maths, that's for sure," said Mason. "There's no doubt that this tech has human origins, but there's no way that thing is from Sol. I've never seen anything like it."

"Look alive, Charlie Team, we have incoming," said Kearney.

"What the hell are they sending at us now?" said Conway.

From their monitoring distance, Charlie Team watched as a circular port opened on the orb, spewed from the depths of the massive ship.

"All Raptor pilots," said Conway, broadcasting to the team and *Vengeance*'s Raptor pilots, "be advised we have eyes on the enemy targets. Nature is unknown; they could be missiles, drones or piloted craft. Stay sharp."

"Like wasps leaving a nest," said Ten.

"Ten? What the hell are you doing in an SEV?" demanded Conway.

"Sightseeing. The Eagle Nebula is breathtaking this time of year, and the wildlife is fascinating."

"Stop pissing about," snapped Conway. "Stay out of the way!"

"We're just here to observe," Ten lied. Conway didn't bother to answer.

"Can you see better than us, *Vengeance*?" said Conway. "What are they, more Sentinel Mines?"

"Negative. I can't say what they are, but the enhanced images are coming in. Sending updates to your HUDs now," said Fernandez.

"They're like some kind of mechanoid," said Mason, peering at his HUD.

Whatever they were, the craft were spewing from the centre of the Firewall Sphere in clusters of ten. As they advanced, and *Vengeance* trained its most powerful visual sensors on them, the HUD images improved.

Each one was a human-size black Mech, mounted on a circular black disc onto which weaponry was attached. They had gun barrels on the disc, built into their arms and at the sides of their heads. As with the Sentinel Mines, the two red lights showed they were activated and armed.

"They look like they're surfing in space," said Ten. "I wouldn't mind a ride on one of those discs."

"You might want to return to *Vengeance*, Hunter, Ten," said Conway. "I'm not sure I'd fancy my chances fighting those things in an SEV."

"Opening my SEV," reported Ten as he activated his helmet. Then he triggered the control and opened the canopy of his vehicle. "Much better," he muttered, checking that his rifle was secure and ready. He reached down into the confines of the cockpit, pulled something out and waved to Hunter, who was pulling up alongside.

"Good idea," said Hunter, following suit. "Those things are fast, they're gonna be hard to shoot."

The first flash of fire came from the forward cluster of Mechs.

"Contact," said Kearney.

"Engage the enemy. Fire at will." The admiral's orders came so quickly, he must surely have been waiting for it.

"You heard the admiral," said Conway. "Happy hunting!"

Admiral Stansfield interrupted angrily, "Negative. Belay that sentiment. All hands, I say again, all hands. That Sphere is the enemy, and our intelligence suggests they will give no quarter. I expect every man Jack of you to do your duty. Britain demands it. The Commonwealth expects it. Every Sol government needs it. We will terminate this enemy with extreme prejudice and give no quarter. For *Colossus*!"

Conway took the initiative. "Roger that, Admiral. Disperse, Raptors, let's see what these metal-heads have got to throw at us. Look after your wingmen, I don't want any mavericks out here!"

The Raptor pilots drew off and began to target the approaching Mech clusters. The red lights of their armaments started to flash across the dark expanse of space, the Raptor missiles trying to get a fix and find something to shoot at.

In minutes the Mechs had closed on the Raptors and begun their attack.

<Raptor down, number 3, they're like ants or wasps or something, they all attack at once> sent Raptor 10.

Conway had noticed the explosion in the distance, but kept her focus on the Mech cluster ahead. Ten of them, swooping in around her, with complete control over movement. She fired missiles – one – two – three – four ... and got one hit, sending a Mech exploding into the stars like a bag of nuts and bolts.

She spun her Raptor round to take evasive action. It felt like the Mechs were trying to mob each Raptor rather than take them down like a conventional fighter.

<Raptors 6, 9 and 1 down. Raptor 1 got clear, but they shot him in his ejector seat> sent Raptor 2.

"We're losing it out here, Admiral. They're all over us, there are far too many to shoot. Request permission to withdraw? I think we're going to need to call backup," Conway said to the bridge team.

"Granted, Conway," said Stansfield. "What's your assessment? Dare we send out the HRs?"

"Send out something with a modern Sol signature, something you can stand to lose," said Conway. "No crew."

"Agreed," said Stansfield. "Get back to Davies and finish off that radio link. Let's have some battery fire on those things."

As Conway engaged her craft to make the turn, two Mechs struck her Raptor and their discs stuck to the side like limpets. The Mechs climbed off the discs and immediately began cutting into the side of the craft with some kind of circular saw that came out of their hands.

"I've got two Mechs on my Raptor, anybody available to help out?" said Conway.

<Raptors 2 and 7 down. *Vengeance*, we're failing–> sent Raptor 8. Then there was a flash as Raptor 8 exploded before the pilot was able to finish her communication.

And still the Mechs came, hundreds of them now, a swarm in space.

"Nobody does this shit anymore," raged Ten as he launched a shoulder-mounted rocket at one of the Mechs on Conway's Raptor as it banked toward him. The missile struck it in the back and detonated, reducing it to a pair of legs that lost their magnetic grip on the Raptor and floated away into space.

Seconds later, Hunter came in below her Raptor, canopy open, and emptied a full magazine into the second Mech's face, pummelling it into scrap metal.

"Screw you, metal-head," said Hunter, reloading his weapn as the remains of the Mech tumbled away from the ship.

"Thanks, guys, loving you and leaving you now," said Conway as she signed off, punching her boosters to return to the launch bay as fast as possible.

<Requesting backup, we're completely outnumbered, *Vengeance*> came Raptor 10's alert.

<Launching a test shuttle now> sent Fernandez from the bay.

Under remote control, the engineering team launched the oldest modern-fitted shuttle they'd got from *Colossus* before she met her untimely end. The moment it emerged from the shadow of *Vengeance*, a massive blue beam shot from the Sphere, striking the shuttle amidships. The shuttle exploded and the beam winked out.

<Test failed> sent Fernandez as the shuttle's debris drifted into space. <No HRs, will launch more Raptors>

<Negative, Lieutenant, you're just going to send more ships to the graveyard. Open SEVs with well-armed Marines are more effective. This is close-quarters fighting> sent Ten.

<I agree> sent Hunter. <We're doing way more damage with assault weapons than the Raptors, but it'll take more than the two of us >

Attacking the Mechs with Raptors was like using a sledgehammer to crack a nut – if the nut was amongst a bunch of other nuts, in mid-air, as they were emptied from a bag.

"Admiral, get the lads out here in SEVs and power armour. Small arms are proving effective. The Mechs want to get in close and go hand to hand for some reason; once they're not moving, a rifle to the face seems to do the job. My rocket launcher has got a few as well," Ten said as he calmly reloaded his launcher, locked a nearby target and fired.

"What in blazes are you doing out there in an SEV?" Stansfield demanded.

"Improvising, sir," said Ten as he launched another missile, "Adapting." He reloaded, locked the closest target he could quickly visualise, and fired. "Overcoming. Happy to listen to other ideas, sir, but we could really do with some support."

"Roger that. Open SEVs it is," said Stansfield. "Despatching reinforcements. Raptors stay wide, provide defensive cover."

<It's just you and me for a few minutes, Hunter, let's see how many of these bolt brains we can take out> sent Ten.

"You've seen them, yes? These things bleed," said Hunter.

"I think you mean 'leak,' Hunter. It's just oil and coolant."

"It was red, I'm telling you," said Hunter. "There was a big splash of it all over Conway's Raptor. That's blood if ever I saw it."

The Marines were in their element, immersed in a battle that required a bit of strategy and brainpower.

"I'll take your word for it. Must be some kind of power armour, then. Either way, this anti-vehicle launcher is targeting them just as easily as an APC or a tank," said Ten. "Okay, we've got two clusters heading straight for us. One each? I'll take left."

"Sure thing, Mr Sharp-Shooter. First to get all ten wins a prize!"

Hunter and Ten dropped back into their SEVs, leaving the canopies open to vacuum. That was the odd thing about space combat; there was nothing out there. An open canopy felt wrong, but there was no wind to tear it away.

They broke to the left and right, outflanking the Mechs. Ten's rocket launcher was useless from within the craft, and he wanted to be able to fight from the cockpit so he could slip away if they swarmed him. He pulled out a bog-standard firearm instead, and Hunter grabbed a carbine.

With their canopies open, the two troopers had a good field of fire, but the Mechs swarmed like a cloud of angry mosquitos, gathering in the dark.

"That's three," said Hunter. "Changing location." He dropped back down into the cockpit and punched the booster, forcing the advancing Mechs to change course. They were nimble, but their acceleration couldn't match the SEVs'.

"Six," replied Ten. "I won't need to move. Seven."

"Fuck off! Four. How have you got seven already?"

"Because I'm not just better-looking than you, mate, I'm older and wiser to boot."

"Old is right, grandad," said Hunter, "and that's six."

"That's what your mum said. Nine."

"Oh, come on!"

"And that's ten, I'm done."

Hunter growled in frustration and finished off the seventh of his targets. Then Ten's SEV pulled alongside as the final three Mechs closed on Hunter's SEV.

Ten clambered onto the nose of his SEV, his power armour's

magnetically-soled boots clamping to the frame of the exploration vehicle. In his arms he cradled a hefty-looking machine gun.

"What the fuck is that?" Hunter yelled as he punched his arm into the face of a Mech wielding a vicious circular saw.

Ten's gun flashed twice, sending short bursts into the other two Mechs and knocking them physically off Hunter's SEV. He followed up with more bursts once they'd drifted clear, reducing them to clouds of bloody metal and ensuring they wouldn't find their way back to do any harm.

"This, my son, is a .50 calibre Bren 2400. It's a successor to the old WW2 gun, if only spiritually," Ten replied. "Found it in a dusty box in *Vengeance*'s armoury."

Hunter was still struggling with the last Mech, but he seemed to have the upper hand. The Mech's sawblade floated free, and Hunter had it off balance. He grabbed it under the chin, wrenching it around in something that looked like an homage to a Judo throw, and broke its neck. He flung it away into space and stood there on top of his SEV, gasping for breath within his suit.

"Nicely done," said Ten. "I thought for a moment you were going to introduce it to your pleasure hand." He made an obscene gesture.

"That's cheating," said Hunter, ignoring Ten's insults and pointing at the machine gun.

"Yeah, well, I told you to tool up. Not my fault if your generation doesn't know what that means. What are they teaching you guys these days? Do I need to go back to teach a refresher course?"

Ten reached down into his cockpit and calmly began reloading his weapons, including the three rifles rifles he'd emptied while Hunter wasn't looking.

"For future reference, mate, in space no-one can hear you shoot," Ten went on, clearly not finished dispensing advice. "Grab the biggest gun you can and fuck up the enemy before he tears you a tiny, tiny hole in your powered armour and your balls freeze into little olive-sized ice cubes too small to chill a martini, okay? Don't ponce about with a carbine trying to be subtle. Stealth out here is all about light, not sound. Except for walking on the hull of a ship, that's a right bastard to do quietly. Magnetic boots clang something fierce from the inside of a ship."

Hunter thought about that as he reloaded his weapon. Then he realised what had been niggling him. "Hang on, what do you mean, 'go back'? You're just a bootneck, right?"

Ten turned to stare at him, and even through the opaque helmet visor Hunter could sense the coldness. It sent a chill down the back of his neck.

"Yeah. That's right, kid, I'm just a bootneck," said Ten in a dead tone. "Don't go letting your head get too big for your diving helmet just because you made it into the SBS, okay?"

Ten fired a few bursts from his machine gun with no apparent effect. Even the closest Mechs were too far away.

"Look, I didn't mean it like that. I just meant it sounded like you weren't always a Marine," said Hunter.

"Of course I wasn't. I went to school, just like everyone else."

Hunter wasn't amused. "Fine, be like that. I'll just look at your file when we're back on *Vengeance*."

Ten snorted. "You go right ahead, sonny. But I'd be surprised if you've got clearance to see the files, let alone access their contents."

Something about his tone stopped Hunter from making a snarky comment. "Bloody hell, what did you do to end up with this sentence?"

"Oh, now that's definitely above your pay grade. Time to focus on the job. You've got some work to do if you want to even the score. Here, you want to try this?" Ten asked, holding up the rocket launcher.

"Sure," said Hunter, taking the launcher, "but I'd rather try the machine gun."

"Yeah, not today. This is a proper antique, mate. Needs careful handling."

"Oh, right, just your speed then," Hunter smirked. "Let's get stuck in."

~

"This is useless," muttered Ten a few minutes later. "There are too many of them." He watched the Mechs gathering, all staring at the dark, distant hulk that was *Vengeance*.

He and Hunter had done some damage. Their technique of opening up a swarm with the rocket launcher and then finishing them off with the Bren gun worked, but it was far too slow.

Even though they'd been joined by the rest of Charlie Team and a squad of Vernon's Marines, they weren't making any progess. A complement of boarding-action trained crew members had joined them as well, but it still wasn't going as well as they'd like.

And then, glancing around, Ten saw something he wasn't sure anyone else had noticed.

"Oh, shit," he said quietly as he realised what was happening. He flipped into *Vengeance*'s bridge comms channel.

"Marine X," acknowledged Commander Vernon. "Report."

"An observation, sir," said the Penal Marine. "These Mechs are built for close-quarter fighting. Out there it makes no sense, but they're a swarm, like locusts."

"Locusts?" muttered Hunter. "What the fuck are locusts?"

Ten ignored him as the certainty of his insight grew, "The Mechs are equipped with short-range anti-personnel weaponry and cutting equipment. It's unconventional, but they tore through the Raptors once they got close."

"And your point is?" said Admiral Stansfield, breaking into the conversation.

"They're not trying to destroy *Vengeance*, sir," said Ten quietly. "They're trying to capture her."

"Capture?" hissed Stansfield.

"They know we're here," said Ten. "If they wanted to destroy *Vengeance*, they'd use the blue beam of death. Deploying the Mechs makes sense only if they plan to board. For all we know, they have racks full of perfectly good railguns they didn't bring with them. They didn't come to shoot us down, they came to take prisoners."

The channel was silent for a moment.

"I think you're right," said Stansfield with a grudging respect. "They have the firepower to snuff us out, so this isn't about destruction. This is a full-scale incursion."

"It's a damned weird way of doing it," said Vernon.

"Life would be dull if nobody tried anything new," said Stansfield. "Prepare to repel boarders."

"Will do," said Vernon grimly, leaving the bridge to prepare his small contingent of Marines.

"Davies, Conway," said Stansfield. "I could really use that radio link back home."

"Working on it, sir," said Davies.

"Well, work faster, damnit," snapped Stansfield. "The situation is deteriorating."

"Oh, shit," said Ten as the Mechs began to move and spread out in waves. "They're heading your way, *Vengeance*."

18

_____

"Status report, Mr Fernandez?" Stansfield's voice boomed from the radio.

"We're seven SEVs down, we count at least thirty more clusters, I don't know how they're able to send out so many of these things."

"And have you managed to trial radio comms yet? How are Conway and Davies doing out there?"

"They're on the other side of the portal, sir, running a relay test to _Kingdom 10_. Based on the last timings, the portal will be closing again soon. We have to sit it out for a while until it opens up again."

"Keep me informed, Lieutenant."

Out in the field, Ten and Hunter were working well with the SEV teams from _Vengeance_. Hunter had taken to battering the Mechs, flying into them to knock them from their discs. His SEV was covered in abandoned Mech discs, held in place by some mechanism that Ten didn't understand. He stared at them for a few seconds, scrabbling to work out what he was missing.

"No remote," he murmured suddenly as realisation dawned. "They need to be in contact. Hunter, get them off the discs and they're helpless."

"I'm way ahead of you, mate, but I don't see how we win this."

"I reckon we can kill the whole group by hitting the Bosses. You up for it?"

"Sounds like a plan. How about those guys over there? The cheeky buggers are trying to break away and head for *Vengeance*."

"You're right, Hunter, they have a strategy. Okay, try not to hit one of the general Mechs, I want a direct hit on a Boss, okay? I'm going in as bait."

Ten's SEV roared across the path of the cluster, and they were immediately on him, turning to follow. Ten slowed, allowing them to catch up. He'd seen what they'd done to Conway, trying to break into her Raptor rather than destroy it. They'd looked like a savage salvage team, setting about her vehicle before he and Hunter had sent them flying into space.

"Careful, Ten," Hunter warned. "I can't shoot if they're on your SEV, I don't want to kill my new buddy."

"You focus on the Boss," said Ten. "Leave his guardians to me."

He closed his canopy, securing the vehicle, then slowed his SEV until he felt the Mech's discs lock onto the side of the craft. They were all over his ship; he could feel the vibrations from their saws as they began to cut their way inside. And for the first time, he got a real close-up look at the enemy through the SEV's external cameras.

"Are you seeing this, *Vengeance*?"

"Following, Marine X, report what you see," said Vernon.

"These things are about ninety per cent Mech and ten per cent human. Can you see the detail on the images you're getting? Some of them have human faces inside their helmets, and some have other body parts too. That one has an eye and an arm inside his suit. They're trying to strip my SEV of parts."

"Confirming your analysis, Marine X, I've never seen anything like it," said Stansfield.

"Hey, I got your Boss," said Hunter. "Do you see any change?"

Ten had. The Mechs had paused, frozen in place for less than a second. The Mech that was just above him, the one trying to remove the glass canopy of his SEV, transformed in front of him, gaining the purple light that indicated its new status. The new Boss went back to its disc and moved to the side of the ship, back into flight, leaving the rest to carry on their work.

"False hypothesis, *Vengeance*," Ten said. "I thought we could disable a cluster by shooting the Boss. Turns out they just elect a new one."

"Say more," said Stansfield. "What do you mean?"

"The Boss Mechs are like cluster leaders, but they're interchangeable. The role is reassigned if a Boss is killed."

There was a heavy thud on the side of Ten's SEV. Hunter had arrived, and the two SEVs were holding station, locked together like lovers in a desperate clinch.

"I don't know if you noticed," said Hunter, "but your SEV's getting stripped by Mechs. Back to work, Marine. On my mark ... three, two, one, open."

Ten and Hunter popped the canopies of the SEVs. One of the Mechs lost its footing and tumbled away, arms flapping as it floated slowly into space.

Its comrades swarmed across the surface of Ten's SEV, some slicing at the metal, others racing to reach Hunter. One reached into the cockpit, leaning in to flail an arm at Ten, groping for something it could seize in its mechanical fist.

"Gngh!" said Ten as he leaned away. The Mech followed him, slithering into the cockpit on its belly. Ten grabbed at his pistol and hammered at the Mech's faceplate, forcing it back far enough that he could place the barrel under the thing's chin. He squeezed the trigger and repeatedly shot the Mech until it crumpled and released its grip on the SEV to float away in a swirling cloud of rapidly-freezing bodily fluids.

"Too fucking close," said Ten as he holstered his pistol and grabbed his rifle, "and these things have brains."

Hunter stood on the outside of his SEV, held in place by the magnetic boots of his power armour. "I dunno, they don't seem all that bright to me," he replied as he shot two of the Mechs, rifle eerily silent in the darkness of the interstellar void. "Hey, robo guts look super cool in space," he said with a grin.

"I meant actual brains. They're definitely not robots. If we weren't in vacuum I'd be splattered with grey matter right now."

"SEV teams, withdraw to *Vengeance*," said Stansfield. "They're sending out more clusters, hundreds of them. Get back to the ship."

"Time to go," said Hunter as he fired at the Mechs swarming Ten's SEV.

"Watch your rear, Hunter," said Ten, struggling to escape his chair, secure his safety line and bring his weapon to bear. "You've got one at your back."

Hunter turned, boots still clamped on the SEV's surface, as three Mechs clambered over him, tightening their grip until he could barely move. His power armour fought against the Mechs but, working together, they were too strong.

"Help," he squealed, rifle firing uselessly into space as the Mechs grappled with him. Then they ripped the weapon from his grasp and tossed it away.

Ten, his line finally secured, pushed himself out of his seat and brought his rifle to bear. He emptied the rest of his magazine into the closest Mech; then his line snapped taut and he floated in space, ten metres from his SEV as the fight played out before him.

"Why aren't they shooting at us?" he yelled, slamming a new magazine into his rifle and trying to choose a target.

Then a new vehicle came into view and, just for a moment, Ten thought *Vengeance* had sent a shuttle to rescue them.

But as its manoeuvring thrusters fired to settle the craft neatly between Ten and the SEVs, he realised it wasn't a Royal Navy ship at all.

Out of sight, Hunter growled and screamed curses at the Mechs. Ten fired on the enemy vessel, hoping to draw their attention from Hunter, but his efforts had no discernible effect.

Then the craft's thrusters fired again, and it slid sedately away before turning to head back to the giant sphere. Ten could only watch as the ship's main engines fired to take it and the Mechs home.

And when he turned back to look at the SEVs, Hunter was gone.

The only indication he'd ever been there was a hole in his SEV, where the Mechs had cut him loose from the surface.

19

On the bridge of *Vengeance*, the situation was hardly any better. Admiral Stansfield watched the vid-screens as alerts came in from across the ship.

"There are hundreds of them," said Vernon from his post in the main bay. "External sensors show them swarming across the hull. They're all over the outside of the ship."

Stansfield would never have believed it if he hadn't seen it for himself. The Mechs were landing in huge numbers and using some sort of magnetic clamps to traverse the hull.

"Brace for breach," said Stansfield. "Secure the bridge, lock down all systems. Mr Yau, I want to know the minute the portal reopens."

"Ay, sir, monitoring for any sign of activity," said Yau.

"Give me a status report on the SEVs," said Stansfield.

"Only two left, sir," said Midshipman Henry. "Trooper Hunter and Marine X. All the others are silent."

Stansfield nodded as he absorbed the news. In all his years of command, he'd never seen anything like it. Hundreds of Mechs were attaching themselves to the sides of *Vengeance*, and the metallic tapping of their fingers could be heard as they crawled all over the outside of the battleship, looking for a way in.

"Close the bays, Mr Fernandez," he said, opening a channel to the main bay, "they're our most vulnerable point."

"We still have SEVs out there, Admiral. And Davies and Conway too, they're stranded on the other side of the portal ..."

"I'm well aware of that, Lieutenant," said Stansfield. "Lock down the bays, that's an order." He switched channels before Fernandez could argue further. "Commander Vernon, report."

"We have squads standing ready to repel boarders in each bay and covering all entrances on every level of the ship. All non-essential personnel are armed and deployed, and the firewall protocols have been enacted on all essential operating systems and power sources. Bridge fortifications are active and ready to be implemented on your order. In short, we're ready for the buggers if they breach the hull, sir."

"What about vents and exhaust systems? These things are every-where, like ants."

"Fernandez has teams on it, sir. Nothing more to do but wait."

"There'll be no twiddling thumbs today, Commander. Keep everyone on their toes, and get me a status report on our pilots – how many still active and how many wounded?"

"Twenty-seven pilots lost with their craft, three wounded, sir. Kearney and Mason from Charlie Team made it back. Conway and Davies are working on the comms link. Marine X's link shows him to be alive."

"And Hunter?" asked Stansfield.

"Nothing, sir, he's offline."

"Keep me informed, Commander," said Stansfield. Then he closed the channel and reviewed the monitors. Things weren't looking good.

"Sir, the sphere is broadcasting," said Lieutenant Yau, *Vengeance's* science officer. "They started when the Mechs were launched."

"Broadcasting, Mr Yau?" asked Stansfield, leaning forward in his chair.

"A slow pulse, sir, not on one of our normal communications frequencies. I believe it's meant to go unnoticed, but we caught it whilst scanning the Mechs to try to figure out how they communicate."

"And your conclusion, Mr Yau?" said Stansfield, trying to keep his frustration in check. Like all science officers, Yau seemed to have a limited appreciation for urgent strategic situations.

"I think it's a pulse given out to mark the position of their main control. It just carries on every fifteen seconds, and doesn't seem to influence the Mechs or the Firewall Sphere in any way."

"Can we make any use of this information, Lieutenant?" said Stansfield. "Maybe by disrupting the signal?"

"Maybe, sir," said Yau with a frown as he thought it through. "But I'm not sure what impact it might have. From a scientific perspective, it's interesting to know that the enemy need to communicate and that they do it in an open way."

"Thank you, Lieutenant," said Stansfield, more calmly than he felt. "If you find a way to disrupt the signal, please go ahead."

"Ay, sir, I'll work on that now."

"Commander Vernon," said Stansfield, dismissing Yau's information as an unhelpful distraction, "can we make contact with Conway or Marine X?"

"Hailing Marine X now, sir," said Vernon. "Open channel."

"Hey, I thought you'd forgotten all about me," said Ten. "You seem to be covered in Mechs, *Vengeance*."

"*Vengeance* fights on, Marine," said Vernon. "What's your status?"

"My SEV is damaged but still usable. Ammunition still plentiful. The flow of Mechs from the Firewall Sphere seems to have stopped, so it looks like that's your lot for now."

"Anything else to report on the Sphere?" said Stansfield. "Our intel is seriously limited."

"Nothing to report, sir. It looks for all the world like a giant spherical dustbin I once saw at a music festival in my spotty youth. I don't suppose that helps much. Difficult to get a sense of size from here, but I'd estimate battleship size."

"We concur," Stansfield replied, looking to Yau for confirmation.

"The Sphere is a little over five hundred metres in diameter," said the science officer, "with an internal volume of sixty-five million cubic metres. There could be thousands of Mechs on the Sphere."

"And it has a main cannon that can destroy a battleship like *Colossus*," said Ten. "Any idea why they haven't just blown us out of space?"

There was a pause before Stansfield replied.

"We concur with your earlier suggestion that they wish to capture *Vengeance* rather than destroy her. Do you have a sit rep on Hunter?"

"The Mechs took him. They cyborg-napped him, as it were," said Ten. "Did something to his armour, bundled him into a transport, and returned to the Sphere. He was alive when I last saw him."

"Capture it is, then," said Stansfield quietly. "Hunter is lost, defending *Vengeance* until the portal reopens is our priority. Return immediately."

"Sorry, sir," came the voice of Ten, suddenly quiet and wobbly. "You're breaking up. Can you rep–"

"Marine X? Marine X, answer," snapped Stansfield. He glared at Midshipman Staunch at the comms desk. "What happened?"

"Running diagnostics, sir," said Staunch with a confused frown. "Nothing wrong at all, sir. We're still linked to Marine X's SEV, he should be able to hear us."

Stansfield stared at the monitors, shaking his head as the view showed a lone SEV powering toward the Sphere.

"Bloody Marines," muttered Stansfield. Then he turned his full attention to the Mechs that crowded the hull of his ship.

"Sorry, sir," whispered Ten. He paused to make clicking noises with his tongue. "You're breaking up. Can you rep."

He stopped and muted his microphone. It was an old trick, and he knew the admiral wouldn't fall for it, but there was no way he was getting back to *Vengeance* alive, not with all those Mechs crawling outside it.

Not that he blamed the admiral. He understood that Stansfield's only choice was to order his return to the ship, but even if he survived the journey and fought his way to a door, they couldn't let him in without also admitting the Mechs, and that was never going to happen.

"Sphere it is," he said to himself, looking back at his SEV as he floated on the end of his line. He switched his HUD to take stock. An alert from the SEV warned of low power and oxygen reserves. "Shit."

He tugged on the line and floated back to the SEV. Hunter's craft sat alongside, dormant and open, and in much better condition than Ten's vehicle.

"Time to move, Marine," said Ten. He activated his magnetic boots and manoeuvred himself into his SEV. "Ammunition, weapons, oxygen," he muttered as he pulled items from his craft and attached them to his armour or gathered them in his arms.

Then he stepped out of the SEV, walked carefully across the hull to Hunter's less damaged craft, and slipped into the seat. The canopy slid closed, and he gave the controls a little nudge to get clear of the other SEV.

Ten looked across the void at the Sphere that now held Hunter. The likelihood of death out here, so far from home, was high whatever he did, and there was little chance of his backup ever being found. If that happened, he would eventually be redeployed, but with no idea what had happened since he'd left New Bristol.

For a few long seconds, Ten stared at *Vengeance*. The only humans for hundreds of light-years were in there, safe at the moment, as far as he could tell, but outmanned and outgunned and a long way from help. The Mechs would get in eventually, and when they did, the small teams on *Vengeance* wouldn't last long.

If he was going to die in the cold void of space, he may as well try to pick up a little intel before he croaked.

"Fuck that shit," said Ten to nobody in particular. He pushed away all thoughts of death and focussed on the Sphere. "One problem at a time," he muttered. "Hold on, Hunter, I'm coming for you."

He punched the SEV's controls and felt the gentle kick as the engine fired, starting him on his voyage to the Sphere.

"Marine X, come in," said a voice. Ten almost opened his mic, but he didn't need new orders at the moment. He said nothing and concentrated on the Sphere.

"This is Mason," said the voice. "If you're out there, there are still three Marines in damaged SEVs. We don't know if they're alive, but you're their only hope. Good luck." Then a file landed in his HUD: a flight plan with coordinates of the three unfortunates.

For a few moments, Ten ignored the file, trying to wish away the blinking alert in his HUD.

"Fuck," he said loudly. He pulled up the file, checked the locations, and ran the numbers. It would take time, but he had enough oxygen and power to check all three and still make it to the Sphere. It meant leaving Hunter with the Mechs for even longer, but what choice did he have?

"Sorry, Hunter," said Ten as he pushed the new flight plan into the SEV's nav-computer, "you'll have to hold out a little longer."

The SEV fired its manoeuvring thrusters and veered away from the Sphere, heading for the coordinates of the closest of the three casualties. The enemy had gone, but the fight zone was littered with Mech parts, SEV debris and the weird black discs the creatures had flown on.

The first Marine was in good shape, but his SEV was dead and cold when Ten drew alongside. He opened a private channel. "You all right in there?"

"Better for seeing you," said a relieved male voice. "Thought I'd been abandoned out here." There was an overtone of fear in the man's voice, the fear of being left to a slow death in a cold craft. "Can you give me a tow?"

"I'm not going back to *Vengeance*," said Ten. "There's only one way out of this."

"The Sphere? You're mad," said the Marine.

"Ay, onwards to glory."

"There's no way we survive this."

"Maybe," admitted Ten, "but they've got Hunter, and *Vengeance* won't last long."

"Shit," said the Marine, and Ten could hear the change in his tone as he made his decision. "Can't leave him behind. I'll come to you."

Ten watched as the canopy of the damaged SEV shattered and floated in pieces into space. The Marine pulled himself out, a rifle slung on his back, then steadied himself against the outside of his craft.

"Catch," he murmured, then he launched himself at Ten's craft. A few seconds later there was a clang as the Marine's magnetic boots caught on the outside of the hull. "Good to go."

"Two more SEVs to check," said Ten, "then we go in. You okay out there?"

"Hell of a view," said the Marine. "I'm Jackson, for what it's worth."

"Call me Ten," said Ten as he guided the SEV to the next set of coordinates. "You see anything alive in there?" he asked as they drew close to the SEV.

"Shit. It's Franklin, and she's dead," said Jackson. "Headshot."

"Roger," said Ten through gritted teeth. "This day extracts a heavy toll." Ten could feel his optimism draining away as the SEV approached the third casualty on Mason's list.

"Company," warned Jackson, readying himself for action. There were five Mechs on the outside of the prone SEV, still hacking at its hull even though their comrades had long since left to attack *Vengeance.*

Ten opened a channel to the Marine in the remaining SEV.

"Hey, Marine, need some help?" he said, staying just far enough away from the other craft not to place himself in direct danger of a Mech attack.

"Am I pleased to see you! Have you seen what these pricks are doing? They're stripping my ship for spare parts," said a woman's voice. "It's bloody outrageous!"

"What's your name, Marine?" Ten asked.

"Irsia Gray. They're almost in, so now would be a good time to act."

"Good to meet you, Gray. Jackson's here as well, get ready to attack."

"Roger," said Gray. "What's the plan?"

"Shoot them in the face till they're dead," said Ten. "Fifteen seconds, mark. Stand ready, Jackson."

20

Ten brought the SEV to a halt ten metres from Gray's vehicle. He popped the canopy, raised his rifle, and when the timer hit zero, he opened fire. Jackson swore and fired as well.

The first two Mechs died in seconds, their bodies drifting slowly away under the impact of the bullets as they lost their grip on the outside of Gray's SEV.

Gray was struggling with her canopy, punching at the heavy glass with a power-armoured fist and shouting incoherently. A Mech reached into her SEV through a hole in the hull, arm disappearing up to its shoulder as it reached for the Marine.

"Fuck," said Gray as she was yanked back into the SEV. "Get off me, you fucking fuck," she yelled.

"Jackson, you have a shot?" Ten fired on a Mech that was cutting into Gray's canopy.

"On it," said Jackson as the body of a third Mech collapsed under the weight of his fire. He shifted position, targeted the Mech that was trying to pull Gray's arm off, and shot it in the back.

The final Mech, perhaps realising that it was suddenly alone, turned to bring its weapon to bear on Ten's SEV. The barrel spat fire and stitched a neat line of holes in the hull.

Then Gray managed to pull herself free from the wreck of her vehicle and pointed her pistol at the remaining Mech.

"Die, fucker," she said with a tone of quiet triumph as she emptied her magazine into the Mech at short range. It went still, head a bloody ruin, and spun away into the void.

"You okay, Gray?" said Jackson.

"They're tough buggers, aren't they?" she said, out of breath as she reloaded her pistol. "And my SEV is dead. Did you see how easily they cut into the hull?"

"Time to worry about that later," said Ten. "We need to deal with that Sphere."

"Wait, what?" asked Gray. "You want to attack it?"

"It's the only way," said Jackson. "And we're the only ones who... shit, look out!"

A sixth Mech had appeared, clambering around the outside of Gray's SEV to grab her from behind. Its arms slid around her neck, and it wrapped its legs around her waist as it tried to twist off her helmet.

"Help," yelped Gray, struggling to bring her pistol to bear.

"I don't have a shot," said Jackson, moving across the hull of Ten's SEV as he sighted down his rifle. "Can't get it."

Ten opened the canopy on his SEV and heaved himself into space.

"Hold on, Gray," he said, holding the edge of the craft and getting his feet beneath him, "hold on."

"I fucking heard you," said Gray as she scrabbled for purchase on the Mech's arm, trying to pull it away from her neck.

Ten breathed out to steady his focus, then pushed off with his legs to launch himself across the gap between the two SEVs. As he flew, he drew his pistol and reactivated his power armour's magnetic boots.

"Gah," said Gray as she saw Ten approaching.

Then Ten slammed into her, almost knocking her loose. He pulled himself around to stand on the hull of the SEV, then put his pistol against the Mech's faceplate and pulled the trigger.

"Weirdly quiet," said Gray as the Mech stopped struggling. "Can't get over the lack of noise."

"You okay?"

"Yeah, just about. Get it off me, would you?"

Ten unwrapped the Mech's legs and arms and pulled the corpse away from Gray.

The Mech had a name etched into its metal frame. *Wachowski.* Was that Russian origin? Eastern European? Total coincidence, maybe?

Ten tossed the Mech into space and turned to check on Jackson and his SEV.

"Looking good," said Jackson, waving. "What the hell is that?" he asked suddenly, pointing at Gray's vehicle as his ride twisted slowly, turning to carry him out of view.

Ten turned and clomped across the hull. "Just cuts where they were trying to get in," he said. Then he stopped and looked again, and now he saw what Jackson had seen: a message scratched into the hull by the Mechs.

D*EATH TO SOL*

"W hat the hell...?" said Ten, capturing images through his HUD camera. The letters were crudely cut into the outer hull of the SEV, ugly and ill-formed but as clear as the stars. "A message. A message for us in English, and not a friendly one."

"Admiral Stansfield isn't going to like this," said Gray as she moved to stand beside Ten. "They know where we're from. We need to tell *Vengeance.*"

"You need to hold that thought a little longer, Gray. We're ordered back to *Vengeance*, but we need to take the fight to the enemy. They took our cyborg mascot, and I want him back. Are you with us?"

Gray was a young Marine, unversed in the etiquette of order-dodging, but familiar with the 'get it done' doctrine of the Commandos.

"*Vengeance* is my first combat posting," she said after a moment's hesitation. She glanced across the void at the battleship. Its surface seemed to be moving as the Mechs crawled all over it, and she shuddered.

"Funny you should say that," she said carefully, "but I've been having comms problems with my HUD. Must be the Mechs... Ten, watch out!"

Ten turned fast, and a Mech smashed into him. The cluster Boss wrapped its arms around him so that he couldn't move. And then it began to squeeze, locking his arms against his sides so that even with the power armour, he couldn't break free.

Ten could see the thing's eyes glinting behind its faceplate, mere inches from his face. He leant back, trying to pull free, but the thing held him tight. There was an ominous creak from the armour, and a pressure warning appeared in his view.

"Watch its head!" warned Gray, and Ten blinked at a row of spikes that had appeared on the Mech's forehead. He squirmed and pulled but couldn't break free. All he could do was watch as the Mech pulled its head back, then slammed it forward into Ten's helmet. The spikes skittered across the surface but didn't puncture the helmet. The Mech pulled back and headbutted Ten again.

And now it was Ten's turn to call for help. He tried to shuffle around to give Gray a clear line of sight, but the Mech smashed against his helmet again, and Ten saw sudden lights in his vision as his head was rammed back and forth.

Again and again, the Mech pounded Ten's helmet. Between strikes, Ten felt vibrations through the hull of the SEV, as if someone were banging it like a drum.

Then the Mech went limp and fell back, pulled clear by something.

Ten blinked the lights from his eyes and shook his head to clear it.

Gray was in front of him, holding the shattered corpse of the Mech in one hand and her pistol in the other.

"Did you get him?" said Jackson. Ten and Gray looked over to see Jackson coming back into view as Ten's SEV continued to revolve. "Is it dead?"

"Gray got it," said Ten gratefully. "That's got to be the last of these buggers for now, right?"

"Yup, they come in tens," said Jackson.

"So, what were you saying about that Sphere?" said Gray. "I'm up for the trip, but my SEV is fucked."

"Are you sure?" said Ten. "Are you wearing a clone?"

"Of course," said Gray in a tone that suggested any other option was utterly insane. "And so is Jackson, and the rest of our company. Who isn't, these days?"

"The rest of Charlie Team," said Ten darkly, "and most of the crew of *Vengeance*, it seems."

"Yeah, well, they're properly weird and old," said Gray. "We arrived on *Colossus* and were off-loaded to *Kingdom 10* while we waited for *Vengeance* to arrive from wherever she'd been."

"Have you died before, Gray?" asked Ten quietly.

"No," said Gray.

"Me neither," said Jackson.

"Well, this isn't the time to start practising, okay?"

"*Vengeance* doesn't have cloning bays yet," said Gray, as they watched Jackson take control of Ten's SEV and guide it carefully across the short gap, "but I think *Colossus* delivered new equipment to *Kingdom 10* at the same time she dropped us off. You've got a mix of cloned Marines and *Vengeance* original crew on board. So if you're asking if I mind joining you on a one-way suicide mission, my answer is 'yes'. I'm too raw to have lost a skin yet, but there's got to be a first time, right?"

"Definitely," said Ten as Jackson brought the SEV close enough for them to step across the gap between the craft. "And this is as desperate a situation as you could wish for."

They were quiet for a few moments as Gray and Ten stowed the gear they'd rescued from Gray's SEV and arranged themselves on the outside of the hull.

"The comms with *Vengeance* are dead," said Jackson as he triggered the thrusters to move them clear of Gray's SEV. "The ship has gone completely dark. We're on our own."

21

A breach warning was the first sign the Mechs had penetrated *Vengeance*'s hull. The klaxon wailed throughout the ship until someone hit the override control.

"External comms are offline, sir," said the midshipman at the communication console. "Internal channels still functional."

"Give me an update, Commander," said Stansfield.

"Three breaches, Admiral," said Vernon. "Two in the bays, one in the vents."

"Damn it, Ed. I ordered the vents to be sealed."

"They cut their way in and past the seals, sir, nothing we could do to stop them."

"Refresh my memory, Fernandez," said Stansfield. "The bridge uses a separate venting system, yes?"

"We're going to get a breach in this bay any moment, sir! The Mechs are forcing the doors, there's no stopping them."

"An answer to my question, please, Fernandez," said Stansfield calmly.

"You're secure, sir. The bridge has its own life-support and venting systems, and all security, power and essential services can be diverted to the bridge."

"Thank you, Lieutenant. Keep me briefed, and make sure you're ready to send those Mechs packing if they breach your bay."

"Ay, sir, we'll be ready," said Fernandez, sounding anything but prepared and ready.

"Report from Bay Three, sir," said Vernon. "Defensive teams pulling back, the bays are too large to defend, and they're at risk of being overrun by Mechs. A similar report from Bay Ten."

Vernon was beginning to show signs of stress. He looked like a man with the troubles of the world on his shoulders.

"Thank you, Commander," said Stansfield, scanning the data flowing through the command centre. This was the most alive he'd felt since coming out of stasis. This is what made life worth living.

~

In Bay Seven, Kearney and Mason watched the inside of the outer doors with Lieutenant Fernandez and a small team of Marines. All wore power armour, and they'd thrown together a defensive position behind a bank of packing crates and half-assembled cloning equipment.

"Kearney, Mason," said Stansfield in their HUDs. "I want regular updates and a visual feed."

"Will do, sir. Any news on Hunter and Ten?" said Kearney.

"No news," said Stansfield. "And I want you to catch one of those things alive, find out what makes it tick, understood?"

"Ay, sir," said Mason, "but what about Davies and Conway?"

"Safely on the other side of the portal," said the admiral before he cut the channel.

"Love you too, sir," said Mason with a heavy dose of sarcasm.

"How long till they get the bay doors open?" asked Kearney. "Have I got time to update my will?"

Mason snorted. "What do you own that anyone would want?"

"I'll have you know I have an excellent collection of primitive 3D films from the early twenty-first century depicting a team of heroes as they struggle to–" Kearney's reply was lost behind a squeal of tortured metal as the bay door was finally levered open. The atmosphere howled out, sweeping past the Mechs that crawled across the hull.

"Stand by," said Kearney, aiming her rifle across the top of their improvised fort.

"Bay doors breached, sir," said Mason, back on the line to the admiral. "They literally prised them open, hundreds of them."

And then the firing began. It was noisy at first, but grew quickly quieter as the last remnants of the bay's atmosphere blew out into space until the two sides were fighting in total silence.

"Eerie," said Mason as he shot a Mech that was clambering along a wall.

"They're all over the place," said Kearney. "They move so fast in here."

With the bay doors open, the Mechs crawled in through the gaps like an ant nest on the move. They swarmed between the doors, and the moment they stepped into *Vengeance*'s artificial gravity field, they sped up.

Mason updated the bridge crew. "They're incredible. Even at speed, they're laying down accurate fire. We're hardly slowing them."

"We need to fall back," said Kearney. "We'll never hold them here."

"The Admiral wants one alive," said Mason, firing at the Mechs that ran across the open bay.

"Any idea how we're supposed to do that?" yelled Kearney, her own rifle firing continuously.

"Not a fucking clue," said Mason. He tossed a grenade across the bay, then ducked back behind the crates to reload his rifle. "Where's Ten when you need him?" he muttered to himself.

"We need a different strategy, Lieutenant," said Kearney. The Mechs had taken cover amongst the vehicles in the bay, and now the two sides were standing off taking potshots at each other. "It's only a matter of time before we run out of cover and they kill us all," she said as the crate to her left disappeared in a cloud of splinters.

"Agreed," said Fernandez. "Admiral, we're withdrawing from Bay

Seven," he said, waving at Mason to give the order. "Evacuate the atmosphere behind us. Have any other bays been breached?"

"Bays One and Nine are lost," said Stansfield. "Capture me one of those things alive, there has to be a way of disabling them. They're just tech, and that means they'll have an off button."

"Fall back into the corridor, Marines," ordered Kearney, hurling grenades over the barricades. "Me, Mason and Fernandez are going to try and capture us a souvenir. Give us cover when we come out."

The Marines moved towards the door, firing as they went, and slid out into the corridor beyond. The door closed behind them and, just like that, the firing stopped.

"They think they've won," said Mason, peering cautiously between the crates as the Mechs moved across the bay floor. They were gathering near one of the other doors, lining up.

"Why do you want me?" hissed Fernandez. "I'm no Marine. I fix things made of metal."

"Exactly," Kearney said, "and now you need to break things as well. Stick close to me and Mason. Have you got a hover lift in this hangar?"

"Yes, what do you need it for?"

Kearney grinned inside her helmet. "We're gonna disable one of those bots and get it out of here on a lift."

"Disable it how?" asked Fernandez sceptically.

"You're the engineer, sir," said Kearney. "Figure it out."

"And quickly," added Mason. "They're assembling over there, lining up, and we ain't got long before they're ready to move out. How many you reckon, three hundred? And the same in the other bays?"

"Okay," snapped Fernandez, "you've made your point. We can't shoot all of them, they outnumber us completely. Stansfield is right, there has to be a tech solution to this."

"They're gathering in the bays," said Commander Vernon in the command channel. "We're holding them off at the vents, but they learn quickly, and the launch bays are our biggest vulnerability, so that's where they're focussing their efforts."

"Same number in each bay?" asked Kearney.

"Looks that way," said Vernon. "They seem to be gathering for an assault."

"I have a plan," said Fernandez in the local channel. "Look. See that device over there? It creates a massive magnetic field in a concentrated area. We use it for testing. If we can lure one of those Mechs over, it should be able to contain it, if nothing else."

"Are you sure?" said Mason. "Because we're going to have to stick our heads out to lure one over."

"They travel in clusters, remember?" said Kearney. "We should try for one of those purple bosses, they seem most important in the hierarchy."

"They're on the move," said Vernon in the command channel.

"This is it," said Stansfield. "We're fighting for *Vengeance* now."

Kearney, Fernandez and Mason watched as the assembled Mechs moved move towards the bay exit, proceeding in a stately, unhurried fashion.

But they didn't all leave. One cluster remained behind as if guarding the bay.

"Perfect," said Kearney, staring out at the Mechs. "Here's our chance. Only ten of them, so how are we going to catch our mouse?"

Then there was movement from across the bay.

"There's a Marine over there," said Mason, planting a flag in his HUD to indicate the location. "Must have been isolated from his unit. It's Foster, he's on his own."

"Fernandez, we're going to give him backup, then loop the Mechs round here. Make sure you're ready," said Kearney.

Kearney and Mason moved off, leaving Fernandez to build his trap.

Foster was yelling something now on the local channel as the Mechs swarmed over him. They disarmed him, then began cutting into his armour, working to remove the arm at the shoulder.

"Help me!" he yelled, struggling against the Mechs as they began to unscrew his helmet. His screams were suddenly cut off as the helmet came free and was tossed across the bay.

Kearney and Mason watched in horror as Foster gasped for breath in the vacuum. Then a Mech produced an extraction instrument from its hand and, with complete precision, removed the Marine's right eye. Foster's body went limp, and the other Mechs moved like a team of mechanised surgeons to open his armour and strip him of body parts.

"Shoot him," said Kearney, appalled at the torture.

But Mason had already done it. They couldn't save Foster, but a clean shot to the head ended his pain.

"Standard RMSC clone," said Mason. "We'll buy him a drink once he's been redeployed, okay? Fuck, though, I've never seen anything like that."

"Move, you idiot. They know where that shot came from!" said Kearney, diving away behind a Raptor that stood on stubby legs in the middle of the bay.

"Fuck," said Mason in horror, "they're storing the body parts in some sort of freezing device. I don't like this one little bit," he said as he joined Kearney.

Shots followed him, ripping past his head and pinging off the Raptor. Kearney returned fire and downed two of the enemy as Mason shifted position.

Mason opened fire as well, taking three more as they crossed the open bay towards the Raptor.

"Getting a bit hot over here," said Kearney, looking around for a way to circle behind the Mechs. "Go that way," she said, moving in the other direction.

"They're intent on getting Foster's body parts," said Mason as he crouched low to run across the bay. "Let's take the two on refrigeration duty, then lure the others to Fernandez."

"Not quite ready yet, guys," said Fernandez.

"Work faster," said Kearney as she shot at the remaining Mechs, "because we're out of time."

"Three to go," said Mason. "Okay, Fernandez, we're heading your way."

"Still not ready," snapped Fernandez.

The three remaining Mechs circled Kearney and Mason, edging unknowingly toward Fernandez's position.

"They're stalking us," said Kearney, "trying to get close. I think they're after our bits and pieces to...you know. What the hell do they want with it?"

"They're not getting their cold metal hands on any of my choice cuts of meat," said Mason with feeling. "This is a limited-edition body, and it's not for sale!"

"Limited edition?" snorted Kearney. "Remaindered, water-damaged stock, you mean."

Mason said something under his breath, but kept moving.

"Almost there," said Kearney. Mason couldn't see her anymore, but her position showed in his HUD. "Firing."

A Mech collapsed, shot through the head, and its comrades changed direction, heading towards the source of the firing.

"Wow, I forgot that was your speciality," said Mason, genuinely impressed. "Nice work. I still can't work out how you do that, but–"

Before he'd finished, Kearney popped out of cover and riddled the second to last Mech. Then she ducked away into cover as Mason jogged across the bay.

"How do you even do that?" he asked, shaking his head as he ran.

"Now, guys," shouted Fernandez, "move now!"

The lieutenant popped up from behind his crates and waved wildly at the final Mech, trying to lure it into his trap. Taking their cue, Kearney and Mason advanced on the Mech, dodging between cover and firing as they came, careful not to hit it as they herded the creature towards Fernandez.

"Help," cried Fernandez as the Mech lunged at him. It reached out and grabbed him, pulling him close, and Fernandez slammed the magnetic device into the middle of its back above its spinal column.

The effect was immediate. The Mech jerked back, frozen in position, and fell to the floor. The thing was paralysed: alive, but unable to move.

"Gotcha," said Fernandez quietly, standing over his fallen enemy. Mason joined him.

"Ugly little fucker, ain't he?" said Mason, nudging the Mech with his foot.

"Get him loaded," said Kearney as she guided the hover lift to a halt beside the fallen Mech. They heaved the body onto the lift, checked that it really was as incapacitated as it appeared, then looked at each other and grinned inside their helmets.

"So what now?" asked Kearney.

Fernandez looked again at the Mech, trying to work out what to do next.

Then the lights went out, and the bay was plunged into complete darkness.

22

With only a couple of kilometres to travel to the Firewall Sphere, the SEV ran out of power and died.

"That's going to make life a bit tricky," said Jackson stoically as he prodded at the unresponsive controls. "I'm guessing we'll glance off the Sphere and float away into the darkness," he said with gloomy resignation, "there to freeze to death when our suits run out of power, lost to the deep dark of the interstellar void, so close to our destination but, ultimately, so far away."

"Poetic," said Ten. "Is that all you've got?"

"I'm not ready to give up yet," said Gray.

"To be honest," said Ten, "I hadn't figured out how we'd get from the Sphere back to *Vengeance* in any case." Living in the moment was great, but only when it all worked out.

"What about the discs?" said Gray, looking at the outside of the vehicle. "The ones the Mechs rode. Could we use them?"

There were several of the black discs stuck to the outside of the SEV, but whether magnetically adhered or chemically bonded, Ten couldn't say.

"It's gotta be worth a try," he said. "How long until we reach the Sphere?" he asked, looking up at the huge ship.

"Maybe ninety seconds," said Jackson as he clambered out of the SEV's open canopy, a grab bag of ammunition slung over one shoulder, a rifle over the other. "These things ain't the fastest, but the Sphere isn't far away, so we're going to get there pretty soon."

"Better move fast, then," said Ten. "We don't want to be stuck on this thing when it strikes home."

Gray strode across the hull of the SEV to the nearest disc and climbed aboard, looking ridiculous as her boots clamped onto the matte black surface.

"How do you think those things work?" she asked, crouching down to peer at the surface.

"Mech power? Robo fuel? Recycled cooking oil?" offered Ten.

"They probably have some sort of biometric security," said Jackson miserably, "or a token-activated ignition of some sort. Maybe a thirty-two-character password with voice recognition."

"Whoa," said Gray as her disc detached from the SEV and began to float slowly away. "Looks like you just need to hit the standby button."

"This'll never work," said Jackson as he found his own disc. "Probably a fluke, or it's damaged," he went on, prodding at the black surface of the disc until his also floated free. "Maybe the whole batch is defective," he said as Ten found a ride and cleared the SEV.

"Nice," said Ten, nodding appreciatively.

"Controlled by leaning," said Gray as she demonstrated. Her disc moved forward, powered by some mechanism hidden in the rim. She tilted back, and the disc came to a stop relative to the SEV.

"We're still going to crash into the Sphere," pointed out Jackson. "It's going to sting, even at thirty kilometres an hour, and that'll leave us stuck on the outside with our new toys."

"This is going to be fun," said Gray, enjoying herself. "You lean into it, it's a bit like a surfboard as far as I can tell. I'm going to come back to you at the SEV."

Gray leaned gently forward, and the disc began to move. She pushed slightly to her right, and the disc began to spin on its hub.

When she faced the SEV, she straightened up, and the disc began to move back towards Ten and Jackson.

"It's quite easy once you get the hang of it," she said, pulling to a halt alongside Jackson. "It must have onboard guidance doing all the real work, interpreting your movements."

"Forty seconds," said Jackson, reading from his HUD.

"Ready?" said Ten as they drew closer to the Sphere.

"Chocks away!" said Gray, turning to face the oncoming Sphere.

"Do we even have a plan?" asked Jackson as he unshipped his rifle and leaned back to slow the disc as the Sphere loomed up before him.

As they pulled in closer, they slowed and levelled up, their thoughts turning to business.

"What do you think, go in the same way the Mechs came out?" said Gray, looking for openings.

"That's got to be favourite," said Ten from just behind her as he checked his rifle.

"Hey," said Gray in alarm, "I've lost control." She leaned back and forth on the disc, but it was now heading straight for a gap in the sheer wall of the Sphere.

"Me too," said Ten. "Looks like they're on auto-pilot for the final approach. Jackson, you ready?"

"Not really," said Jackson as he lost control of his disc and began to follow the path that Gray and Ten were locked onto.

"I'm slowing down," said Gray, as she knelt and aimed her rifle ahead.

Up close, the Sphere was huge, about the same diameter as *Vengeance* was long. From a distance, it had looked smooth and rounded like a billiard ball, but now they could see it was made up of all sorts of parts, as if it had been constructed from scrap metal taken from a giant salvage yard. There were lights across the surface and inside the structure, and they seemed to flicker as the Marines flew past.

"There's the bay," said Gray, pointing at a huge hatch, still open but poorly lit and difficult to see from a distance. "That's where they're taking us."

"Damn, they're like small moons," said Ten as the stars disappeared behind the bulk of the Sphere. "No wonder they made such short work of *Colossus*."

"They'll probably shoot us before we reach the bay," said Jackson.

"I think they'd have shot by now if they were going to," said Ten. "I reckon they think we're Mechs, as we're riding on these discs."

"Maybe they plan to shoot us once we're inside," said Jackson.

And then they passed through the huge doorway into the bay beyond.

"It's just a hangar entrance," said Gray, looking around for threats, "same as *Vengeance*. And the gravity works," she said as she crossed the hangar threshold.

Whatever was guiding their discs took them deep into the bay and across to the left-hand side, where a long series of landing platforms was waiting. Beside each landing platform there was a human-sized pod, open and ready to receive the returning Mechs.

"Stay sharp," said Ten as the discs slowed and landed, one after another, on the docking mechanisms.

There was no movement in the bay, and for several long moments they stayed on the discs, scanning the huge room. They appeared to have the place to themselves.

"All quiet," said Ten, scanning the area. "Let's take a look around. Follow my lead." He jumped down to the deck and headed for the edge of the bay, Jackson close behind.

"Do they sleep in these things?" asked Gray, frowning at the pods as she followed the others. The pods just sat there, looking not at all inviting, canopies open as if their residents had merely stepped away and might return at any moment.

"These ones are occupied," said Ten when he reached the edge of the hangar. "They have Mechs in them, sleeping, I reckon."

"Let sleeping Mechs lie," said Jackson ominously. "We should keep moving."

"Agreed," said Gray, "these things are super creepy. At least we know we can jack the discs and escape with Hunter once we find him."

"*If* we find him," said Jackson quietly. "They'll probably kill us before we get anywhere close."

"This entire place looks like it's automated," said Ten. "Let's head for the door."

They moved towards one of the exits from the bay, a huge, heavy hangar door. They looked at each other.

"We'll never get that open," said Jackson. "Probably needs a security pass or DNA-sequenced ID verification."

"It's an airlock," said Gray as she peered at a panel beside the door. "Ready?" She tapped a button without waiting for a reply, and a pair of doors slid back to reveal a large airlock.

"It's a trap," hissed Jackson, but Ten and Gray were already inside.

"Or it's just an airlock," said Ten, who was beginning to find Jackson's negative attitude a little annoying.

Jackson sighed and followed them in. The door closed behind them, and there was a hiss of returning atmosphere.

"Any suggestions?" Gray asked. "My suit's telling me the atmosphere is breathable. Shall we risk it?"

"Poison gas," warned Jackson.

Gray stared at him for a moment, then looked at Ten. "My readings say breathable atmosphere, but Jackson's right. Helmets stay on, even if the Mechs are human-based and have the same requirements for pressure, air and temperature."

The inner door opened, and they crept out into a silent corridor.

"Where the fuck are they?" asked Ten as they padded down the corridor.

"Armoury," said Jackson. The others stopped and stared at him. "This is the armoury," he repeated, pointing at a door. "That's a gun icon, that's a stylised grenade, that's a lock. Armoury."

"Okay," said Gray slowly, as if tasting the idea. "So how do we get in? Shoot the door down?"

"Hold on," said Ten, "let me see what I've got in this tool belt." He rummaged around for a moment, then realised that this wasn't the right approach. "Humans, right?" he said, putting away his tools. "But all in those pods, asleep. So maybe we just need to–" he reached out to the control panel and tapped it "–make our presence known."

There was a clunk from inside the wall, and the door slid open.

"No fucking way," whispered Jackson.

"Sheesh!" said Ten, mock outraged. "Their security's terrible. I guess they didn't expect us to just wander in and help ourselves."

"Told you it was an armoury," said Jackson smugly. An open area inside the door held tables, and beyond them, a set of shelves held a huge assortment of weapons and ammunition in neatly stored and labelled crates.

"This stuff is all made for human hands," said Ten as he cracked open a crate of heavy pistols.

"We should keep moving," said Jackson. "Time is not on our side."

"Yeah, good point," said Ten, turning away from the pistols. He jogged down the aisles between the shelves, looking for something larger, and stopped when the crates changed shape. He dragged one off the shelf and flipped open the lid to expose a heavy weapon that looked like a cross between an assault weapon and a bazooka.

"It's like a shopping mall for commandos," said Ten as he slung his rifle and pulled the new weapon from the crate. "I like this one," he said as he searched for the right ammunition.

Jackson stood guard at the door, peering suspiciously into the corridor as Ten and Gray systematically ransacked the armoury. Ten loaded his new toy and slung a bag of ammunition over his shoulder.

Gray had found a multi-barrelled machine gun with a matching pack of ammunition and a heavy-duty belt feed. She tossed her rifle to Jackson and slid the pack onto her back. The gun was weighted for easy carrying, and it clicked ominously when she armed it.

"You look ridiculous," said Jackson. "Do you even know how to use that thing?"

"I guess we'll find out," said Gray, "and if it all goes wrong, you'll just have to save me, right?"

"Time to go, kids," said Ten.

"That way, I think," said Gray, turning away from the hangar and heading deeper into the Sphere.

The corridor ended at a T-junction. To the left and right, the corridor stretched into the distance. Ahead, a door blocked their progress.

"It's got to be that way," said Ten, nodding at the door.

Gray stood to one side, and Jackson stepped forward, muttering something about traps as he peered at the control panel.

"Easy," he said as he tapped the panel and the door slid open. He stepped through the doorway into the dimly-lit chamber beyond, then swore as his HUD adjusted to the light and showed him what the room contained.

"Mech pods," said Ten quietly, "hundreds of them."

Then an alarm sounded, and the pods began to light up and open as the Mechs awakened.

"Bollocks," said Ten. "I think they're onto us."

23

"Hey, Davies, how does it feel to be stranded in space?" said Conway.

"I've been abandoned in worse places," said Davis, calm and focussed. "How long until that portal opens again? It's beginning to get a bit quiet out here. I mean, not that I don't appreciate the conversation, but it would be nice to have my other pals back."

"Could we make it to *Kingdom 10*?"

"Good question," said Davies, running the figures in his HUD. "Hmm, sort of. Probably."

"Probably?"

"It's fifty thousand kilometres, or thereabouts. If we load into your Raptor, point it in the right direction and burn half the fuel, we'll hit maybe two thousand kilometres per hour. We have oxygen for about fourteen hours."

"So our corpses would get to *Kingdom 10*," summarised Conway.

"Most likely we'd miss by a few kilometres and vanish into space, or get caught in the planet's gravity and burn up before crashing into the surface."

"You're all joy today, Davies."

"Better hope the portal reopens, or *Kingdom 10* can send a shuttle."

They hung in space for a few moments, staring at the view. Then Davies shrugged and decided that he might as well get on with the work. "Okay, I'm going to run a test to *Kingdom 10*," he said. "If this works, I'll eat my hat."

Conway was close by in her Raptor, ready to carry Davies to safety when the portal opened again. He was tethered to the framework of the old shuttle they'd used for their previous test. As a temporary solution, it wasn't the worst satellite ever launched, and it would be worth it if it enabled the planned signal hop.

"Nothing from *Vengeance*," muttered Conway, not that she expected there to be. *Vengeance* was thousands of light-years away, stranded and unable to help. "I wish the freakin' portal would open again. Those Mechs were formidable."

"Marine Davies to *Kingdom 10*, this is *Vengeance* crew calling *Kingdom 10*."

A mess of scrambled static came over the speaker, but nobody answered.

"Keep trying, DD. They might be distracted, and I bet they don't get a lot of callers at a shitty outpost like that."

"I'm going to push the booster unit a bit harder," said Davies, digging through the menus in his HUD. "It might cause it to fail, but I may as well give it a good thrashing since the bloody thing isn't working anyway. Marine Davies to *Kingdom 10*, is anybody receiving this?"

More scrambled noises, but nothing that sounded like speech.

"So what do we do if we can't make this work?" asked Conway. Davies was silent for a moment as he thought through the implications.

And then there was a voice from the darkness.

"*Kingdom 10* to *Vengeance* crew, authenticate, please."

At last, they'd made contact.

Davies pinged his authentication code to *Kingdom 10* and relaxed.

"It's good to talk, Marine," said *Kingdom 10*. "We lost comms with *Vengeance,* are you all good out there?"

"Negative, *Kingdom 10.* The portal has closed, and we encountered a formidable enemy. *Vengeance* is stuck on the other side of the portal, requesting immediate help and backup to contain the enemy."

"What's your plan, Davies? We can't risk another mistake like *Colossus.*"

"I want to rig this signal for data transfer," said Davies. "If we can pull the archived Marine mind states from *Vengeance,* you'll be able to deploy them to clones and begin building an assault force. All we need is old enough ships to send back across the portal. Doesn't have to be anything fancy."

"We can accept mind states," said *Kingdom 10,* "but our cloning facilities aren't yet online, and we don't have any stock."

"Shit. I thought *Colossus* delivered new equipment?"

"She did, but it takes time to install. Even if it were all running, we have only enough supplies for a dozen clones. After that, we need to await deliveries."

"What about ships?" said Davies, although he already had a pretty good idea of the answer.

"On their way," said *Kingdom 10* without offering any details at all, "but the Admiralty insists they're to stop anything crossing the portal, not to provide assistance on the other side."

"We're abandoning *Vengeance?* After all they've done?"

"Careful, Marine. *Vengeance* is unique, there aren't many like her now, but she'll have to manage on her own."

"Then *Vengeance* had better still be in one piece when the portal reopens," said Conway angrily, "because she's all that stands between *Kingdom 10* and obliteration."

~

In the bay, Fernandez, Kearney and Mason waited in the dark with their hostage.

"Bridge, this is Fernandez. The lights have gone out in Bay Seven. Bridge?"

"The Mechs are trying to hack our power and security controls," said Stansfield. "Hold tight, we're re-routing at the moment."

They waited, and then a number of lamps came back on, casting a dim light across the bay.

"That's as good as it gets, Lieutenant," said Stansfield. "Do you have a captive?"

"Ay, sir," said Fernandez, "we're heading to the medbay and workshops on deck two now."

"Be aware that decks five and four are held by the Mechs with little to no ongoing resistance. Fighting is fierce on deck three, but we still hold decks two and one."

"Roger," said Fernandez, "understood. Fernandez out." He turned to Kearney and Mason. "You heard that?"

"We're on deck six, right?" said Kearney.

Fernandez nodded, his helmet exaggerating the gesture.

"So we just fight our way through three enemy-held floors, dragging a captive, so that you can take it apart and work out what makes it tick?" said Mason.

Fernandez nodded again.

"What a day to be alive," said Mason with a sigh. "Better just to get on with it, then," he said, hefting his rifle. "Besides, I'm getting sick of this fucking bay."

⌇

"Commander Vernon, an update, please," said Stansfield, his voice dominating the bridge.

"All bays are completely overrun, but the flow of new Mechs has stopped. Can't tell if they've despatched their full force or if they just think they have enough to do the job," said Vernon with a grudging respect.

"Decks four and five are mostly quiet, as far as we can tell. None of our people left alive, or at least active, on those decks. We have maybe ten minutes before we lose deck three. We're organising a retreat and placing traps on deck two as we concentrate our efforts on protecting deck one and the bridge."

"Any sign of that portal opening yet?" Stansfield asked, seeking a chink of light in their current darkness.

"No movement, sir. We're outside the regular activation cycle. It looks like the Mechs don't want to give us a way to get out of here."

"How about Marine X and Hunter? Any updates, Mr Staunch?"

"Negative, sir. Complete radio silence after we lost their signal, no way to know where they are or what they're doing."

Stansfield sat in his command chair and glared at the small number of monitors that still functioned, almost daring them to give him more bad news. Then he brought up the command screen on his data slate and scrolled to the option that would destroy *Vengeance* if no other escape were possible.

He stared at it, unblinking, then flicked it away.

"Not yet," he said to himself. "Not quite yet."

"Are we nearly there yet?" said Mason as he leaned out to peer down the long corridor. A burst of gunfire caused him to yank his head back in. "Not even close," he muttered.

They had made it to deck five, but now they were trapped in a narrow engineering access corridor, with only emergency backup lighting to help them see the enemy. A squad of Mechs was advancing down the corridor, firing on their position and clearing side rooms as they came.

"Thorough little buggers," said Mason. Behind him, Fernandez was struggling with the hover lift.

"It's not designed for this," he said, yanking at the controls to get it around a tight corner.

"Not much we can do," said Kearney, shouting to make herself heard above a sudden burst of gunfire. "No cover, no help, no way out."

A burst of fire tore through the wall above their hiding spot, blasting great holes in the steel.

"Now would be a great time to be somewhere else," shouted Mason, firing blindly down the corridor.

There was a sudden burst of rapid and intensive fire, then silence.

"Take a look," said Kearney.

"Thanks," muttered Mason sourly. He slid across the floor, power armour scraping at the metal, until he saw a squad of *Vengeance* Marines coming rapidly down the long corridor.

"We're here to support you up to the medbay," said the sergeant, a dour-sounding man named Weston. He'd scraped together a team of half a dozen Marines from the company that had been deployed across deck three, and had fought his way into the bowels of the ship.

"The engineering elevators are still operational," said Weston as his troops fanned out to provide cover as Fernandez manoeuvred the hover lift. "The Mechs don't seem to have found them yet. Risky, but the fastest way to deck two."

Kearney looked at the Marine. His face was bloody, and he was carrying some sort of leg wound.

"No more suits?" asked Kearney, feeling slightly guilty that this group of unarmoured Marines had been sent to save them.

"Bullet-proof vests," said Weston with a sad shake of his head, "and the best helmets money can buy. And we're low on ammo, so if we could get moving...?"

The Mechs seemed unstoppable, and they were inflicting heavy casualties on the crew of *Vengeance*, but it wasn't all going their way. The Marines looked worn out, but they'd left a trail of Mech corpses everywhere they'd gone, and now they swept the deck again as they backtracked towards the elevators.

"Linked up with Weston's squad, now heading for the engineering elevators," said Kearney as she checked in with Vernon. "Get ready to receive, Commander."

"Roger that. Tech and med personnel are standing by."

"Come on," said Weston, waving them on from further down the corridor, where it widened into a chamber big enough to host the engineering elevators that carried heavy equipment between decks.

Kearney, Mason and Fernandez ran down the corridor to the engineering elevator and squeezed into the small space.

"You couldn't have found us a smaller lift?" asked Mason as they crowded in.

"Go," said Weston, "but send the lift back down for us. We'll hold them here if we have to."

Kearney looked at Weston, then nodded her thanks and pushed herself into the elevator so that the doors could close behind her.

It was a tight fit. Fernandez had flipped the hover lift so that the Mech was upright, and they stared at each other as the creature strained to break free from the magnetic field. As the lift began to move upwards, Fernandez studied the Mech.

"A cyborg," he said, making notes in his HUD as he began his inspection, "comprised of both custom human-like body parts and what appear to be real human organs, all encased in a vacuum-resistant armoured suit analogous to, but clearly different from, our own power armour.

"The brain appears to be human and is housed in a transparent container that is mounted in a metal framework that forms the head," Fernandez went on. "This subject has artificial eyes, but–" he paused to lean across the Mech as the elevator shuddered slowly upwards "– yes, the spine is also encased in a translucent conduit clamped into the back and protected by a metal framework. Two human legs, also encased and supported within an exoskeleton."

He paused as something banged against the roof of the elevator.

"It's like nothing I've ever seen before," he said finally.

"Coming up on deck two," said Mason. "Why is this thing so bloody slow?"

"It's a bloody freight elevator," snapped an exasperated Fernandez. "Cables and wheels. It doesn't need to be quick."

There was an explosion somewhere in the shaft beneath them, and the entire elevator rocked.

"How safe is this thing?" said Kearney.

"It won't drop, if that's what you're asking," said Fernandez. "Worst case scenario, we get stuck between floors and burned alive by some incendiary device."

"Cool, that's put my mind at rest," said Kearney.

"Deck two," Mason announced. "Hardware, children's wear, ladies – what the fuck?"

The elevator had stopped, but the door hadn't opened.

"It's jammed," said Mason, "help me force it." He could hear movement on the other side, and moments later, the doors slid slowly open as the Marines heaved.

"I'm Smith," said the Marine who was waiting to escort them to the medbay. She and her team were wearing utterly inappropriate combat fatigues and what looked like desert-ready body armour. "Where's Weston?"

"Smith and Weston?" asked Kearney with a frown.

"Make a joke about it, I fucking dare you," snarled Smith. "Where is he?"

"Next elevator, or coming up the stairs," said Mason. "He was guarding our back."

"Shit," said Smith as the sound of gunfire and explosions drifted up the elevator shaft. "Fuck it, we're not going to hold this deck much longer, but we've got you a route to the workshop."

"Let's go," said Kearney, moving out into the corridor to cover their exit.

Two Marines flipped the hover lift and ran with the captive Mech to the right-hand side of the corridor. Mason and Fernandez followed as a huge ball of flame rushed up the elevator shaft, turning their previous transportation into an inhospitable inferno.

"This is it," Fernandez shouted as they turned a corner toward the workshop. From further down the corridor came the sharp sound of the Marines' rifles and the heavy *crump* as the Mechs returned fire. In the workshop, a med-team were waiting with equipment, and a pair of welders stood ready to seal the doors.

"Get in here," shouted Fernandez as he pulled off his helmet and unlocked the gauntlets of his power armour so that he could work. "The Mechs are just around the corner."

Kearney looked at Mason, who shrugged and shook his head.

"Seal the door, Fernandez," said Kearney from the corridor. "We'll buy you the time you need to do the job."

"Get in here," yelled Fernandez, "you'll never survive the firefight."

Mason pressed the button to the side of the heavy workshop door and waved at Fernandez as it began to close.

"Thought we'd never get rid of him," said Mason as he checked his weapon.

Then the corridor was quiet, and Mason and Kearney were alone with only the pissed-off Sergeant Smith and her squad of unhappy Marines for company.

"Time to go to work, troopers," said Kearney . "Let's kill some Mechs."

24

"Time to move," shouted Ten as the Mechs began to stir in their pods.

"Do you hear that?" said Gray.

"I see lots of Mechs getting ready to kick our arse. I'm not sure if we have time for a hearing test."

"Listen," insisted Gray. "There's some kind of pulse sound. It's running through the sphere. It's everywhere, like a heartbeat."

"Can't hear anything," said Jackson.

"I don't care," snapped Ten. "This way, run!"

"Do you even know where you're going, Ten?" said Gray as they ran through the huge chamber. All around them the pods were racked to the ceiling, hundreds of them, and it looked like they were all being activated.

"I haven't got a freakin' clue," admitted Ten, "but we can't stay here, and it seems to me like we need to get deeper into this thing."

Ten skidded to a halt in front of a huge door. Behind them the Mechs were clambering or jumping to the deck and beginning to look for the intruders.

"Hurry up," said Gray, hopping nervously from foot to foot as she pointed her gun into the chamber.

"Patience is a virtue," said Ten as he struggled with the controls.

"It really isn't," said Jackson, "not today."

"Got it," said Ten as the door slid open. He dived through and found himself in another corridor, sparse and darkly functional.

"Close it," said Gray, still covering their retreat but unwilling to fire until it was absolutely necessary. Jackson punched the controls, and the door slid closed.

"It won't hold them," he said, "they'll be through in moments."

"This way," said Ten, leading them down the long corridor. After thirty metres it opened out into a huge open space.

"The middle of the Sphere?" suggested Gray.

"They're coming," said Jackson, staring through the sights of his rifle as the door of the pod chamber opened.

"There's an elevator," said Ten doubtfully, punching what he hoped was a call button. Gray joined him, and was equally unexcited by the prospect of the hole in the floor.

"Run or fight," said Jackson as he backed towards them. Mechs were boiling along the corridor, and they could all hear the pounding of metal boots on steel floors. "Either option works, but make a decision now."

"Looks like we're taking the elevator," said Ten.

"This place is crazy. There's virtually nothing here," said Gray as the elevator arrived from the depths.

"Jackson, come on," said Ten as he joined Gray on the platform. It was big, but it didn't fill the shaft like a normal lift, and it lacked rails and doors.

"Coming," said Jackson, backing toward the elevator and firing as he came. He emptied a magazine and ejected the empty cartridge as the elevator began to drop. Then he took one more step back into thin air and toppled backwards.

"Shit," said Jackson as he fell. He bounced on the elevator platform and slid over the edge, one hand scrabbling at the smooth surface.

"Got you," said Ten, diving across the elevator platform to grab Jackson's wrist. For a moment he lay there, stretched across the platform as Jackson dangled in the shaft. Then Gray reached over and heaved them both to safety.

"Too close," said Jackson as he reloaded his rifle. "Thanks."

The unenclosed elevator gave them a chance to get a good look inside the interior of the Sphere. "There's hardly anything here," said Gray as the platform floated downwards. "That's got to be the bay we landed in," she said, pointing at a huge structure near the Sphere's equator, "and that bit looks like engineering or tech. "

"Gun emplacements all over," said Jackson, shaking his head. "They have a lot of firepower, more than *Vengeance*. Look at that lot up there. They circle the whole ship."

"And that looks like the main reactor core," said Gray, ignoring Jackson to point at a huge structure that hung near the centre of the Sphere. It was dark and encased in steel, held in place by a framework of metal girders and looped in cables and fuel lines.

"I have a bad feeling about this," said Jackson.

"You have a bad feeling about everything," said Gray with a snort.

"This feels like a fortified outpost," said Ten. "It can't be their main base. It's like a troop deployment station. Pretty fearsome, but I'll bet that whatever it protects is worse."

Gray and Jackson nodded their agreement.

Then the elevator slowed and stopped. A pair of doors opened in front of them, and they stepped out into an area built to a much more human scale, with proper floors, walls and ceilings again.

"Best not destroy the elevator," said Ten, one hand on the doors to stop them closing. "I'm not sure if we'll be able to make it back up again if we do. Can we jam it?"

"There, look," said Gray. "I'll shove that container halfway through the door, see if that stops them for a while."

"It probably won't," said Jackson, "and if we go back that way, we have an army of Mechs to fight our way through."

With the elevator door jammed, they moved out to look around the level. It was sparse, just a short corridor with three rooms, one at the end, one at either side.

"They're really not into decorating, are they?" said Gray. "This place could do with a makeover."

"Yeah, right. Some flowers over there, a couple of paintings hung on the wall. I'm guessing these Mechs don't get too hung up about that kind of thing."

"Do you hear that pulse? What is it?" said Gray, obsessed with the recurring sound.

"I hear only the cold metal fingers of Mechs making their way down the lift shaft to rend us limb from limb," said Jackson.

"Yeah," said Ten, creeped out by Jackson's poetry, "let's find Hunter and get out of here."

They moved ahead. The room on the left was empty. It had all the appeal of a freight container, but had no discernible use.

The room on the right was packed with parts and tech. A door in the far wall led to a vast warehouse of Mech spares. Shelves were lined with metal head frames, legs, arms, containment shells for brains and spinal columns, liquids, chemicals, circuit board parts and anything else that might be needed to create some technical monstrosity.

"Well, that's where they keep the nuts and bolts," said Gray. "I wonder where they do their biological bits and pieces?"

They got their answer behind the third door.

"An operating theatre?" said Ten as they ghosted into the room. It was white and spotlessly clean. In the far corner, three robotic arms were working silently on something that was laid out on an operating table. There were nine such areas, all identically equipped with robotic arms. Between them, an automated parts truck moved, shuttling back and forth to the spare parts room to collect bits and pieces for repairs.

"Hunter," said Ten as he recognised the figure strapped to the far table.

"Help!" yelled Hunter as the arms moved around him. "They're taking my arm!"

Gray and Ten opened fire, riddling the robots and surrounding equipment with bullets. The arms collapsed in a smoking heap as Ten jogged over.

"Shit, what have they done to you?" whispered Ten, opening his helmet to talk to Hunter as Gray joined him beside the table.

Ten had seen some nasty stuff in his time, but this shocked even him. Hunter was laid out on the operating table, strapped tightly down with bands of steel on his legs, waist, neck, forehead and remaining arm. The three robots had removed his cybernetic arm, and it sat now on the floor, still gripped in the jaws of one of the robots.

Hunter was fully conscious, and he gave them a sickly grin. "Hey, shake my hand," he said weakly, "it's around here somewhere." Hunter's arm had been reduced to a stump. A circular metal attachment point protruded from the bone. "Damn, I'm glad to see you."

"Incoming," said Jackson from the doorway, "and I don't think they're looking to make friends." He fired down the corridor, then retreated into the room. "Time to go."

Gray hefted her weapon and faced the corridor. "How many?"

Jackson looked at her and grinned from within his helmet. "Couple o' dozen, maybe."

"Fun times," said Gray, and she pressed the trigger. The gun whined, and for a moment it looked like nothing was going to happen.

Then it spat fire at the wall and tore it apart. Gray played the barrel from left to right, all the way across the room, and shredded the wall, the Mechs in the corridor and the wall on the other side. Spent shell casings fountained across the room, spraying the operating theatre with hot brass.

In seconds it was over, and Gray released the trigger.

"Come on," said Ten, slinging his rifle so that he could release Hunter's restraints and help the man to his feet.

"Need my arm," hissed Hunter as he stumbled across the floor. He put one foot on a robot, grabbed his cybernetic arm, and yanked it free. "Okay, let's go."

"More incoming," said Jackson. "Looks like the trick with the lift didn't hold them." He fired a burst through the remains of the wall, then another.

"Hey, Ten, do you hear what I hear?" said Hunter. From above came the thud of boots on metal panels. The Mechs were on the roof, and as one, the team turned to stare at the ceiling.

Then there was an explosion at the other end of the room, and the ceiling crashed down to give them a sudden view across the interior of the Sphere. Mechs began to swarm into the med area, dropping through the hole in the ceiling.

Jackson dived away from the door, firing at the Mechs as he slid into the meagre cover offered by the operating tables.

Then the room was filled with the rumble of gunfire and the tinkle of falling brass as Gray's weapon chewed on the Mechs. She played the weapon across the room, shattering the Mechs as they tried to organise themselves, carving out the wall and the ceiling at the same time.

When she stopped, the remains of the room were suddenly quiet, except for the sound of cooling steel as the barrels of her gun smoked in the dim light.

"Right, yes," said Ten, looking around at the destruction wrought in only a few seconds by Gray's overenthusiastic weapon. "Time to call base. I think I've figured out how we're getting back to *Vengeance*."

25

"Davies, the portal is back," said Conway. She'd been lounging in the Raptor for hours while Davies tinkered with the comms setup and enjoyed his spacewalk. Now, with the threat of imminent action, she sat up and paid attention.

Davies looked up from his spot on the outside of the shuttle they'd cannibalised for their communication platform. "Oh, at fucking last. Let's test this thing and go home." He flicked channels. "Davies to *Kingdom 10*, we have a portal opening. Repeat, the portal is opening."

"Affirmative, Davies, we see that too. Our teams are on standby. Awaiting your instructions."

"There's something different about this one, DD," said Conway, dragging Davies' attention back to their private channel. "Look, it's not like the other times."

The portal opened more slowly than it had before, and it stopped growing well before reaching its previous size.

"It's not opening fully," said Davies, frowning within his helmet as the portal's growth slowed further, then stopped completely. "Well, that's about as much use as a three-legged horse in an arse-kicking contest. *Vengeance* will never get through that."

"Plenty of room for the Raptor," said Conway as she absorbed the information on her instrument panel, "I'm just a bit jittery about it closing on us. Have you ever been in a collapsing wormhole?"

"No, but I can bore you with the science if you want."

"Thanks, Davies, I'm too busy dusting my cockpit, so I can't fit that in. Are you ready to try hopping a signal through the portal to *Vengeance*?"

"Yeah, we're ready to go."

"Hailing them now," said Conway. She took another look towards the portal and knew something was off. The previous openings had been colourful and spectacular affairs, but this time the portal was dull and small. It didn't matter until they had to pass back through, and it would be good enough for a test, but it worried her all the same.

"*Vengeance* here," came Vernon's voice. "Tell me you've got some good news, Conway?"

"We have a high-bandwidth connection to *Kingdom 10*, sir, and can pass through full mind states whenever you're ready. What's your status, *Vengeance*?" said Conway, eager to catch up with developments.

"It's not good," said Vernon, his tone grim. "Everything below deck one has been completely overrun by Mechs. We're on our last legs here, Conway, throw us a bone, won't you?"

"Working on it, sir," said Conway, although she really wasn't sure that they'd get very far. "We're linked to *Kingdom 10*, testing comms now."

"We've got our ears open on *Vengeance*, Marine, send us some audio, please," said Yau.

"*Kingdom 10* here, are you receiving this, *Vengeance*?"

"Anything?" Davies asked.

"Nothing here, sorry," said Yau.

Davies inspected the panel again, then swore under his breath. "Rookie error, try again now."

"*Kingdom 10* to *Vengeance*, are you receiving us?"

"We hear you loud and clear, *Kingdom 10*, loud and clear." There was a small cheer from the bridge crew of *Kingdom 10*.

"Good to hear you too, *Vengeance*. How are you holding up?"

"In need of some TLC, if I'm honest," said Yau.

"Davies, I take it this link is encrypted, yes?" snapped Stansfield, injecting himself into the conversation.

"Yes, sir, all encrypted. Everything from *Vengeance* to the shuttle and then on to *Kingdom 10* is secured using the Navy's normal security protocols."

"Then get back to *Vengeance*," said Stansfield. "There's work to be done here."

"Roger, on our way, sir," said Conway.

"I need to take a look at the cloning bays on *Vengeance*, sir," said Davies as he waited for Conway to collect him.

"The cloning bay is on deck three," said Vernon, "and we no longer have access to that area of the ship."

"Is there a bay on deck three? Is there a way onto the ship without going through the front door?" Davies was reaching, but he needed to be in the bay to work on the cloning machines.

"There's a small maintenance bay on deck three, identification BAY3/12," said Yau. "That's the closest we can get you to the cloning area."

"Can you dock us remotely?" said Conway.

"Yes, ma'am," said Yau confidently. "Just shout when you need us."

"Roger, Conway out," said Conway, closing the channel. "Coming to pick you up, Double-D. Are you done?"

"Yup, let's get out of here."

"Our first cloning bay is operational, *Vengeance*," reported *Kingdom 10*. "Manufacturing has begun, first deployments in eight hours. We'll have a second bay online in four hours or so, and the next two eight hours after that."

"What about ships?" asked Stansfield. The news that cloned

troops would soon be available was welcome, but *Kingdom 10*'s numbers and timeline weren't going to make any real difference. "If these things make it through the portal, you're next in line. What's the Admiralty sending?"

"This is Captain Orwell, Admiral. I can confirm that *Resolution*, *Conqueror* and *Orion* are on their way."

Stansfield frowned as the details of the incoming ships appeared on his data slate. "Those are all new ships, Captain. Is there nothing of Astute19 Class? Are there no old ships left? Surely we haven't been gone that long."

"I'm sorry, sir, *Vengeance* is the only Astute19-class still in service. Her sister ships have either been decommissioned, scrapped or lost. Astute19s are museum pieces now. There were some older ships being recommissioned, but they've been sent to Commodore Cohen at New Bristol."

"I know how they feel," grumbled Vernon under his breath.

"Too little, too late," muttered Stansfield, shaking his head. *Vengeance* might be the last ship of her class, but he was damned if he was going to lose her. "Send everything you can. We need supplies, weaponry and attack craft. And Marines, lots of Marines. If you have any ex-military personnel willing to put up a fight, send them too."

"Ay, sir," said Orwell. "We're going as fast as we can."

"Keep me informed," said Stansfield. "*Vengeance* out."

There was a rumble from below that sent the bridge crew clutching at the seats for support and rattled the fittings.

"What the hell was that?" demanded Stansfield, glaring at his monitors.

"Some sort of explosion on deck two, sir," said Yau. "No reports of hull breaches, but some of our systems are offline."

"Defensive teams on deck one are being pushed back, sir," said Vernon. "Maybe ten minutes till the Mechs have unopposed access to the bridge doors."

"What about the other decks?"

"Only isolated pockets of resistance," said Vernon, shaking his head. "There are just too many Mechs."

"This is not how I had wanted to end the day, Commander," said Stansfield, as if the boarding of his ship and the imminent loss of his command were mere inconveniences at the end of a trying afternoon.

"No," agreed Vernon, brushing dust from his shoulder. "Permission to have a bash, sir?" he asked, patting his pistol.

"Denied, Commander," said Stansfield with an apologetic shake of his head. "I need you here, and one gun won't make a difference against this horde."

For a moment, it looked like Vernon would protest, but then he holstered his pistol and nodded.

"Plenty of time for a glorious last stand, old friend."

Vernon looked a little uncomfortable at that, and Stansfield raised an eyebrow, prompting him to lean in for a private word with his commanding officer.

"I know we were in stasis for a long time, but if we're old, then so are the midshipmen and the ratings," Vernon whispered.

Stansfield considered this for a moment. "Good point. Well made, my dear friend."

"'Dear friend'? You're going soft in your old age, sir. Shall we sort these buggers out, then?"

Stansfield barked a laugh, "We're not done yet, Commander Vernon."

∿

"Do we fly the discs back to *Vengeance*?" said Gray, looking at Hunter's half-naked body. "Because that ain't gonna work."

"We'd never be able to capture them," said Jackson as they stared out at the inside of the Sphere from the remains of the operating theatre. "They'd kill us before letting us leave."

"I'm going to call a taxi," said Ten. "I know just the pilot for a desperate last-minute rescue in the face of certain death." He opened a channel to *Vengeance*. "This is Marine X, calling home."

"This is *Vengeance*," said a voice Ten didn't recognise. "Good to hear from you, Marine X."

"Likewise, *Vengeance*. We've found Hunter, but we're on the Sphere and need a ride home."

"A ride?" growled Stansfield.

"Ay, sir, on account of us being stuck inside an enemy station with no way to escape. I wondered if Conway might swing past and pick us up."

"At least your HUD is working again," said Stansfield.

"Ah, yes, sir. A bit of percussive maintenance and it was right as rain. I'll have an engineer check it out when I'm back on board."

"Do what you must to survive, Marine," said Stansfield, "but I want the Sphere intact, understood?"

"Understood, sir," said Ten, "no problem at all."

"Don't let me down," barked Stansfield. "Conway's on her way. *Vengeance* out."

"Sorted," said Ten.

"He wants the Sphere intact?" said Gray, shaking her head. "The man's mad."

"They're coming to us," said Jackson, looking up through the shattered roof at a host of Mechs on discs that were descending towards them. They came as a wave, spread out and with weapons raised.

"I don't think they're looking to take prisoners anymore," said Gray, backing away.

"Yeah," said Ten as he aimed at the incoming discs. "I think you're right. Head for the warehouse."

With Hunter's good arm around Jackson's shoulders, the Marines made a dash for the ruined corridor as Ten opened fire. The Mechs broke formation like a flock of birds fleeing before a hawk, and Ten ducked into cover as they swarmed towards him.

"Go, go, go," he yelled as he ran down the corridor. Behind him the ceiling of the operating theatre collapsed further as the Mechs began to crash into it, leaping clear of their discs to continue their pursuit.

Ten turned at the door that led to the warehouse and opened fire as the first of the Mechs appeared in the corridor. A second Mech blazed away from within the wrecked theatre, shooting blindly into the corridor through the drifting smoke. Rounds pinged from Ten's power armour, knocking him back before he could swing around to face the new enemy.

Then Jackson was beside him, calmly returning fire and cutting down the Mechs.

"Get inside," said Jackson. "Hunter's in trouble."

Jackson covered their retreat as Ten ducked through the door into the room they'd searched earlier.

"Through there," said Jackson, nodding at the warehouse door.

Ten hurried on through the door, then pulled up sharp as Gray pointed her monstrous gun at him. She quickly lowered the weapon; then Jackson came into the warehouse and slammed the door shut behind him.

Ten wedged a splinter of packing crate under the door, then piled more crates against the door before backing further into the warehouse. The walls here were sturdier, but neither they nor the barricade would hold the Mechs back for long.

"We need to keep moving," he said, eyeing the door with suspicion. "Where's Hunter?"

"Here," replied Hunter from along one of the aisles. He was on the floor, struggling to refit his cybernetic arm to the mounting plate in his stump. "This ain't as easy as it looks," he said through gritted teeth as he failed to get the plates to line up correctly. He almost dropped the arm and slumped back against the shelves he was leaning on.

"Is this really the time?" said Ten taking in Hunter's grey face and shaking limbs. "You've had a rough day."

"Need my arm," hissed Hunter. "Just need to align it properly." He made an effort to lift it again, but his exhaustion was obvious.

"We don't really have time for this, mate," said Ten with a calm he didn't feel. "Let's just get you back to *Vengeance* and let the docs put you back together."

"No," said Hunter firmly, pulling free from Ten's helping hand.

"Need my arm." He nodded at something on the other side of the aisle. "Look."

Ten looked across the aisles at the items on the shelves, but he wasn't sure what it was he was supposed to be noticing.

"Looks like boxes of computers," he said, as there was a bang from the warehouse door, "but they're about as much use to us as a chocolate teaspoon."

Hunter let his head flop back so that he could glare up at Ten and give him a sickly grin. "Computers in crates here means computers on networks somewhere else, right? Find the computers, find the commanders."

"Time to move again," shouted Gray, "they're knocking on the door." She had retreated into the aisle with Jackson, and now the two Marines stood guard, waiting for the Mechs to break through their improvised barrier.

"Okay," nodded Ten in broad agreement with one eye on the door. "And you need the arm because...?"

"I have skills," said Hunter simply. "Direct neural coupling via the arm. Might be able to hack their systems and slow them down," he explained when Ten looked sceptical.

"Fine," said Ten, slinging his rifle and shaking his head. He squatted down on the floor beside Hunter. "How does it attach?"

Behind him, the crates piled against the door screeched as they were pushed back across the floor. Jackson opened fire, aiming for the narrow gap between door and frame, and something fell back.

"Just slap it on the mount and hold it in place," whispered Hunter, his eyes closed. "It'll do the rest itself."

"Right," said Ten doubtfully as he crouched down beside Hunter. He offered the cybernetic arm up to the mounting plate, squinted at the alignment, then pushed it home.

"Argh!" said Hunter as the arm reattached to the mounting plate and clamped itself against the battered flesh of his stump. His whole body tensed as the arm settled into place; then there was a gentle ping and the arm came alive.

"Help me up," he said, holding up his cybernetic arm.

Ten looked at the metal hand for a moment, then grabbed it and heaved Hunter to his feet.

"What's that way?" asked Hunter, nodding at the far end of the warehouse.

"No idea," said Ten as Jackson fired again on the Mechs trying to gain entry to the warehouse.

"Pretty busy here," yelled Gray as she and Jackson backed up towards Ten and Hunter. "Can we go now?"

"That way," said Ten, pointing down the aisle. "Hunter has a plan to stop the Mechs. Take him, find a terminal, then get out of here."

"Where are you going?" asked Gray as Ten's helmet closed around his head.

"We need more time, and I know where to find it. I'll catch you up." Then he unslung his pilfered weapon and strolled down the warehouse towards the Mechs.

G ray watched Ten walk calmly towards the door; then Jackson grabbed at her arm and pulled her away. She took a step back, wondering if she should stay and help, but Jackson pulled again.

"Okay," she snapped, knowing that she should be helping Ten but really not wanting to get caught in another firefight. She hurried after Jackson to find that Hunter was staggering along the aisle, leaning heavily on the shelves and dragging one foot.

"Grab him," said Gray, glancing over her shoulder as the sound of gunfire floated up the aisle. "We don't have much time."

Jackson wrapped his arm around Hunter's waist and half-carried the injured Marine down the warehouse. At the end of the aisle was another door, this one wide enough for three people to stagger through. To the left, in the warehouse's other wall, stood another set of doors that appeared to open onto a freight conveyor of some sort.

"That could be interesting," said Gray, but Jackson ignored her and triggered the control that opened the doors ahead of them. As they slid open, they revealed a wide concourse running left to right.

At either end of the huge space were more doors, but it was the open area ahead that caught the attention of the Marines.

On the far side of the concourse, three steps led up to large open room set with a huge display that ran thirty metres across the wall. It showed video feeds from two dozen or more Mechs, as well as a long-shot of *Vengeance* and various charts and infographics. In front of the main display sat a rank of consoles, each with their own display and, at each station, a Mech.

Gray froze, head whipping left and right as she looked for signs that they'd been seen.

Nothing.

"Ten, are you seeing this? Looks like we've found the command room," said Gray, whispering inside her helmet.

"Thanks for getting in touch, Marine X is not available to take your call right now."

She could tell by the strain in his voice that Ten was dealing with something unpleasant. She closed the channel and focussed on the room ahead.

"Do we...?" Jackson hefted his rifle and nodded at the bank of seated Mechs, all seemingly oblivious to the threat behind them.

Gray shook her head slowly, then opened her helmet so she could talk more easily to Hunter.

"They don't have legs, their torsos are just mounted on those stool things," she hissed, the creeping horror making her skin crawl.

"Hard-wired? What is this place," said Jackson, "some sort of high-tech terror palace?"

"Can you work around them?" said Gray.

"Yeah, but get closer," said Hunter quietly, "need to get closer."

Gray and Jackson exchanged a look, and then both closed their helmets. The Mechs looked peaceful enough, but looks could be deceiving, and neither Marine wanted to be left exposed when the firing began.

Gray went left to keep a clear arc of fire across the consoles, while Jackson helped Hunter to close on the nearest Mech. Even when they stood right behind it, looming over it, the Mech gave no sign of being aware of them.

"What's wrong with them?" said Hunter, prodding at the nearest Mech. It ignored him and focussed on its display, utterly engaged by the feeds it was analysing.

Gray made 'get on with it' motions as the sound of gunfire and crashing metal floated across the concourse from the warehouse. Hunter nodded wearily and held up his hand. He closed his fist as his middle finger changed shape. Gray blinked in surprise as the finger became a long, prehensile cable.

Hunter leered at her briefly and gave her a wink. Then he reached past the Mech, closed his eyes, and plugged himself into the console.

For a moment, nothing happened. Then Hunter's eyes flicked open.

"Shitloads of information," he said, then he shuddered and shook his head. "We have a lot of problems, but I know how to deal with that death ray thing."

"Focus on the Mechs," said Gray firmly. "Can you shut them down?"

There was another burst of fire from the warehouse, louder and closer, and a stream of explosions.

"Not from here," said Hunter with a grimace of pain. "They're on a different system. But I reckon I can disable the Sphere's weapon systems, shut them down and flag them as in need of repair. That'll slow them down."

"Good, because we're going to need that time soon," said Jackson. "I think they're coming for us."

Gray turned to look across the concourse as Ten emerged from the warehouse, backing through the open doorway and firing as he came. The Mechs were firing back, and even as he retreated Ten took multiple rounds to the chest.

"Shit," said Gray, closing her helmet and dashing down the steps to the concourse. Ten staggered back, still firing. His power armour was battered and creased from the abuse it had received, and covered in scorch marks.

"Move," said Gray as she raised her weapon towards the warehouse, but Ten just waved her back.

"Almost done," he said. A Mech appeared in the doorway and Ten emptied the remains of his magazine into it, leaving it slumped across the threshold. Then from inside the warehouse came another round of explosions and the terrible screech of tortured metal and collapsing shelves. There was a long, drawn-out rumbling crash, and a spray of spare parts bounced through the open doorway and across the concourse.

The noise rolled away, and nothing moved for a few seconds. Then Ten tossed away the empty weapon and unslung his rifle.

"Is Hunter finished? Because I'm about ready to get out of here."

26

"They're coming again," said Mason, slamming another magazine into his rifle. He and Kearney were at opposite ends of the short corridor that ran alongside the medical bay where Fernandez was working on the captured Mech. "Persistent little fuckers, ain't they?"

"Clear at this end," said Kearney as she peered around the bulkhead she was using for cover. Beyond, the Mechs were scurrying around, but she couldn't work out what they were doing. "Better keep them on their toes," she muttered, then she launched a grenade down the corridor.

"Drums in the deep," she warned, ducking back behind the bulkhead. There was a rumbling crash as the grenade exploded, and a cloud of debris blew down the corridor.

"How's it going in there, Lieutenant?" said Kearney in the brief lull that followed the explosion.

"It's difficult to work with all the noise," said Fernandez, "but we make progress."

"Anything we can use yet?" said Kearney, squeezing off a few more rounds at the Mechs.

"Not yet," said Fernandez testily. Then he closed the channel.

"Prick," muttered Kearney as the Mechs gathered again at the nearby junction.

"Come on!" yelled Mason, firing at the oncoming enemy. Then he dodged away as the Mechs boiled down the corridor, firing blindly as they came. "Small calibre, high volume, spray and pray," he murmured, back to the wall.

The first Mech charged past, and Mason shot it in the back. The second and third Mechs, moving too quickly to stop, went the same way, but the fourth turned to face Mason, struggling to bring its weapon to bear.

"Back, fiend," said Mason, slamming his rifle into the Mech's head. The thing staggered back into the path of the following Mech, and both stumbled. Mason reared up, then punched down with all the force his power armour could muster. His fist crumpled the Mech's helmet and crushed its skull. It fell senseless to the floor.

"And one for you too," said Mason, slamming his heavy boot into the second Mech's faceplate. The head snapped back; then Mason stomped down, crushing his enemy's skull.

He stepped back and looked around, suddenly aware that no more Mechs had charged up the corridor. "Still alive," he muttered to himself, peering around the bulkhead in search of enemies to fight. They were still there, twenty metres away, firing intermittently along the corridor, but they weren't in a hurry to advance.

"Fine by me," said Mason, firing a few rounds in their general direction to let them know he was still there.

"You okay?" said Kearney from the other end of the corridor. She still fired her rifle, keeping the Mechs clear.

"Not dead yet," replied Mason as he pushed a new magazine into his rifle. "Running low on ammo, out of grenades." He paused to check his HUD. "Suit power not looking too clever either."

"Won't have to worry about it much longer," said Kearney. "Here they come again!"

And then Mason was too busy fighting to talk as the Mechs charged his position once more.

On the bridge of *Vengeance*, the atmosphere was tense. Unable to play a direct role in the defence of the ship, the crew could only watch as their colleagues were cut down or forced back. All around the bridge, monitors showed reports and feeds from helmet and static cams. None of it looked good.

"That's it," said Stansfield as the last of the defenders outside the bridge doors was killed. "The enemy is at the gates."

"Permission to open the bridge armoury, sir?" asked Yau.

"Granted, Mr Yau," said Stansfield. "One final stand." He looked around as the crew began to move, and Yau started handing out rifles and ammunition from the bridge's small store. "It has been an honour to serve with you all," he said, taking a rifle and slamming in a magazine, "but every glittering summer must have its rainy day."

"And that rainy day is here, I'm afraid," said Vernon, looking up from his console as the dull sound of metal being cut reverberated across the bridge. "Because the only thing now standing between us and the Mechs are those four doors. Once they break through, the Mechs will have the ship."

"That's it," said Hunter, unplugging his arm from the terminal. "I've downloaded everything I can find and disabled their weapons." He paused, frowning. "At least, I think I've disabled their weapons. Difficult to be sure."

"Good enough," said Ten, looking around the command room. "We need to get out of here. This place is giving me the creeps." He opened a channel. "How's it looking, Conway? You coming to get us?"

"Couple of minutes out, Ten. Are we going to get shot to pieces as we approach?"

"Nope, Hunter's killed their defences, you've got a clear run to the hangar." He sent her an image of the exterior of the Sphere, with the hangar door ringed in pink. "That's where we'll be."

"Got it," said Conway. "Don't hang around."

"Roger, out," said Ten, closing the channel.

"Shall I...?" asked Gray, waving her obscene weapons at the Mechs that still sat, oblivious, at their terminals.

"Waste of ammunition," said Jackson. "It won't help us get off the Sphere or back to *Vengeance*."

"Maybe not," said Ten, nodding his agreement, "but anything that hinders the enemy is a good thing right now." He stepped back down the steps, away from the consoles, as Jackson helped Hunter. "Fill your boots, Gray."

She looked at him, nonplussed, and Ten sighed. "Just get on with it," he said in a weary tone, waving his hand at the screens and terminals.

Gray nodded and pressed the trigger on her weapon. There was a momentary pause as the barrels spun, then the gun roared as it spat bullets. Gray played the stream of fire across the Mechs and their terminals, then across the screens and consoles. For twenty seconds she sprayed the command room, splattering every surface with blood and shattered componentry.

Then she took her finger off the trigger, and the monstrous weapon wound down and was silent.

"You're having way too much fun," said Ten with a shake of his head. "Right, how do we get out of here?"

"Freight elevator, that way. Takes us right back to the hangar," said Hunter. The Marines all stared at him. "What? I download a partial schematic," he said. "Let's not fuck around here any longer."

"Starting to sound like your old self again, mate," said Ten as he led the group along the corridor. It was quiet, as if the Mechs were silent or absent or somehow avoiding the Marines.

"Feeling a bit better," said Hunter, "but I'd kill for a steak. My stomach thinks my throat's been cut."

"It might yet happen," said Jackson as they hurried along the corridor. From behind them came the sound of an elevator, and then a squad of Mechs burst out onto the far end of the corridor.

"Run!" shouted Gray. The Marines sprinted down the corridor, with even Hunter putting on a decent turn of speed. The Mechs opened fire as they gave chase, and rounds pinged off walls, ceiling and armour.

"Turn and fire," yelled Ten as he skidded to a halt, taking what little cover was offered by a buttress in the wall. Jackson took cover in an alcove on the opposite wall, while Gray and Hunter barrelled into the open elevator.

Ten fired down the corridor, not bothering to aim as the Mechs charged toward the elevator, firing as they came, heedless of the risk of death or injury. Jackson fired as well, precise controlled bursts to take down the nearest enemies.

Then Gray's weapon spun up and filled the corridor with lead. The Mechs disappeared in a cloud of blood and sparks and shattered metal, and when she stopped firing there was nothing left alive apart from the four Marines.

"Move," yelled Ten, chasing Jackson the rest of the way to the elevator. "Go," he said as they reached the elevator. Gray punched the control and, as more Mechs rushed into the corridor, the elevator rose smoothly through the Sphere toward the hangar.

"They'll be waiting for us," said Jackson as he fitted his last magazine into his rifle. "There's no way they won't have seen this coming."

"Gimme a weapon," said Hunter, standing unaided but still sounding less than entirely healthy.

"Take this," said Gray, passing over her pistol and a pair of spare magazines. She handed a rifle magazine to Jackson, who nodded his thanks and slipped it into his webbing.

"Get ready," said Ten as the elevator approached the hangar level. He crouched down with Hunter behind, and aimed ahead. Gray stood to his side, weapon raised and trigger-finger poised, and Jackson took a stance to her left.

"It's been nice knowing you," said Jackson, "but this isn't going to work."

The elevator came to a halt behind a pair of steel doors. There was a pause, the Marines all tensed, then the doors swished open to reveal an empty corridor.

"Move," hissed Hunter, nudging Ten with his knee. "Before they get here."

Ten nodded and moved into the corridor, the others following closely behind. He swept the open space with his rifle, but there was nothing there. The Mechs were nowhere to be seen.

"I've got a bad feeling about this," muttered Jackson as the team moved quickly towards the doors at the far end of the short corridor. "I don't think this is the way to the hangar."

"Hush," said Ten in an annoyed tone. He stopped at the end of the corridor where it branched left and right, and peered carefully in each direction before stepping into the open area. He moved cautiously to the doors and triggered the controls. The control panel flashed red several times, as if the doors were trying to work out if opening was really such a great idea; then they slid back into the walls to reveal the room beyond.

"Told you," said Jackson in a smug voice as they Marines piled into the room. It was huge, a cavernous space with terminals along one wall near the door. In the middle of the room, suspended by gantries that linked it to the walls, floor and ceiling, was a complicated cylindrical machine from which great bundles of pipes and cables emerged to loop out to ports in the walls.

"What the hell is it?" said Gray, side-stepping across the room as she checked for Mechs and clues as to the machine's purpose.

"No idea," said Ten, "but I know a man who might." He opened a channel. "Davies, are you out there?" He played his helmet cameras across the machine. "I need to know what this is and whether we can use it to disable the Sphere."

"Hey, Ten," said Davies, "good to hear from you. We're on our way, coming in wide, fast and hot to try to avoid the Sphere's defences, but the odds–"

Ten cut him off. "No time. What is it?"

"Oh, right," said Davies. "Ahem. Looks like a fusion reactor."

"Fine, we'll pull the plug. You almost here?"

"Close by, but the guns, Ten, the guns," said Davies.

"Working on it. Be in the hangar in ninety seconds. We'll need a suit for Hunter. Ten out." He closed the channel and looked around at the rest of the crew. "Any suggestions?"

"Shoot it?" said Gray, offering the long-preferred solution advanced by fighting forces everywhere for millennia.

"Or I can just switch it off," said Hunter. He'd plugged his arm into the computer terminal, and his eyes flickered beneath their lids as he ransacked the Sphere's files. "Here goes," he said, grabbing the edge of the bench with his free hand.

For a moment, nothing happened. Then the artificial gravity failed, and all the lights went out.

"Shit," spluttered Ten as he flicked on his helmet lamps and groped for something to hang on to.

"Think I'm going to hurl," said Gray as Jackson grabbed her and heaved her towards the wall.

"Can't say I'd advise it," said Ten as he swam slowly back to the door. There was a hum, and a load of dim red lights came on.

"Emergency lighting," said Hunter as he unplugged from the terminal. "I think I gave it a hard reset, so that thing'll be down for an hour at least, maybe more if their backup isn't up to restarting it," he said, nodding at the reactor.

"Can't hurt to give it a tickle," said Ten, firing a few short bursts into important-looking parts of the reactor and its peripheral equipment. The other Marines followed suit, laying waste to the delicate parts of the machine.

"That'll do," said Ten as he switched out his empty magazine. "Either they're screwed now, or we'll never do enough damage to have an impact."

"Let's get out of here," said Gray, floating cautiously out into the corridor. "Shit," she said, heaving herself back through the doorway as rounds ripped past and ricocheted off the walls and ceiling. "Mechs."

"No, really?" said Ten, floating across to the other side of the doorway. He nodded at Jackson, then looked at Gray. "Top, middle, bottom," he said, pointing at them in turn and then himself. "And remember to hold onto something if you don't want to float away."

"This isn't going to go well," muttered Jackson.

"Three, two, one, go!" said Ten, and then the Marines leant out through the doorway and opened fire on the Mechs in short, controlled bursts.

A couple of the Mechs fired back. As Ten sought targets and fired down the corridor, the Mechs milled aimlessly. Where previously they had acted as one entity in awesome unity of purpose, now they seemed to be isolated and separate, as if each was struggling to determine its role.

"What's wrong with them?" asked Gray. "What's changed?"

"No power," said Jackson as he drilled a Mech as it swam towards them through the air. "No comms, no guidance."

"Like new recruits," said Ten to himself as realisation dawned. "They're directed via the Sphere, and we've broken the link to their controllers."

And the Mechs weren't prepared for zero-G combat.

"Rookie mistake," said Ten as he gunned down a Mech that was firing wildly and spinning in mid-air. The thing kept firing long after the recoil from its weapon had made aiming impossible, spraying bullets into the floor, walls, ceiling and its fellows.

And then more Mechs began to fire, and half of them floated free. The Marines ducked back and waited as the Mechs, in their panic, emptied their magazines.

<Charlie Team> sent Ten. <This is Marine X. Anyone there?>

<Kearney here. Good to hear from you, Ten>

<You too. Listen, the Mechs here are in trouble, and yours might be too. It won't last long, but now's your moment to act>

<We'll take anything we can get right now> sent Mason. <It's been busy here>

<Good luck. Out> sent Ten. He closed the channel and listened for the shooting to stop, then signalled the Marines to advance into the corridor.

"Zero-G will get you every time," muttered Ten as he pushed away a slowly revolving corpse. The corridor was filled with spent bullet casings, body parts, weapons and shattered fittings.

"What a mess," said Gray as the team made their way to the hangar airlock.

"We're at the airlock, Conway," said Ten, reopening the channel. "Where are you?"

"Coming in hard and fast, Ten. Thirty seconds."

"Roger."

"Oh, shit," muttered Hunter as he stared back down the corridor through the cloud of debris from their last firefight. "What the hell is that?"

27

<G ood luck. Out>
    Kearney looked down the corridor for a moment, wondering if Ten might be right about the Mechs. "Only one way to find out," she muttered to herself.

<I'm going to take a look> she sent to Mason as she checked her magazine. Then, before Mason had a chance to talk her out of it, she eased herself around the bulkhead and walked cautiously down the corridor, letting her rifle swing left and right as she searched for Mechs.

<What's the story?> sent Mason, but Kearney ignored him and focussed on her work. There was a Mech in the corridor, staring blankly at the wall. It felt almost underhanded to shoot it, but Kearney put a tight burst in its chest nonetheless.

She paused at the next bulkhead, checking for movement. A Mech wandered past, oblivious to her presence, weapon pointing at the floor. Kearney shot it in the head, and the thing slumped to the floor.

Around the corner, three more Mechs were huddled. One raised its weapon as Kearney approached, but there was no snap to its actions, no vigour. The purpose and drive that had characterised the Mechs' attacks on *Vengeance* was gone.

Kearney shot them all, then turned to check behind her. Nothing. The corridor was quiet.

<Ten was right> Kearney sent to Mason. <Attack>

<Roger> acknowledged Mason.

"Sir," said Kearney, opening a channel to Vernon as she prowled down the corridor, killing every Mech she found. "There's something wrong with the Mechs. They're defenceless."

"Repeat that, Kearney," said Vernon with a note of astonishment in his voice.

"I'm on deck two, clearing the Mechs. Something must have happened, they're offering no resistance," she said as she mowed down two more non-threatening enemies and reloaded her rifle. "Ten said it might not last long. Now's the time to attack with everything we have, sir."

"Are you sure about this?" said Stansfield, butting into the conversation.

"Don't know how long it'll last, sir," said Kearney as she carefully drilled bursts into a brace of somnolent Mechs, "but at the moment it's like shooting fish in a barrel."

"Welcome news, Trooper," said Stansfield. Then the channel clicked off, and Kearney was left alone to hunt her incapacitated enemies.

"*Vengeance*, this is Stansfield," said a voice over the ship's announcement system. "The Mechs are suffering a technical problem," he went on, clearly struggling to keep the triumph from his voice, "and we have an opportunity to retake the ship. Give them hell, *Vengeance*."

Kearney grinned as she worked her way back toward the medbay to link up with Mason and Fernandez. Finally, something was going their way.

"We have a problem, sir," said Fernandez as he worked on the Mech laid out on the table before him. Around the room, the remains of his party were checking their weapons as the welding team worked to reopen the doors.

"What is it, Fernandez?" said Stansfield.

"About five minutes ago, the Mech I've been analysing changed, sir. It went limp, and its chest is now lit by a bright blue matrix."

"Mason reported seeing two like that, sir," said Vernon.

"And?" asked Stansfield. "What's your conclusion?"

"It's dormant," said Fernandez. "All power seems to have been diverted to the matrix. If you asked me to speculate, I'd say it's sending a message or backing up – maybe both."

"And that means?" said Stansfield. "Hurry it up, Lieutenant. We don't have all day."

"Sorry, sir," said Fernandez, tearing himself away from the matrix. "I think they're packing up and backing up, sir. The Sphere's been disabled, and the Mechs think they're beaten. I think they're sending every bit of data they have on *Vengeance* back to the core. And from there, who knows where it's going? It's a massive data backup, and they're saving everything they know about us for a rainy day."

28

"Ten, you there? This is Conway, coming in hot. Keep your heads down."

Outside the airlock, Ten floated in the shadow of a bulkhead with Hunter behind him and Gray and Jackson on the other side of the corridor. Thirty metres away, a nightmare in steel and ceramic armour picked its way towards them, long brass-encased legs stretched out to tap against floor, ceiling and walls.

"Can't come too soon," said Ten, bracing himself to fire. He squeezed off a short burst, then another, but the beast kept coming. "What the fuck is it?" he said in frustration. "Just die already, you bastard, it's been a long day."

He fired again as Hunter popped away with his pistol and Jackson emptied his magazine into the monster. Then there was a hum of spinning barrels, and Gray opened fire, spraying the creature with rounds. It stopped, holding position against the walls as bullets bounced from its armour and carapace.

For a moment, it looked like it would be forced back, but then the firing stopped, and Gray's gun fell silent.

"That's inconvenient," she muttered as shook the weapon in the vain hope that more ammunition would magically appear. "Fuck."

"I'm out," said Ten, letting go of his empty rifle to draw his pistol. "Are you seeing this, Conway? Anytime right fucking now would be great!"

"Almost there, calibrating," said Conway, and Ten had no idea what she was talking about.

"That's not good," said Jackson, and Ten's attention whipped back to the armoured Mech. Two arms had unfolded from behind the armour, each holding a pair of multi-barrelled guns exactly like the one that Gray was struggling out of.

"Duck," advised Ten needlessly as the barrels began to spin. Jackson grabbed Gray and pulled her back into cover as the Mech began to fire, and suddenly the corridor was filled with noise and smoke and a deadly hail. There was nothing the Marines could do but hide in cover and trust their armour.

"Conway!" yelled Ten, unable to hear anything in his helmet over the noise. <Where are you?> he sent.

<Ten seconds> came the response, but Ten couldn't tell what she planned.

The Mech crawled closer, firing as it came, and now it was only metres from their hiding place. Ten thought small thoughts and tried to press himself into the metal wall of the corridor as the bulkhead began to disintegrate under the weight of fire. Behind him, Hunter cowered under the diminishing protection of Ten's armoured bulk.

<Ten, pull your socks up> sent Conway.

"What the fuck?" muttered Ten, emptying his pistol into the oncoming Mech.

Then came a series of whining thuds and spine-shattering bangs as something tore through the walls. The Mech seemed to scream, then the corridor fell briefly silent.

Ten peered cautiously around the bulkhead as a wind began to build behind him. The Mech was clearly dead, shot through with a dozen large holes, armour shattered and useless, weapons floating free. One great leg was torn free and tumbling along the corridor.

"What the fuck?" said Ten again, subconsciously fitting a new magazine into his pistol.

But the wind was growing stronger, and now an alarm began to sound, whining out over the rapidly thinning atmosphere as air bled through the huge holes Conway had punched in the hangar wall.

<Airlock, now!>

The airlock inner door hissed open, and a figure reached out to pluck Hunter from his hiding place and drag him inside. Then the door closed again, and when Ten turned around, there was nothing to show that Hunter had ever been there.

"Where's Hunter?" Ten yelled, looking desperately around. The wind was roaring now, tumbling debris along the corridor as it raced past the Marines into the vacuum of space. "Hunter!"

The whine of the alarm was fading now as the last of the atmosphere escaped into the hangar, and suddenly the corridor was silent. Ten looked at Gray and Jackson, still huddled on the far side of the corridor behind the remains of their bulkhead.

"Time to go, Ten," said Conway's voice. "Airlock."

Ten turned back to the airlock as the door slid open. Inside, Davies was waiting in his power armour. Hunter was with him, now safely encased in an emergency environment suit. He gave a wave and grinned weakly through the faceplate of his helmet.

Ten stared for a moment, then grinned back and hauled himself into the airlock. Gray and Jackson followed, and the inner doors closed behind them.

"We're out of here," said Davies, triggering the outer door. The view opened onto the hangar and there, not ten metres away, hung Conway's Raptor with doors open and ready to receive.

"Go, go, go," said Davies, pushing the Marines through the airlock doors into the hangar. "This isn't a healthy place to be."

Hunter and Jackson went first, crossing the open space and floating into the Raptor's small crew compartment. Gray followed, leaving Ten and Davies at the edge of the airlock.

"After you," said Davies, gesturing to the Raptor's waiting door.

"No, please," said Ten, with a slight bow, "after you."

Then the airlock doors closed behind them, and the lamp lit to indicate a transit cycle. The Mechs were coming.

"Fucking move!" yelled Conway. Ten and Davies shared a look, then, as one, pushed themselves out into the hangar. They were halfway across the deck when the airlock doors opened, and Mechs began to stream out into the hangar, firing as they came.

"Get in there," said Davies as he gripped the edge of the airlock and swung around, pushing Ten through the open doorway as he went. "We're in!" he said, slapping the control to close the door as bullets left dents and scars on the hull of the Raptor.

"Roger," acknowledged Conway. Then the Raptor spun on its axis and the nose swung around to face the airlock. The ship's railguns spat, chewing through the airlock and ripping apart the Mechs as they tried to organise themselves.

"Hang on to something," said Conway, "manoeuvring thrusters then main engines, we're not hanging around." The Raptor spun again, then shot forward towards the open hangar doors.

Seconds later, they burst out of the Sphere into the vastness of space, and the Marines breathed freely again.

"*Vengeance*, this is Conway. Package retrieved, on our way home."

"Acknowledged, Conway. Happy flying."

"Manoeuvring, then a ten-second burn," said Conway. "We'll be safely back on *Vengeance* in a few minutes."

"Negative," said Hunter, squeezing himself past Davies into the cockpit, "we have to finish this now, before we return."

"Finish what?" said Ten from the crew compartment. "You want to go back?"

"That weapon, the starship destroyer," said Hunter, "the one that did for *Colossus*."

"What about it?"

"We have to deal with it, or *Vengeance* is toast as soon as the Mechs fix their fusion reactor." He had removed his helmet, and now he looked at Conway. "If we don't do this, we can't win." He held up his arm. "I have the data."

"Well, shit," said Davies. "Are you sure?" Hunter gave him a flat look, and Davies nodded. "Yeah, I guess you are."

"How do we do this?" said Conway.

"The solution of the ages, updated for modern tech," said Hunter. "Shoot it until it dies, railguns and missiles," he went on when the other just stared blankly at him. "It's the only way to be sure. Turn around, I'll guide you in."

Conway shook her head, but her hands flew over the controls as she changed the flight programme and span the Raptor around until it pointed back at the Sphere. The enemy ship hung in space like a vast ball of evil, its dark face rising up before them as the Raptor drifted slowly away.

"There," said Hunter, pointing at a protrusion from the Sphere's surface. "That's the weapon. Hit it with everything you've got."

"Will that destroy the Sphere?" asked Conway as she prepared a firing solution. "Stansfield wanted it intact."

"Dunno," shrugged Hunter. "Does it matter?"

Conway bobbed her head, as if the breaking of a direct order was merely a minor breach of protocol.

"Mechs," said Davies, who was monitoring the Sphere from the crew compartment and watching for threats. "Half a dozen, maybe, on those bloody discs, heading this way."

"Later," said Hunter urgently as the targeting computer picked out the incoming Mechs and displayed them on the monitor with yellow highlights. To Ten, they looked like angry wasps buzzing in to attack a picnic. "If we don't destroy that weapon, this'll all have been for nothing."

"Ready," said Conway. She looked at Hunter. "You're sure about this?" He nodded, exhausted. Conway took a deep breath and gave the order. "Firing now."

The Raptor vibrated as the railgun battery streamed rounds toward the Sphere. With its reactor shutdown and its weapons offline, the Mechs had no response, and the railgun rounds tore through the great weapon's components, shredding its power delivery mechanisms and delicate innards.

"And a light sprinkling of high-explosive missiles," said Conway as the targeting computer activated the launchers. Six pairs of missiles accelerated through the void, and all struck home. The face of the Sphere seemed to ripple as the explosions tore a great hole in its side.

More explosions followed, then a gout of flame blew out from within the Sphere to spray debris into space. The few lights that had shone from the hangar went out, and the Sphere began to turn gently under the impulse from the attack.

Nothing more happened for a few seconds; then Ten, leaning into the cockpit with his helmet off, sniffed loudly.

"That ought to slow them down a little," he said softly. "Home, Conway, and don't spare the horses."

"Report," barked Stansfield as he stood alone on the bridge of *Vengeance*. The bridge crew had taken the chance to exact their revenge on the Mechs with relish, and had barrelled out across the main deck with a bloodthirsty aggression that had swept away the remaining Mechs.

"Just cleaning up now, sir," said Vernon. "I'm on deck two with Mason and Kearney. Sergeants Smith and Weston are taking the remnants of their squads to deck three, but it's all over. The Mechs aren't putting up any sort of resistance."

"Good work, Commander. Keep it going, I want my ship back."

"Ay, sir, it'll be a pleasure."

Stansfield switched his attention to a monitor that showed the view from the hangar on deck three, where Conway's Raptor was landing. He watched with no small degree of satisfaction as six figures disembarked and pressed forward, shooting Mechs as they went. In moments, the hangar was free of the enemy, and Charlie Team had moved on.

"Most satisfactory," murmured Stansfield, flicking through the camera feeds from the rest of the ship and watching as his diminished crew methodically cleared the Mechs and re-established control.

"*Vengeance*, this is *Kingdom 10*," said a voice. "Thought you'd like to know that we're deploying the first of your reinforcements as we speak."

"This is Stansfield. Acknowledged, *Kingdom 10*, looking forward to meeting them."

"Roger, *Kingdom 10* out."

"Better late than never, I suppose," muttered Stansfield, "but a win is a win."

"Did we do it?" Davies asked as he dropped into an empty seat.

"It isn't over," said Jackson as he sadly shook his head. "I can feel it in my bones."

The team had completed their sweep of *Vengeance*, and now they waited in the mess on deck one for Kearney and Mason, who were coming via the armoury on the sound principle that a break in the fighting was the best time to restock.

"Nonsense," said Ten, grinning at the morose Marine. "Time for a hot wet, and then home for medals and promotions." He paused, head cocked to one side. "Medals and promotions for you lot, at least. I might get a reduction in sentence, unless I'm lucky."

They all looked at him as if he'd gone mad, and he shook his head.

Stansfield's voice came over the ship's address system, as steady as it had been throughout the crisis. "I can confirm the Mechs that boarded *Vengeance* have been eliminated. The ship is secure."

"See?" said Ten, arms spread wide. "What could possibly go wrong now?"

EPILOGUE

F ernandez whistled tunelessly under his breath as he worked. The Mech was dead, of that he was sure, but there was little else he knew for certain, and he had so many questions.

"Why a cyborg?" he muttered under his breath. "Why not just grow a new body, or build a full robot?"

He lifted out a panel that had covered the Mech's abdomen and peered into a mixed mess of human intestines and artificial processors of some sort.

"And why not just replace all the internal systems? What sort of deranged mind comes up with a mess like this?" He teased aside a coil of purple innards and paused as something blinked at him from deep inside the Mech.

"Well, hello there," he murmured, frowning and leaning closer. "What have we got here, then?"

There was a soft *plunk* noise from the Mech's skull, and Fernandez's head whipped toward the noise. Then the top of the Mech's head began to move.

Fernandez took a step away from the corpse, his skin crawling at the sight before him.

"Oh, shit."

THANK YOU FOR READING

Thank you for reading Incursion Book 1 of By Strength and Guile, set in the Royal Marine Space Commandos universe.

We hope you enjoyed the book and that you're looking forward to the next entry in the series, Armada.

It would help us immensely if you would leave a review on Amazon or Goodreads, or even tell a friend you think would enjoy the series, about the books.

Incursion is the first book in By Strength & Guile, a series with our new co-author, Paul Teague. Paul is the author of many books, including the popular series The Secret Bunker & The Grid.

We think you'll love this trilogy that opens the door into the world of special forces operations in our Royal Marine Space Commandos universe.

Armada (book 2) and Devastation (book 3) will be out by the end of 2019 and we hope to have more collaborative efforts in the future.

Jon Evans & James Evans

AUTHOR NOTE FROM PAUL TEAGUE

I had a fabulous time thinking up and writing the trilogy that includes the books Incursion, Armada and Devastation – and it all came about because of a podcast.

I have been the host of a writing podcast at self-publishing-journeys.com since 2016 and I met Jon Evans at a writing conference in the UK as a consequence of him listening to my weekly ramblings.

I invited Jon onto the show for an author interview and, at that time, he hadn't begun publishing his military sci-fi series with his brother Jon.

We chatted in our interview at self-publishing-journeys.com/episode-125-jon-evans about our mutual love of sci-fi and Jon outlined the details of his new universe during our chat.

At the time, I was very resistant to the thought of collaborations, and when he suggested the idea to me in our post-interview chat, I was very non-committal.

However, I loved the sound of the universe that he and his brother were creating.

I can't remember what made me change my mind about co-writing these books, but we ended up agreeing on an initial series of three stories, to be set in the same universe but promising a completely new off-shoot into different worlds and adventures.

I read Commando, Guerrilla and Ascendant very quickly whilst staying in Spain over Christmas and New Year 2018 (yes, those books were read in the glorious Spanish sunshine) and hastily began plotting out three adventures for my new crew.

I'm a huge consumer of sci-fi and have been since I was a kid; I'm old enough to have seen the original Star Wars in the cinema the first time it came out, and no, it wasn't a silent movie in black and white, don't be rude!

That movie was ground-breaking – even as a kid I remember what a game-changer it was in terms of story-telling and special effects.

My sci-fi influences are many and numerous.

I bought the first ever edition of 2000AD as a twelve-year old in 1977 and immediately loved characters such as Judge Dredd, Harlem Heroes, M.A.C.H. 1 and Flesh.

I grew up hiding behind the sofa watching Doctor Who with Jon Pertwee (my favourite doctor) and Tom Baker. My favourite season is The Day of the Daleks (1972), in which the Ogrons featured heavily.

Whatever happened to the brilliant Ogrons?

I always loved the original Star Trek, as well as seventies classics such as Space 1999 (I still have my Dinky Eagle toy), Blakes 7, UFO, Survivors and Logan's Run but not the original series of Battlestar Galactica.

However, skip forward several years, and you'd have found me watching Babylon 5, Star Trek: The Next Generation, the updated Battlestar Galactica and any movie that was set in space or which portrayed a dystopian future.

My first seven sci-fi books were inspired by the likes of The Hunger Games, The Maze Runner, the Divergent series, The Giver, The Running Man and The Terminator, to name just a few.

The worlds portrayed in these books are decaying or have been destroyed already, their plots depict dark forces and deadly plots.

Working with Jon and James has given me the opportunity to shoot my stories into space, spinning off their much-loved and well-established universe in a completely new direction.

Of course, my trilogy had to include Ten, he was an obvious choice for a cameo role in a spin-off series, and I had great fun finding increasingly threatening scenarios to throw at him and put him through his paces.

The trilogy has a strong theme running throughout it too, culminating in the third book and the introduction of that story's super baddie.

I was keen to examine the concept of what makes us human.

As we replace more and more body parts with mechanical or synthetic substitutes, at what point do we cease to be human?

That might sound all a bit deep so worry not, I love a good space battle, exploding ships, a crew set against the odds, and some super tense, high-octane scenarios and those are never in short supply in this series of books.

This first trilogy is set up so that we can explore the story further in the future.

No plot spoilers here, but there's a promise of joining Ten for a drink sometime in the future.

If there's a chance of a free drink, there's no way the ship's crew aren't fighting their way through whatever horrors lie ahead just to make sure Ten can buy them that pint!

It's been great fun being allowed to play in Jon and James' universe, and I hope you like these stories enough for me to pay another visit in future.

I loved creating this crew, and I can't wait to deploy them on another set of adventures deep in space.

If you liked this trilogy, you'd find more of the same sort of sci-fi shenanigans in my other two series.

All seven books are linked, I'd suggest starting with The Secret Bunker Trilogy, then reading Phase 6, and finally moving on to The Grid.

And if you enjoy reading thrillers, I've got another thirteen books written as Paul J. Teague.

My thrillers have plots which are just as fast and furious as these books – you just won't see any laser guns or aliens there 😊

All the best,

Paul Teague

SUBSCRIBE AND GET A FREE BOOK

Want to know when the next book is coming and what it's called?

Would you like to hear about how we write the books?

Maybe you'd like the free book, Ten Tales: Journey to the West?

You can get all this and more at imaginarybrother.com/journeytothewest where you can sign up to the newsletter for our publishing company, Imaginary Brother.

When you join, we'll send you a free copy of Journey to the West, direct to your inbox*.

There will be more short stories about Ten and his many and varied adventures, including more exclusive ones, just for our newsletter readers as a thank you for their support.

Happy reading,

Jon Evans & James Evans

We hope you'll stay on our mailing list but if you choose not to, you can follow us on Facebook or visit our website instead.

imaginarybrother.com

* We use Bookfunnel to send out our free books. It's painless but if you need help, they'll guide you through so you can get reading.

facebook.com/ImaginaryBrotherPublishing

ABOUT THE AUTHORS PAUL TEAGUE

Paul Teague is the author of The Secret Bunker Trilogy, The Grid Trilogy and the standalone sci-fi novel, Phase 6.

He's a former broadcaster and journalist with the BBC but has also worked as a primary school teacher, a disc jockey, a shopkeeper, a waiter and a sales rep.

The Secret Bunker Trilogy was inspired by a family visit to a remarkable, real-life secret bunker at Troywood, Fife, known as 'Scotland's Secret Bunker'.

It paints a picture of a planet in crisis and is a fast-paced story with lots of twists and turns, all told through the voice of Dan Tracy who stumbles into an amazing and hazardous adventure.

The Grid Trilogy takes place in a future world where everything has gone to ruin.

Joe Parsons must fight for survival in the gamified Grid, from which no person has ever escaped with their life.

The standalone novel Phase 6 bridges the worlds of The Secret Bunker and The Grid, revealing what happens between Regeneration and Fall of Justice.

It depicts the world as we know it falling under a dark and sinister force - things will never be the same again.

Paul has been enjoying sci-fi since he was a child, cutting his teeth on Star Trek, Doctor Who, Space 1999, Blake's 7, Logan's Run and every other TV series that featured aliens, space ships and futuristic landscapes.

This collaboration with Jon and James Evans has allowed Paul to unleash his love of space ships and their crews.

He's a lover of Battlestar Galactica, Babylon 5, most iterations of Star Trek and Red Dwarf, and this series of books incorporate influences from all of those franchises and more.

Paul has also written thirteen psychological thrillers, including the best-selling, Don't Tell Meg trilogy and the brand new Morecambe Bay trilogy.

The Secret Bunker website can be found at **thesecretbunker.net**

The Grid website can be found at **thegridtrilogy.com**

You can find out more about Paul's sci-fi and thrillers at **paul-teague.net**

Follow Paul on Facebook: **facebook.com/paulteagueauthor**

 facebook.com/paulteagueauthor

ABOUT THE AUTHORS JON EVANS

Jon is a sci-fi author & fantasy author, whose first book, Thieftaker is awaiting its sequel. He lives and works in Cardiff. He has some other projects waiting in the wings, once the RMSC series takes shape.

You can follow Jon's Facebook page where you'll be able to find out more about the first five books of the Royal Marine Space Commandos series.

If you join the mailing list on the website, you'll get updates about how the new books are coming as well as information about new releases and the odd insight into the life of an author.

jonevansbooks.com

- facebook.com/jonevansauthor
- amazon.com/author/jonevansbooks
- goodreads.com/jonevans
- bookbub.com/authors/jon-evans
- instagram.com/jonevansauthor

Printed in Poland
by Amazon Fulfillment
Poland Sp. z o.o., Wrocław

53802270R00139